NIGHTMARES!

JASON SEGEL
KIRSTEN MILLER

NIGHTMARES!

~ ILLUSTRATED BY KARL KWASNY ~

DELACORTE PRESS

Copyright © 2014 by The Jason Segel Company

All rights reserved. Published in the United States by Delacorte Press, an imprint of Random House Children's Books, a division of Random House LLC, a Penguin Random House Company, New York.

Delacorte Press is a registered trademark and the colophon is a trademark of Random House LLC.

Visit us on the Web! randomhousekids.com

Educators and librarians, for a variety of teaching tools, visit us at RHTeachersLibrarians.com

Library of Congress Cataloging-in-Publication Data is available upon request.
ISBN 978-0-385-74425-6 (trade) — ISBN 978-0-375-99157-8 (lib. bdg.) —
ISBN 978-0-385-38403-2 (ebook)

The text of this book is set in 12.2-point Sabon MT.
Book design by Stephanie Moss

Printed in the United States of America
10 9 8 7 6 5 4 3 2 1
First Edition

To Al, Jill, Adam, Alison, and my friend R.B.
—J.S.

NIGHTMARES!

CHAPTER ONE

THE STEPMONSTER'S LAIR

It was five minutes past midnight, and a boy was gazing down at Cypress Creek from the window of an old mansion on the town's highest hill. It was an odd-looking building. The front porch was overrun by a jungle of potted plants. Thick green vines crept up columns, and lady ferns and blood flowers fought for every patch of moonlight. An octagonal tower sprouted straight from the house's roof, and the entire structure was painted a dreadful shade of purple. Anyone who saw it might assume that the mansion's occupants were a bit on the strange side—and yet the boy at the window appeared perfectly normal. He had

sandy blond hair and no visible tattoos, scars, or hideous warts. But judging by the miserable expression on his face, something was terribly wrong.

His name was Charlie Laird, and he'd lived in Cypress Creek all twelve years of his life. He and his little brother, Jack, had grown up in a house just down the street. In fact, Charlie could see the old place from his new bedroom window. A different family of four owned it now. Every night, Charlie watched the lights in his former home go out and imagined the kids snuggled up nice and safe, tucked into bed by their mother and father. He would have given almost anything to trade places with them. It had been three months since he'd moved to the purple mansion on DeChant Hill with his brother and father. And it had been three months since Charlie Laird had gotten a good night's sleep.

Charlie took a step back from the window and saw his reflection in the glass. His skin was the color of curdled milk, and dark bags sagged beneath his red-rimmed eyes. He sighed at the sight and turned around to start his night's work. Thirty-eight heavy boxes sat in the center of the room. They were filled with video games and comic books and Little League trophies. Charlie had unpacked nothing more than a few changes of clothes. The rest of his belongings were still stowed away in their cardboard boxes. And every night, before he lay down in his bed, he would move them. Nineteen boxes were used to block the door to the hall. The other nineteen were pushed against the bathroom door, though that often proved *quite* inconvenient.

It would have seemed ridiculous to anyone else. Even Charlie knew the barricades couldn't stop his bad dreams. But the witch who'd been visiting him every night for three months wasn't like other nightmares he'd had. Most dreams faded, but he couldn't forget her. She felt just as real as the nose on his face. So when the witch swore that one night soon she'd come drag him away, Charlie figured he should take her threats seriously. He just hoped all the boxes could keep her out of his room.

She'd already gotten as far as the hallway. The first time he'd heard someone sneaking through the house, Charlie had just woken up from a nightmare. The sun's rays were peeking over the mountains, but the mansion was still and quiet. Suddenly the silence had been broken by the creak of rusty door hinges opening. Then the floorboards groaned and there were thuds on the stairs. The footsteps were heavy enough to be an adult's. But when Charlie worked up the nerve to investigate, he found his father and stepmother still asleep in their bed. A few nights later, he heard the same thing again. *Creak. Groan. Thud.* His father said that old houses make noises. His brother thought the place might be haunted. But Charlie knew there was no such thing as ghosts. He'd been searching for almost three years, and if they'd existed he would have seen one by now. No, Charlie Laird had far bigger problems than ghosts.

The thirty-eight boxes were waiting. Charlie stared at the daunting task in front of him and wondered where he'd find the energy to complete it. His nightmares had gotten worse—and every night he fought a losing battle against sleep. Now his eyelids were drooping and he couldn't stop yawning. As usual, he'd stood by the window until midnight, waiting for his father and stepmother to go to bed. He didn't want them to hear him sliding the boxes across the floorboards or grunting as he stacked them against the doors. But staying up was growing harder and harder. He'd tried taping his eyes open, but Scotch tape was too weak and duct tape pulled out his eyebrows. Pacing just made him dizzy. And while he'd heard that a full bladder could keep sleep at bay, every time he tried chugging water at bedtime, he ended up frantically shoving nineteen boxes away from the bathroom door. So a few weeks earlier, when all else had failed, Charlie had taken his first trip to the kitchen for a cup of cold, leftover coffee. It always made him gag, and sometimes he had to hold his nose just to get it all down—but the coffee was the only thing that kept him awake.

Charlie tiptoed to his bedroom door, opened it slowly so the hinges wouldn't squeal, and took a peek outside. He was relieved to see that the hallway was dark. He preferred it that way. The walls were lined with old paintings that were far creepier when the lights were on. He listened closely for signs of movement and then sock-skated awkwardly toward the stairs. Past his brother's room. And his father and stepmother's. He was almost outside the last door on the hall when he heard it—a high-pitched laugh that nearly sent him sprinting back to his bed. Behind the last door lay the stairs to the tower. And at the top of those stairs was a room known in the family as Charlotte's Lair. The door was open a crack, and Charlie heard the sound of a fat cat's paws padding down the wooden staircase. A pale golden light leaked out into the hall.

His stepmother was still awake.

CHAPTER TWO

THE MAGIC TOWER

Long before Charlie had become a prisoner of the purple mansion, he'd been bewitched by its tower. The mansion sat in the center of sleepy Cypress Creek, perched on top of a hill. Below it lay streets lined with tasteful houses painted white and beige. Downtown, there were flower-filled parks and charming shops. It would have been a picture-perfect village if not for the purple mansion's tower. No matter where you were in Cypress Creek, you could always glance up and see it. With wooden shingles like dragon's scales and a steep, pointy roof that resembled a witch's hat, the tower would have been right at home in a fairy tale. It had two windows—one facing north and one facing south. Neither had a curtain or shade. And at night, when the rest of the house disappeared in the darkness, the tower windows appeared to glow. It was a faint and flickering glimmer. Charlie's little brother, Jack, used to joke that someone must have left a night-light plugged in. Charlie had a few ideas of his own.

Whenever Charlie walked around town, his eyes were drawn to the tower. He was certain that some kind of magic was taking place there each night. The house was supposed to be empty, but late one evening, he thought he saw a figure standing at one of the windows. After that, his fascination was mixed with fear. At school he wrote stories about the tower. At home he drew pictures of it. His father taped the drawings to the refrigerator and said Charlie had been blessed with a vivid imagination. He couldn't understand what his son found so interesting. And as far as Charlie was concerned, that was the strangest thing of all. Most people thought the purple mansion and its tower were just eyesores—warts on the face of Cypress Creek that they did their best to ignore. But not Charlie. Charlie knew better.

There had been *one* other person who'd known about the tower's magic. Every time a new drawing appeared on the family fridge, Charlie's mom had seemed a little more worried. Then one day, when he was eight years old, his mother confessed that she had visited the purple house several times as a kid. In those days, she'd said, the tower room had belonged to a girl her age.

"What was the tower like?" Charlie had asked breathlessly. "Was it creepy? Was it cool? Was it haunted, was it . . ."

"It was . . . *unusual,*" his mom had replied, and her skin went pale, which told Charlie there had to be more to the story—something dark and dangerous. He pleaded for details, but his mom would only say that the mansion was probably best avoided. Charlie must have looked heartbroken when his mom wouldn't reveal more, because she sat him down and made him a promise. She said she would tell him everything she knew about the tower when he got a bit older. But that ended up being a promise Charlie's mom couldn't keep. She fell ill a few months later—and died four days and three hours before Charlie turned nine.

After his mom passed away, Charlie's fascination with the tower had continued to grow like a noxious weed. He asked his teachers about it. He interrogated the town librarian. He even cornered the mayor at the town's annual radish festival. But no one in Cypress Creek seemed to know much about the old purple mansion—aside from four simple facts:

1. The mansion was older than the rest of the town.
2. It had been built by Silas DeChant, a millionaire hermit and notorious grouch.
3. Silas's wife had painted the house purple herself.
4. The mansion had been vacant for years.

Charlie's dad said that the last person to live there had been an elderly woman. A teacher claimed that an old lady dressed in purple used to hand out grape-flavored lollipops on Halloween. One of Charlie's neighbors said he'd heard that the mansion's owner had gone to live with her daughter in a faraway state. The neighbor's wife swore that the old lady in question had to be at least 110.

One Saturday morning, Charlie discovered that the purple house was the talk of the town. The postman delivered the big news with the mail: the mansion's elderly owner had passed away. Remarkably, she had died just two days short of her 111th birthday from injuries she sustained in a gin rummy accident.

At the coffee shop where the Lairds went for pancakes, a waitress told Charlie's dad that the old lady's granddaughter had inherited the mansion and was moving in. And a man at the next table knew that the new owner's name was Charlotte DeChant—and he'd heard she was opening a store on Main Street. The way folks gossiped about Cypress Creek's newest resident, Charlie figured

Charlotte DeChant might turn out to be interesting. And the first time Charlie laid eyes on her, he was certainly not disappointed.

It was a cool autumn day, and Charlie was riding his bike to his friend Alfie's house when he saw a moving van pull up in front of the purple mansion on the hill. A tall, wiry woman climbed out of the driver's seat. She had bright orange hair with curls that seemed to be blowing in a breeze—even though the air was perfectly still. Her black skirts billowed and swirled around her boots. She wore a white T-shirt emblazoned with a logo in blood-red and forest-green. It read HAZEL'S HERBARIUM.

The woman opened the back door of the van, and from where Charlie had stopped, he could see that there were no boxes inside. Only plants. In fact, it looked like an entire

garden had been uprooted, potted, and driven to Cypress Creek.

"Hey, you! Give me a hand with this stuff and I'll give you five dollars," the woman called down to Charlie.

Against his better judgment, Charlie walked his bike up the hill for a better look. "What is all that?" he asked.

"An enchanted forest," the woman replied matter-of-factly.

"What?" Charlie took a step back. It was an odd thing for an adult to say. She was probably joking, but it did look like the van could hold a few gnomes and a wood sprite or two.

The lady's laugh took him by surprise. It was high-pitched and unpleasant—more of a cackle than a chuckle. "Don't you know when someone's pulling your leg? It's just a bunch of plants. I'm opening a shop downtown."

Charlie and his friends had wondered about the shop opening up next to the ice cream parlor. They'd seen workmen painting the interior multiple shades of green. His friend Paige thought it might be a place to buy seeds and unusual vegetables. Rocco was hoping it would be a reptile emporium. "So it's going to be a plant store?"

"More like a magic shop," the woman replied, and Charlie perked up. Then she pointed at her shirt. "It's going to be called Hazel's Herbarium. I'm an herbalist. That means I use plants to treat sick people."

For a moment Charlie felt a surge of hope. Then heart fell when he remembered that his mom was long past treating.

He looked back up to find the strange woman studying his face. "What's your name?" The way she asked made Charlie wonder if she already knew. He glanced down at his bike. His gut was telling him it was time to leave. This woman was *not* normal—at least, not the kind of normal *he'd* ever met. But he laid down his bicycle and held out a hand.

"Charlie. Charlie Laird," he'd said. The woman took his hand, but she didn't shake. Instead, she held it between her palms as if it were a little creature she'd been clever enough to capture.

"Charlie Laird," the woman repeated, her lips stretching into a toothy smile. "I'm Charlotte DeChant. I've been looking forward to meeting you."

A chill ran down Charlie's spine, and he pulled his hand away. "Why?" he asked a little too quickly. How could she have been looking forward to meeting him? She shouldn't have known he existed.

"If I'm not mistaken, you must be related to Veronica Laird," Charlotte continued.

It felt like the woman had shoved a hand into his chest, grabbed his heart, and squeezed. "She's my mom."

"I knew her once, a long time ago," Charlotte said. "I was sorry to hear that she passed away."

"It's okay," Charlie said. Though it wasn't. And it never would be. He wished the lady would change the subject. He could already feel his cheeks burning.

And just like that, it seemed as if Charlie's wish had been granted. Charlotte raised her eyebrows and nodded at the moving van. "So what do you say? Want to earn a few bucks?"

"I don't know. . . ." Charlie hesitated. He'd always been warned not to talk to strangers—and this woman with her blazing orange hair and portable jungle was nothing if not *extremely* strange.

Charlie looked up at the house behind her, his eyes drawn as always to the tower. The lady was weird, but he hadn't been this close to the mansion in years. Everything he'd always dreamed about was on the other side of the front door. It would be torture to simply walk away.

"Then maybe I should sweeten the offer," Charlotte said with a sly grin. "Five bucks—and I throw in a tour of the house."

It was like she'd read his mind. Charlie's curiosity was an itch he was desperate to scratch. Was the house as ugly inside as it was on the outside? Why did the tower glow at night? And who was the person he'd seen standing at the window? A thousand questions bounced around in his brain.

"What's in the tower?" Charlie asked eagerly.

Charlotte cackled again, and Charlie had to resist the

urge to stick his fingers in his ears. "Things that go bump in the night."

Charlie should have turned away as soon as he heard that. He should have hopped on his bike and hightailed it to Alfie's house and never looked back. He'd never had such a bad case of heebie-jeebies before. But Charlie didn't leave. He couldn't. He didn't know if it was curiosity or some kind of magic that pulled him inside, but he moved the woman's plants to the porch. He accepted five dollars for his trouble. And then he followed Charlotte inside for his tour.

An overfed tabby cat met Charlie at the door. It took one look at him, hunched its back, and hissed. Charlie stepped over the orange beast and caught up to Charlotte just as she was pointing out the mansion's parlor and library. The heavy old sofas and sagging armchairs in both rooms were upholstered in lilac, magenta, or mauve. Even the shelves in the library were painted the color of ripe eggplant.

"Wow. Your place is really grape." The word slid out of Charlie's mouth before he could stop it. The closer he got to the tower, the more jittery he felt. "I mean *great*. Your place is really great."

"Good one," Charlotte replied, cracking a grin. "The crazy furniture came with the house. But I'll probably have everything painted or covered. I had my fill of purple when I was a kid."

She reached a wide wooden staircase that twisted up
toward the top of the house and started to climb. Charlie
found himself stalled on the first step, his eyes fixed on a
portrait that stared down at him from the landing. It
showed a young man dressed in an old-fashioned jacket
and a high white neckerchief. He looked rich, and he would
have been handsome if not for his hollow eyes and anxious
expression.

"Who was he?" Charlie asked his guide. He'd seen circles that dark around his own mother's eyes, and he suspected the man in the portrait had been sick.

Charlotte paused on the stairs. When she turned to face Charlie, she seemed to study him for a moment as if he were a scientific specimen. "That's one of my great-great-grandfathers. His name was Silas DeChant," she said. "He's the man who built this place."

Charlie shivered. He had been searching for Silas for years. The lady who ran the Cypress Creek library had sworn there were no paintings or photos of the town's mysterious founder. And yet here he was—and he'd been here all along.

"What was wrong with him?" Charlie half whispered, gripping the banister. He was feeling a bit wobbly—like his knees had gone soft and the ground was made of Jell-O. "Was Silas sick?"

"Let's just say he was stuck in a very dark place," Charlotte replied. "But he found his way out. My grandma told me Silas had that portrait painted to remind him that there are places some people go where they aren't meant to stay."

"Like where?" Charlie asked.

"Vegas," Charlotte said with a wink. Then she turned her back to him and began climbing the stairs again. "Are you coming?"

Charlie had to take several steps at a time to catch up with the mansion's new owner.

On the second floor, the pair passed through a small door and climbed a set of stairs so narrow that even Charlie felt squeezed. When they finally reached the top, Charlotte stepped aside and held her arms out wide. "Welcome to my lair," she said proudly.

The place was every bit as magical as Charlie had hoped. And so much bigger on the inside than it looked on the outside. Most of the room's walls were cluttered with shelves and pictures, but one had been left entirely bare. Sunshine poured in through the lair's two large windows, turning millions of dust motes into glittering specks of gold. Glass jars lined the room's shelves, and every container was filled with a different kind of seedpod or dried flower or shriveled mushroom. A huge wooden desk took up most of the floor space. Its surface was cluttered with colored pencils, paint tubes, and drawing pads.

An illustration stuck out from beneath a pile of crumpled paper. Charlie could see only a bit, but a bit was enough. Three snakes—one brown, one red, and one emerald green—looked ready to slither right off the page. He could almost swear he heard them hiss—and then, when he began to look away, the green one seemed to bare its fangs.

"Those snakes are amazing," Charlie breathed. "Did you draw them?"

Charlotte snatched the picture and slapped it facedown on the desk.

"That's just a rough draft," she said, sounding oddly embarrassed. "What do you think of the room?"

"It's . . ." Charlie struggled to find the right word.

"The perfect place to work, right?" She finished the sentence for him. "You know, I just started a little project, and I might have a use for a kid your age. . . ."

Might have a use for? Charlie shivered. Why did it sound like she was going to grind up his bones to make paint? He felt something soft brush against his ankle and looked down to see the giant orange cat weaving between his legs, staring up at him wickedly as if she had a few plans for him too.

The doorbell chimed, and Charlie jumped. Thankful for the interruption, he watched Charlotte rush down the stairs. He should have taken the chance to escape, but he stayed behind, too overwhelmed to move. It felt as if he'd been frozen in place. Two floors down, he heard the front door squeak open.

"Hiya!" Charlie heard Charlotte say.

"Ummm . . . hello, my name is Andrew Laird, and this is my son Jack. This may sound a bit odd, but is my other boy, Charlie, here? I was driving by and I saw his bike out front. I hope he hasn't been causing trouble."

"Absolutely not! No trouble at all. You've got a great

kid there, Mr. Laird," Charlotte replied. "He just helped me move a few things, and now he's upstairs. Would you like to come inside for a cup of coffee?"

Charlie was certain his dad would say no. He never went anywhere but work anymore. Since his wife's death, sadness had turned him into a hermit. Once, Andrew and Veronica Laird had been the most popular couple in town. Now Charlie's father turned down all invitations. He never seemed to run out of excuses. Charlie waited to hear what the latest one would be.

Then came the word that sealed Charlie's fate.

"Sure."

Eleven months later, Charlotte DeChant became Charlie's stepmom. And by then, Charlie had vowed to never set foot in the tower again.

CHAPTER THREE

THE MIDNIGHT MEETING

In the three years since his mother had passed away, Charlie Laird had learned not to trust appearances. His mom had *looked* healthy—almost up to the month she died. Charlie himself appeared totally normal—while the truth was, his life was anything but. And everyone thought Charlotte DeChant made a perfect stepmom. Only Charlie knew that she wasn't who she appeared to be. He could tell it was all a disguise.

Charlie stood in the doorway of the mansion's kitchen, hunting for the blinking green light on the coffeemaker. He let his eyes adjust and scanned the rest of the room.

It looked safe enough, but seeing wasn't always believing these days. He took a cautious step inside. The only light in the room came from a weak blue flame that flickered beneath Charlotte's favorite black cauldron. The kitchen had been renovated, and the brushed-steel stove was brand-new, but Charlotte's pots and pans looked like they'd been forged in the Middle Ages. And whatever ointment or potion she was cooking smelled like a mixture of dead rodents and dog farts. Charlie didn't need the light to know that the floor was probably slick with roots and leaves that hadn't made it into the bubbling pot.

Everywhere Charlotte went, messes seemed to sprout up behind her. The jungle of plants on the mansion's front porch made leaving the house seem like a trek through the Amazon. Inside, the rooms were all cluttered with half-empty herb jars and gunky old beakers. You couldn't sit on a couch without squishing a mushroom or being poked in the rump by a shriveled root, and it drove Charlie crazy. He'd tried tidying up once or twice, but Charlotte's cat, Aggie, would just follow him, knocking everything over. In Charlotte's world, Hazel's Herbarium was the only place where order was allowed to rule. Charlie's stepmother kept her shop perfectly organized. Every pod, seed, or fungus that nature produced was stored in a glass container and labeled precisely. More than a thousand such jars lined the store's many shelves.

Hazel's Herbarium was a sight to behold—and no one in Cypress Creek had ever beheld anything like it. For a few weeks after the store's grand opening, some of the older kids at school had teased Charlie about his dad's weird girlfriend, who dressed in black and cooked up smelly potions. The jokes ended when Charlotte cured one of the bullies of the pimples that were eating his face and helped the mayor get rid of his goiter. After that, Hazel's Herbarium was always busy, and nobody whispered when Charlotte walked by. The whole town had fallen under her spell.

The kitchen was too dark to navigate, so Charlie opened the refrigerator for a little light. Stepping over a mysterious puddle on the floor, he made his way to the coffee machine on the far side of the room. There was usually a bit of coffee left over from breakfast, but today, someone had gone and cleaned out the pot. Charlie dragged a chair to the counter and climbed up to grab grounds from the top shelf of the cabinet. He put a filter into the coffeemaker, the way he'd seen Charlotte do. He added ten scoops of coffee and a potful of water. He'd just pressed start when something warm and hairy brushed against his legs.

Charlie's heart nearly flew out of his chest. Stepping back from the counter, he tripped over the creature lurking behind him and landed with a thump on the floor.

"Meow," said Aggie triumphantly. She lifted one paw and gave it a leisurely lick.

Charlie had always liked cats, but Aggie was a demon in an orange fur coat. "You evil little . . . ," he growled. Then he heard footsteps on the stairs. In an instant, Charlie was on his feet.

"Charlie? Is that you?"

The stepmonster had appeared in the doorway, her phoniest grin in place. She wanted Charlie to think she was surprised to see him, but the glimmer in her eyes gave her away. She'd been waiting to catch him.

Charlotte came closer, and her nostrils twitched as she sniffed the air.

"Does your father know you drink coffee?"

In the dim light cast by the refrigerator, Charlotte's features looked perfectly ghoulish. Her cheeks were hollow, her nose seemed to have grown pointier, and her curly hair stuck out like a clown wig. Charlie's friend Rocco said Charlotte was pretty. Charlie thought she looked like a . . .

"Whew! That smells pretty potent. How much coffee did you put in there?" she asked, peering into the pot.

Charlie expected her to switch off the machine. Instead, she grabbed a mug from the cupboard and placed it on the counter in front of him. "Probably won't kill you, but it's gonna taste like mud."

World's Best Stepmom was printed on the front of the mug. The cup had been his little brother's Christmas present to the woman who'd stolen their father. There were a million regular mugs in the cupboard. Charlotte had picked this one on purpose.

"Really?" Charlie asked carefully. "You're going to let me drink coffee?"

"Would it do any good if I tried to stop you?" Charlotte asked. "Besides, I started drinking coffee when I was right around your age."

While the coffee was still brewing, the stepmonster poured them both a mug. "Care to join me?" she asked, pulling a stool up to the kitchen island.

Charlie didn't budge. He stared at the coffee. He wanted it more than anything in the world, but he wouldn't give her the satisfaction. And who knew what she might have slipped in it. He'd watched Charlotte haul crates of little

glass bottles upstairs to her lair. Strange liquids sloshed in some of them; others contained powders or pills or goopy gels. These were her special concoctions—the ones she didn't sell in her store. Only Charlotte knew what they really were. She *claimed* the bottles held herbal remedies. But Charlie was willing to bet that at least one of them was filled with some kind of stepson remover. He was pretty sure Charlotte wanted him out of the way.

"Have a seat," Charlotte said. "It's time we had a heart-to-heart." There was still a smile on the stepmonster's face, but her eyes were serious. It wasn't a request. It was an *order*.

Charlie snorted to cover his nervousness. "You think we're going to be best friends if you let me drink coffee?" It shocked him a little to hear himself be so rude. He used to be able to keep his feelings hidden under the surface, but lately his anger seemed to have a mind of its own. He called it the darkness. It felt like black tar—the kind that swallows up anything that it touches. It had started bubbling up inside him around the same time the nightmares began. Now he couldn't seem to keep it inside.

"What's the deal, Charlie?" Charlotte asked. "What's got you acting so prickly?"

He could have recited a list of the stepmonster's crimes, but they would have been there all night.

"You'd be prickly too if someone stole your family," Charlie replied.

Charlotte took in a sharp breath. Her eyes were narrowed when she spoke. "I haven't *stolen* anyone. I don't want to replace your mom, Charlie."

She'd said it before and the words still got under Charlie's skin. "You *couldn't*. No matter how hard you tried. My mom was the nicest, smartest—"

Charlotte held up a hand in surrender. "Yes, I know. You've told me a hundred times. I remember her too." She paused and stared at the contents of her cup. "I'm guessing a heart-to-heart isn't in our cards, but there's still a question I need to ask you, Charlie. Why do you keep coming down for coffee every night?"

Charlie crossed his arms. He refused to say a word.

For a moment, Charlotte studied him silently—the same way she sometimes did when she thought no one was looking. "You know, you're just like Veronica. She could be every bit as stubborn as you."

When he heard his mother's name, Charlie couldn't hold his tongue. "Stop pretending that you knew my mom."

"I never told you this before because I know the subject is sensitive. But for your information, Veronica and I met right here in this house when we were both twelve years old," Charlotte shot back, her green eyes daring him to disagree. "Didn't she ever tell you any stories about the mansion?"

"What kind of stories?" Charlie replied, faking a yawn. He wanted to look bored, but the conversation had taken a turn for the weird, and Charlotte had him hooked.

The stepmonster leaned forward with an arched eyebrow. "If you'd heard your mother's stories, you wouldn't have forgotten them."

The answer rattled Charlie. He remembered his mother warning him to stay away from the house. Then it hit him. Something must have happened to his mom in the mansion—something bad enough to scare her for years. And it had to be Charlotte DeChant's fault. "What did you do to my mom?" he demanded.

Charlotte sat back with a huff and a roll of her eyes. "Did she *say* I did something to her?"

Charlie leveled his eyes at the stepmonster. "She never got the chance, *Charlotte*. But she did tell me to stay away from this mansion, and now I know why. There's something very wrong with this house."

Charlotte was so still that Charlie wondered if she'd suddenly frozen solid. "What exactly do you think is wrong with the house?" she finally asked.

Charlie considered telling her everything—but caught himself before he did anything stupid. "You're in it," he said with his meanest smile.

He could have been mistaken, but Charlotte seemed almost *relieved*. "Look, I don't know much about kids, and

I've never been good at the warm, fuzzy stuff. So forgive me if this sounds a bit blunt, but it's time for you to pull it together. Otherwise things in this house could get worse than you ever expected."

Charlie laughed at that. "How could things possibly get any worse? I live in the town dump with a crazy woman and her evil cat."

Charlotte flinched, and Charlie could see that his insults had hit their mark. But he didn't care. He hated the stepmonster. And he hated her most for turning him into someone so horrible. Charlie could remember being a nice person once. Now he was always mad. Sometimes he didn't even know why. It was as if his heart had shriveled up inside his chest the day he'd moved into the purple house.

Charlie slid down from his stool, picked up his coffee cup, and dumped its contents in the sink. "Look, I don't want to talk to you. I just came down for some coffee. Now you've managed to ruin *that* too."

"Charlie, coffee won't help." Charlotte reached across the kitchen island to grab Charlie's arm, but he ducked away. "If your problem is what I think it is, there's no point in staying awake."

Before Charlie could ask what she meant, she was on her feet. "Wait right here a sec while I run upstairs," Charlotte said, as if struck by inspiration. "I have something in

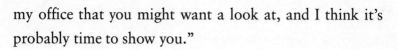

my office that you might want a look at, and I think it's probably time to show you."

Charlie didn't want to see anything the stepmonster wanted to show him. As soon as he heard Charlotte's footsteps on the tower stairs, he sprinted up to his room and quickly pushed a half-dozen boxes against the door. Then he crawled into bed, pulled the covers over his head, and hoped his anger would keep him awake.

CHAPTER FOUR

THE WITCH

"Look who's here," something purred. "And just in time for dinner!"

"Splendid!" said a second voice. The words were followed by a familiar cackle. "So glad you could join us, Charlie. Aren't you looking just *scrumptious* tonight?"

A jolt of fear made Charlie's eyes snap open. He was no longer in his room. His bed was shoved up against a crumbling stone wall that was splattered with patches of moss and mold. He'd been to the witch's dungeon before, but this time he could see the cavernous space even more clearly. A roaring fire had been built in the center of the room. A cloud of smoke rolled above him.

Charlie struggled to sit up, only to discover that he'd been tied down, as usual. Ropes chafed his wrists and ankles. He could lift his head just high enough to see the witch seated beside an enormous cauldron, chopping up a slab of meat. The contents of the pot belched every time she dropped a hunk in. As the witch rose from her seat, she tossed a handful of scraps onto a rubbish heap in the corner. Charlie spotted a doll-sized skull and a broken bat wing sticking out of the pile.

Still clutching her cleaver, the witch glided over to where Charlie lay. A giant black cat the size of a panther trotted beside her. Then it crouched and jumped up on Charlie's chest.

"Oof!" Charlie wheezed as the wind was knocked out of him.

"He's still awfully puny." The cat sniffed Charlie's face and then ran her tongue up the side of his head. "He doesn't taste very good either."

"The bitter ones never do." The witch sighed. "But we'll eat him if we have to. I stocked up on that sauce we like just in case."

The witch was dressed in the ankle-sweeping black dress she always wore. Her masklike face was a sickly green, and her hair, if she had any, was tucked beneath a sleek black hat. But it was her eyes that made her so terrible to behold. The lenses were silvery mirrors. Whenever Charlie looked at the witch, he was forced to see himself.

Just when it was becoming difficult for Charlie to breathe, the cat hopped off his chest and wound around the witch's legs. Charlie drew in a deep breath. "Get these ropes off me, you nasty old hag!" he shouted.

The witch gasped. "Oh dear. Did you hear that? I think he's trying to hurt my feelings!" She bent down until her nose was only inches from Charlie's. He could see his revolted expression reflected in her eyes. "Don't waste your breath, boy. 'Hag' is a *compliment* in this neck of the woods. So let's get down to business. Where do you want to spend the night? My cage or the cat's belly? The choice is yours."

Charlie trembled at the thought of the cage upstairs. It swung in the open air at the top of the witch's belfry, where a giant bell might have been. Old and rusty, the cage looked like it was built to house a monstrous bird. The first time Charlie had seen it, a skeleton had been curled up in one corner. He'd watched with horror as the witch had pulled the cage down and swept out the bones.

Now the cage belonged to Charlie. In most of his nightmares, that was where the witch put him. Frigid winds always blew through the bars. Sometimes rain would pelt him. Other times he'd be buried in snow. But the weather wasn't the worst part. Charlie's time in the cage was so lonely that just a few hours could feel like a week. Still, Charlie never once tried to escape. For a long time, he told himself there was nowhere to go. The truth was, he was terrified of the forest that surrounded the bell tower. He felt there was something waiting for him down there. Something much, much worse than a witch.

"Do what you want to me," Charlie growled at the witch. "As soon as it's morning, I'll wake up in my bed."

"So rude!" the cat said with a yawn as she nuzzled against her mistress's side.

"Isn't he?" The witch pretended to pout. "Such a nasty little thing. No wonder nobody on the other side wants him back. They must be sick of him too."

The words stung. They hurt all the more because Charlie suspected they were true. Lately, the only people who'd been spared his anger were his three best friends. And who knew how long that would last.

"We'd be doing everyone a favor if we left the boy in the cage for good," the cat said.

"But think of the work!" the witch groaned. "I'd have to bring him water every day and change the newspaper once a month and—"

"Then perhaps," the cat interrupted, "it would be best if we eat him."

"I couldn't agree more," the witch said, shuffling away. "I'll get the sauce. You set up the spit."

Charlie closed his eyes and tried his best to stay calm. "This is a dream," he whispered, trying to convince himself. "I'm having a nightmare, and nightmares aren't real."

The witch turned back and shoved her nose in his face. Her breath smelled like she'd been nibbling at the rubbish pile. "What was that?" she asked with a cackle. "Sounds like someone's been lying to you—telling you nightmares aren't real. I'll show you how real I am. Tomorrow I'll pay you a visit in *your* world."

Could she make good on her threats? Charlie wondered. Could she come to the mansion and drag him away? "Go ahead and try," he said, doing his best to sound brave. "You'll never get into my room."

The witch cackled while the cat howled with laughter.

"We'll see about that. I wouldn't be much of a witch if a few stupid boxes could stop me."

"How do you know . . . ?" Charlie blurted out.

The witch plopped down beside him on the bed. Her dress reeked of mildew and mothballs.

"About the boxes in your room? I know a lot of things." She combed her clawed fingers through Charlie's hair. He squirmed with disgust, but she barely seemed to notice. "Do you know why people think nightmares aren't real?"

Charlie was too confused to answer. Something had changed. This nightmare was different from the rest. The witch had never spoken to him like this before.

"Because most people wake up," the witch continued. "Their spirits come here when they sleep and their bodies stay safe and sound in your world until morning." She leaned in closer. "But you know what I've figured out? I've figured out how to bring your body here to the Netherworld too."

Charlie stopped struggling. Dread wrapped around him like a straitjacket. "How?" he asked.

The witch brushed his cheek with the back of her hand. "If your fear is powerful enough, your body can travel to the other side," she told him. "And I've never seen *anyone* as scared as you, Charlie Laird."

Charlie might have been scared. But he was angry too. "Don't flatter yourself," he spat. "If you and your cat are the most terrifying things this place has to offer, then I'm gonna be just fine."

The witch smiled, and Charlie could see the rotten nubs of her teeth. "Oh, I think we both know that I'm not your worst nightmare. There's another nightmare out there that scares you much more than I do. Isn't there, Charlie?"

Charlie's whole body went numb. The other one was never to be mentioned out loud. The other one was a million times more terrifying than the witch.

"Your worst nightmare and I are *very* good friends," the witch continued. "In fact, she's probably waiting for you outside as we speak. Would you like me to invite her in? I bet she's been *dying* for a little chat."

Charlie squeezed his eyes shut. "No," he whimpered. "Please, no. Please, I'd rather be eaten."

"Did you hear that?" The cat sounded delighted. "He told us to eat him. And it *is* dinnertime. Would you mind if I start with a few of his toes?"

"Be my guest," said the witch. "He won't need them once he's in the cage."

The cat stretched her mouth open, and Charlie screamed as she bit down, but her fangs passed right through his foot.

"Blast it, he's fading!" the cat howled. "Quick, chop me off a piece!"

"Not this time," said the witch with a grin. "But he'll be back. Charlie knows he can't get away."

⚘ CHAPTER FIVE ⚘

MONSTERS

"Aaaaaaaaaaaah!" Charlie could hear himself scream-ing, but he couldn't stop.

Someone was shaking him. He forced his eyes open.

"Aaaaah!" There was just enough daylight in the room for Charlie to see a person in a cardboard mask leaning over his bed.

"It's me!" a kid squeaked.

"Jack," Charlie gasped, and relief washed over him. The figure at his bedside pushed its mask up. Charlie's eight-year-old brother was wearing the Captain Amer-ica costume he'd discovered while snooping around in

Charlie's boxes. For the past two weeks, he'd worn it practically every day. Charlie had pitched a fit, but their father had taken Jack's side. The Captain America suit was too small for Charlie, he'd said. And costumes were meant to be enjoyed—not folded up and hidden away. No one cared that it was the last Halloween costume Charlie's mother had ever made for him. Sometimes it seemed like Charlie was the only one who still remembered his mother at all.

Jack's face was so close that Charlie could count every freckle on the kid's pug nose. Charlie had turned out fair-haired, but Jack was a miniature copy of their father, with an unruly mop of brown hair and dark eyes full of mischief. He was always pulling little stunts that would get any other kid grounded for weeks. But everyone just laughed when Jack gave the cat a Mohawk or dug up the yard searching for pirate booty. He was cute enough to get away with murder.

"You okay?" Jack asked.

"Yeah," Charlie said, still struggling to catch his breath.

"Were you having a bad dream?" Jack whispered. "It must have been really scary."

Charlie winced with embarrassment and flopped back on the bed. "How'd you get in here?"

He glanced over at the door. Jack had pushed the boxes back just enough to slide through a narrow crack. *So much for the barricades,* Charlie thought miserably.

"It's time to get up," Jack announced in his official Captain America voice. "Charlotte made breakfast."

It wasn't even eight in the morning and Charlie could already feel the darkness brewing inside him. It was going to be a very bad day. "Since when does the stepmonster make *breakfast*?" Charlotte was usually at Hazel's Herbarium by the time he and Jack left for school.

"Since today, I guess," Jack replied. "Hurry up and get ready. I'm starving to death. And I found something downstairs that you *gotta* see."

As soon as Jack had squeezed around the boxes and out the door, Charlie pulled the covers back up to his chin and thought about what the witch had said. *I've never seen anyone as scared as you, Charlie Laird.* Was it true? Were his nightmares so much worse than everyone else's? He'd never been the kind of kid who was easy to frighten. It was something he'd always been proud of. But that was before he'd drifted off to sleep one night and found himself in a damp, gloomy forest.

It looked like a place he knew very well. Just south of Cypress Creek lay a vast forest. Those who visited usually traveled by foot, using trails worn into the ground by hunters and hikers. Charlie had walked the paths with his mom when she gathered wildflowers in the spring, berries in the

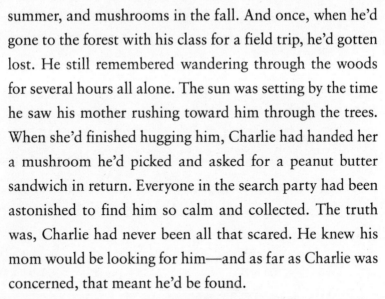

summer, and mushrooms in the fall. And once, when he'd gone to the forest with his class for a field trip, he'd gotten lost. He still remembered wandering through the woods for several hours all alone. The sun was setting by the time he saw his mother rushing toward him through the trees. When she'd finished hugging him, Charlie had handed her a mushroom he'd picked and asked for a peanut butter sandwich in return. Everyone in the search party had been astonished to find him so calm and collected. The truth was, Charlie had never been all that scared. He knew his mom would be looking for him—and as far as Charlie was concerned, that meant he'd be found.

But the forest in Charlie's first nightmare was darker. The trees there grew taller, and their knurled branches twisted together to block out the sunlight. Charlie's feet sank into the slimy moss floor, and thorn-covered vines tried their best to entangle him. He hurried through the woods, desperate for shelter or something familiar. He sensed that someone was searching for him, but this time he didn't want to be found. Whatever was making its way through the shadows frightened Charlie more than any-thing had ever frightened him before. He began to run for his life—and he didn't stop until he stumbled across an old belfry.

The stone bell tower was at least three stories high. Doz-ens of screeching bats circled a hole where the building's bell should have been, and dense black smoke spewed from one of the windows below. A woman knelt near the building's wall, tending a tiny patch of garden. She was dressed in black, her hair hidden beneath a dark scarf. As Charlie drew closer, he could see mushrooms of every size and description sprouting out of the soil. Charlie recognized puffballs and death caps and the red-and-white toadstools that always pop up in fairy tales. And he remembered that his mother had once warned him that the prettiest mushrooms were often the deadliest.

Something was wrong. Charlie's mouth went dry and his spine began to tingle. He knew he was teetering on the edge of a trap. But he couldn't bring himself to return to the forest. The woman in black might have been bad. But whatever was looking for him in the woods was worse.

"There you are!" The woman's head swiveled around unnaturally. Her face was as green as one of Charlotte's spinach smoothies. And where the woman's eyes should have been, there were two quarter-sized mirrors. "Took your sweet time, didn't you? I've been waiting ages for you to show up!"

"Wh-who are you?" Charlie sputtered. "How do you know me?"

If the witch really had been waiting for Charlie, she already knew what she wanted to do to him.

The witch held out a hand. "I'm your nightmare. Well,

one of them, anyway. You're going to be spending a lot of time here with me."

Charlie had never felt so confused. "Where am I? What is this place?" He was sure he was dreaming, but it all felt real. There was still a stitch in his side and sweat on his brow. He could hear his lungs wheezing and smell the putrid smoke drifting out of the building.

"My kind calls it the Netherworld. But soon, Charlie Laird, you're going to be calling it *home*."

Charlie turned and bolted back through the trees.

"Don't you know those woods are haunted?" the witch screeched. "You're much better off here with me!"

When Charlie had woken from that dream, he'd felt as if he'd been running for hours. His legs were sore and his lungs tight. The pajamas he'd worn to bed were soaked through with sweat. The fear had stayed with him the entire day. He flinched at loud noises. His heart pounded when he glanced out a window and saw the trees in the distance. The fear made Charlie feel helpless, and that made him angry. The darkness inside him began to swell. Over time, things had only gotten worse. Now when he woke, Charlie often peered out his window at the gloomy, cloud-covered sky and wondered if the witch had found a way to trap him in her world. He told himself it wasn't possible.

But the truth was, he wasn't sure of anything anymore. The only thing Charlie knew for certain was that he'd gotten himself into a whole lot of trouble.

"Looks like you've worked up quite an appetite, Captain," Charlotte joked. "Must be hard work protecting the nation."

The miniature superhero was sitting at the kitchen table, shoveling scrambled eggs and green pancakes into his mouth.

"What did she put in those things?" Charlie asked Jack, pointing at the pancakes.

"*She* just added a little kale," Charlotte replied. "*She* swears they aren't going to kill you."

"Kale, quinoa, couscous? Can't we just have bacon like the rest of the world?" Charlie grumbled under his breath.

"Kale is *delicious*," Jack said with his mouth full.

"And you're way too old to wear a costume to school," Charlie muttered as he pulled out a chair next to his brother. He knew they'd all say he was picking a fight. Maybe it was true. But being angry felt better than being scared.

Charlie was about to sit when he heard a hiss. Aggie the cat was curled up on the seat of his chair. He shoved her off, and she raked her claws down his jeans leg before she stalked away.

"Well, good morning, sunshine!" the boys' father said

cheerfully through the bushy brown beard he'd been cultivating over the last year. Charlie *despised* it. It didn't fit with his dad's chunky black glasses—and it made him seem like a whole different person. "You certainly woke up in a wonderful mood again!"

"I'm serious. Jack can't go to school like that," Charlie said, unable to stop himself. He'd already been teased enough, thanks to Charlotte. The last thing he wanted was another freak in the family. "It's embarrassing. He's not in kindergarten anymore. He's in the third grade!"

"But Cypress Creek Elementary *needs* Captain America!" Charlotte trilled as she placed a heaping plate of

green pancakes on the table in front of Charlie. "Who else is going to punish the wicked and defend the innocent?"

"Yeah!" Jack exclaimed from behind his mask. "What *she* said!"

Charlie glared at his stepmother. But before he could tell her to butt out, his father jumped in.

"What's the matter, Charlie?" Andrew Laird asked gently, though Charlie could hear the frustration in his voice. "You're mean and grumpy, and you look like you haven't slept in weeks. Have you been staying up all night playing video games?"

Charlie caught Charlotte's eyes across the room. She hadn't told his father about their midnight chat, which was weird. Usually he couldn't even belch in the stepmonster's presence without Andrew Laird finding out about it. There had to be a reason she hadn't said anything this time.

"No," Charlie said. He didn't point out that the question was ridiculous. His video games had never been unpacked. He shoved a forkful of pancakes into his mouth. They tasted like grass, but he forced himself to chew.

"Are you *sure*?" His dad didn't believe him. He never did anymore.

"Give him a break, hon," Charlotte said in a voice so sappy and sweet that it almost made Charlie gag. "His video games are still in their boxes."

Jack pulled a black binder out from under the table. "Well, I've got something that will cheer Charlie up!"

He banged the binder down on the table, nearly knocking over the juice jug.

"What is it?" Charlie asked.

"Some kind of story!" Jack announced. "I found it on the counter when I got downstairs this morning."

There was a crash at the sink behind them where Charlotte had been rinsing dishes. "That binder is mine!" she exclaimed, and Charlie wondered if it might be the thing she'd rushed upstairs to get the night before. "It's something I've been working on. Please don't mess with it," she begged. "It's not ready to be read yet. I was just going to . . ."

"Hey, look at this." Jack kept talking while Charlotte searched frantically for a dish towel to dry her hands. The binder was already open, and he was thumbing through the pages. Charlie watched as illustrations flashed by. They reminded Charlie of the picture he'd spotted on Charlotte's desk the day she'd taken him upstairs to the tower. Most of the drawings in the binder were of hideous creatures—monsters and mummies and a man with snakes slithering out from beneath his hat. It seemed the only humans Charlotte had drawn were a pair of young girls—one with blond hair and the other with red. "Isn't this cool?" Jack asked.

"Yeah, cool," Charlie grumbled, turning his eyes back to his breakfast. But his curiosity was piqued. What kind of weirdo spent her free time sketching pictures of monsters and freaks?

"So what's the story about?" Jack asked Charlotte as she took the binder out of his hands. "Can I read it? Can I? Please, please, please?"

"Maybe." Charlotte slid the binder under her arm. "When I'm done."

Why didn't she want Jack to read it? Charlie wondered. Suddenly he was dying for a look. But he wouldn't let Charlotte see he was interested. He'd sneak a peek later when nobody else was around.

"If the story's as good as the pictures, you're gonna be famous," Jack declared earnestly. "Do you think I could get your autograph?"

"You can have more than an autograph." Charlotte grabbed the boy and smothered him with a hug. "You're so cute, I could eat you up."

Charlie gritted his teeth to keep the darkness from spilling out. *What a fake.* It was mean to mess with a little kid like that. Jack could barely remember their mom. He didn't know that Charlotte's love wasn't the real thing.

"I'm not *cute*! I'm a superhero!" Jack protested, but he didn't even try to wriggle away.

Charlie could taste his pancakes coming back up. They were even worse the second time around. When he looked up, he found his father glowering at him.

"Something wrong with the food?" his dad asked. The cheerful fellow who'd welcomed him to breakfast was long gone.

"It tastes like something she found in a cow pasture," Charlie answered.

"Hop up and help me take out the garbage before I drive you to school," said Charlie's father. His meaning was clear: he was demanding a private chat.

"What garbage? The bag in the can is barely half full," Charlie pointed out, just to be difficult.

"Get up and grab it." His father meant business. "I'll open the door for you."

Charlie pulled the trash bag from its can and headed out the door. He threw the bag into the outside bin and wheeled the bin down to the curb. When he had finished with the pointless chore, he turned back toward the house, only to find his father blocking his path. The new beard made his dad look like Paul Bunyan, Charlie thought. All he needed now was a flannel shirt and an ox. A year ago, Charlie might have joked about it. And a year ago, his dad would have laughed.

"What's bothering you today, Charlie?" Andrew Laird asked, sounding like he actually cared. "Whatever it is, you can tell me."

For a brief moment, Charlie wondered if his old dad had returned. The dad who would take him on long walks just to talk. The dad who was always there when he felt scared and alone. The dad he missed more than he could possibly say. Charlie stared at his feet. He wanted to tell his father about the nightmares. He was searching for the right words when his father spoke again.

"Look, I can see you're upset," he said sternly, "but I'm afraid I can't let you behave like this to your family."

The tone of his father's voice made Charlie's hopes crumble. His old dad was gone, and it didn't seem like he'd be coming back. "Charlotte isn't my family," he argued. "I'm not the one who married her."

"No, *I* did," Charlie's dad answered. "And that makes her your stepmother. You know, it hurts Charlotte when you're mean to her. She tries not to show it, but it does."

Charlie kicked at a clump of grass in frustration. "How do you know she gets hurt? Admit it, Dad—you don't really know anything about her! You met Charlotte a *year* ago. And did you see all those crazy pictures she draws? The woman's a wacko. Her pancakes are green, Dad. *Green!* In a few years when you find out she's an axe murderer, you'll look back at those green pancakes and think, *I should have known then!*"

Charlie's dad took off his glasses and wearily rubbed his eyes. "You've got to be kidding."

"How could you fall for someone you barely know?" Charlie argued. "I bet she's been putting some kind of love

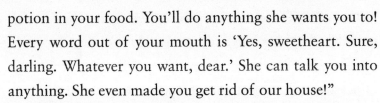

potion in your food. You'll do anything she wants you to! Every word out of your mouth is 'Yes, sweetheart. Sure, darling. Whatever you want, dear.' She can talk you into anything. She even made you get rid of our house!"

"We only needed one place to live, Charlie," his dad explained patiently. "And this house means a lot to Charlotte. It's been passed down in her family for almost two hundred years. I couldn't ask her to sell it."

"Well, *our* house meant a lot to me," Charlie said. Sometimes he'd been able to close his eyes and pretend his mom was still there. "But I guess that didn't matter as much."

Andrew Laird seemed to crumple a little. "I'm sorry, Charlie. I guess I didn't realize you were so attached to the old place. But that's not the real problem, is it?"

Charlie's lips didn't budge. The answer should have been obvious.

"Come on, Charlie," his father said gently. "Work with me here, will you?"

"You don't even remember her, do you?" Charlie could feel the tears welling up in his eyes. "Because Charlotte DeChant made you forget."

Andrew Laird took his son by the shoulders and bent down to look him in the eye. "Nobody's ever going to make me forget your mom, Charlie. I miss her as much as I ever did. But it's not fair to blame Charlotte for everything.

I don't understand what you have against her. Jack gets along with her just fine."

"Jack doesn't know any better. He's *eight*," Charlie said, twisting out of his father's grip.

"That's right," Andrew Laird said, standing up and lowering his voice a few notches. "He's *eight*. And that means he needs a mother."

"So did I. But when *I* was eight, my mom died."

Andrew Laird stared down at the ground and ran a hand through his hair. "I know the past few years have been hard for you. They've been hard for all of us. But Charlotte's not to blame."

"So I guess what you're trying to say is that you're on *her* side now?"

"There are no sides here," his father said with a sigh. "It's been three years, Charlie. You have to find a way to say goodbye to your mom. You know that's what she would want you to do."

"No." There was nothing more to say. "I'll never let Mom go."

"Well, if you're not ready to be a part of this new family, there's nothing I can do about it," his father said. "But while you live here with the rest of us, you'll do your best to be pleasant. And that means you need to stop picking fights with Jack and Charlotte. Be as miserable as you want, but please . . . let them have fun."

❧ CHAPTER SIX ❧

TIMES OF TROUBLE

It was eight o'clock in the morning, but the sun was still nowhere to be seen. Thick layers of dreary gray clouds hovered over Cypress Creek. They hadn't moved an inch in weeks. Charlie sat in the backseat of his dad's Jeep, trying to remember the last real sunny day.

"Look what I've got!" Jack said softly, tugging on Charlie's sleeve. "It's one of Charlotte's pictures." He had unfolded a sheet of paper and was holding it up for his brother to see. But Charlie wasn't interested. Their dad was driving past the house they'd all lived in when Charlie's mom was alive. It looked exactly like it had the day the

Lairds moved out. The front door suddenly swung open, and for a moment, Charlie expected to see his mom step onto the porch. Then two happy little kids rushed outside with their own mother trailing behind them.

"It's a drawing of the mansion, and there are words on the back of it too!" Jack whispered.

"What?" Charlie asked. He turned his attention to his little brother, who was still dressed in the handmade superhero costume. "Can you at least take off the mask?" he begged under his breath, hoping his dad wouldn't hear. They'd arrive at school in a few short minutes.

"They won't know I'm Captain America without a mask," Jack argued.

"They won't think you're Captain America *with* it!" This time, Charlie didn't bother to whisper. No one could get under his skin like Jack.

"Says who?"

"Says everyone who knows that Captain America is over four feet tall. You are not getting out of the car with that mask on!"

"And you're not the boss of me, Charlie!" Jack yelled back. "Dad is."

"That's right!" came the announcement from the driver's seat. "And in my car, nobody messes with Captain America! Leave the family superhero alone."

Maybe I'll leave you all *alone*, Charlie thought as the

school rolled into sight. As soon as the car came to a stop, he got out and took off without saying goodbye. He was halfway to the front entrance before Jack caught up with him.

Cypress Creek Elementary was a four-story brick box with big square windows. The whole building looked like it might have been made of Legos. At eight a.m., the sidewalk out front was packed with kids of all shapes and sizes. There were eighth-grade basketball players who already towered over the teachers—and first graders so tiny that they could have been bussed in from Whoville. For Charlie, it was a relief to slide out of the car and blend in among the crowd.

"Hey, Laird, wait up!"

Charlie whipped around and saw his friend Rocco Marquez waving at him from the front passenger seat of his mom's car. Rocco was the tallest kid in the seventh grade and the best athlete in the entire school. Girls scribbled his name on their notebooks and whispered that he looked like a movie star with his glossy black hair and olive complexion. Wherever Rocco went, eyes followed. He'd hopped out of the car and was headed in Charlie's direction. Which meant Charlie needed to ditch Captain America.

"Go to class, Jack," Charlie ordered his brother.

"Why?" Jack stood his ground. "What if I want to show Rocco my costume?"

"Don't be a dork," Charlie hissed. He hated how horrible he sounded, but it was the only way to make Jack listen. "Get lost."

Jack's face might have been hidden behind a mask, but his padded shoulders slumped and his eyes lost their sparkle. Charlie could see that his brother was hurt. "Why are you so mean?" Jack asked softly.

"Why are you so embarrassing?"

This time Jack didn't say a word. He just hung his head and shuffled away.

"Hey, little Laird," Rocco said cheerfully as the boy passed by. "Awesome mask."

"Thanks" was Jack's sad, muffled response.

"Geez, Charlie. What'd you do to the kid?" Rocco asked.

"Nothing," Charlie insisted, but he couldn't help feeling ashamed of himself. When his mother was in the hospital, he'd solemnly promised her he'd take care of his brother. *The two of you need to stick together,* she'd said. *Never forget that in times of trouble, two will always be stronger than one.* Back then, Charlie hadn't really understood what she meant. The worst trouble he could imagine involved failed tests or bike wrecks. Now he was starting to realize just how bad things could get.

"D'you think I'm too mean to Jack?" he asked his friend.

"Absolutely," Rocco confirmed. Then he grinned. "But that's kinda your job, isn't it? He's your little brother—who else is going to toughen him up? I mean, *my* big brother used to take my underwear and . . ."

Rocco's voice trailed off as a shadow fell over them.

"Gentlemen," barked a deep voice. "It's time to cut the chitchat and get to class." Principal Stearns was new at Cypress Creek Elementary. He'd appeared a few months earlier, at the end of Christmas break. The students had been herded into the auditorium one morning, where they were informed that the principal they'd known for years, a kind woman who kept sugarless candy in her suit pockets, had accepted a job at another school. Her replacement was a giant man with a no-nonsense haircut, the posture of Frankenstein's monster, and the personality of a prison guard. Charlie had grown half an inch since winter break, and yet Principal Stearns seemed even bigger than he had back in January.

Nobody at Cypress Creek Elementary knew where the new principal had come from—or where he went every night. The kids gossiped that the man was the first to arrive at school in the morning, and he was nowhere to be found when the last bell rang in the afternoon. Charlie knew the principal lived somewhere in his neighborhood. Twice he'd spotted him marching down nearby streets. But he couldn't imagine any of the prim little houses that surrounded the mansion being home to someone like him. Actually, Charlie couldn't imagine where someone like Principal Stearns would live at all. Except possibly the mansion itself.

"Don't stand there gawking," Principal Stearns sneered. "Get a move on, you two."

"Yes, sir," Rocco answered. He could tackle football players twice his width, and he'd won the schoolwide arm-wrestling competition in the fifth grade, but his courage deserted him whenever the new principal was around.

"Oh, and Mr. Marquez?" the principal called out as Charlie and his friend started for the school.

Rocco took a deep breath and turned back. "Yes, sir?"

"Make sure you pay close attention in class today." Principal Stearns clapped one beefy hand on Rocco's shoulder. "If your grades don't shape up soon, your parents are going to end up on my speed dial. Now off you go."

"Speed dial?" Charlie whispered as he and Rocco jogged away from the principal and toward the doors. "What was he talking about?"

"Principal Stearns called my mom at work yesterday. To tell her I failed a test."

"Another one?" Charlie was surprised. Rocco had never been the best student, but he wasn't exactly the school dunce either.

"Yeah, I don't know what's wrong with me!" Rocco said

with a helpless shrug. "I'm not getting enough rest, I guess. I just can't seem to focus on anything anymore."

Charlie tried to commiserate, but couldn't stop himself from yawning. He hadn't slept more than a few hours a night in weeks.

Rocco snorted. "Gee, thanks for caring."

"Sorry. I'm just exhausted."

Rocco scanned Charlie's face. "Wow. I'm tired, too, but with bags like that under your eyes I'm surprised you can even stand up straight. I can tell you right now, Laird. There's no way you're ever going to make it through science class."

Charlie stared at the blackboard. The word *GRAVITY* refused to stay in focus. It blurred and faded and disappeared for several seconds. He pinched himself hard for the umpteenth time and tried to train his eyes on Mrs. Webber, a tiny woman with gray curls that sprang in every direction like they were desperate to escape from her skull. For some reason Charlie couldn't remember, the teacher appeared to be holding a Styrofoam ball painted to look like Jupiter.

"Which student can remind me who discovered gravity?"

"*Oooh! Oooh! Oooh!* I know!" called an eager voice from the back of the room. Charlie knew without looking that it belonged to Alfie Bluenthal, class genius and one of Charlie's three best friends. Charlie glanced over his shoulder. Seated in pairs at wooden lab tables, the other kids were all twisted around in their seats, watching Alfie bounce up and down in his blue plastic chair like a bespectacled toad. One girl snickered. Another rolled her eyes. To the kids in class, Alfie was just a know-it-all nerd. They never saw his other side. Having a genius as a friend could come in handy, but it wasn't Alfie's IQ that made him special. You could tell Alfie anything, even your most embarrassing secrets. He never laughed—and you could always be sure that he'd never tell a soul.

"Yes?" Mrs. Webber sighed. "Alfie? Who discovered gravity?"

"Isaac Newton. Though he really didn't *discover*—"

"Excellent! Thank you, Alfie." Mrs. Webber was quick to cut him off. Given the chance, Alfie had been known to take over her lectures. "Now let's get a bit tougher. Which planet in our solar system has the strongest gravitational field?"

"Oooh! Oooh! Oooh!"

"Anyone *besides* Alfie? What about you, Charles? Want to take a shot at the answer?"

Charlie's head had been sinking slowly toward the table. Hearing his name jolted him awake. He lifted his gaze to find that Mrs. Webber had pulled down a map of the solar system, and its blazing orange sun looked hot enough to set her curls on fire.

"What?" His brain was refusing to work.

Mrs. Webber blew her nose into a hankie, as she always did when she was annoyed. "Which planet has the strongest gravitational field?"

Charlie gaped at her. He was so tired that he couldn't even remember the name of the planet he was *on*.

"Have you been listening?"

"Yes, ma'am."

"Well, then who discovered gravity?"

He rummaged around in his head in search of the answer but came up empty. He looked over at the girl in the seat beside him. His lab partner was tiny, blond, and as dainty as a music-box ballerina. Her name was Paige Bretter, and she, Alfie, Rocco, and Charlie had been best friends since kindergarten. Now that they were in the seventh grade, they had absolutely nothing in common except loyalty to each other. Some kids might have thought it was weird to see Rocco hanging out with Alfie—or to see pink-loving Paige spending time with a bunch of boys. But to Charlie and his crew, nothing could have felt more natural. It was as if they'd all been born to be friends.

As usual, Paige had been doodling in her sketch pad. She never took notes, but the teachers didn't mind since she always managed to get straight As. When Charlie caught her eye, she turned her latest picture around so that he could see it. It showed a man with long hair being hit on the head by an apple. *Applehead?* Charlie knew that couldn't be right.

"He just said it," Paige whispered, nodding toward the back of the room.

Charlie gave Paige a little shrug.

"Charles!" Mrs. Webber had finally run out of patience. "Do you know the name of the person who discovered gravity?"

Again, Charlie looked at Paige in desperation. Raising her book to hide her hand, she pointed at Alfie, who had just blurted out the answer seconds before. Charlie nodded gratefully.

"Was it Alfie?" Charlie answered.

The entire class exploded with laughter, but Charlie wanted to crawl under the table. It was only second period and he was already pretty sure that the day couldn't possibly get any worse.

Then, amid all the giggles and guffaws, Charlie thought he heard a cackle. His nostrils caught the faint stench of decay. And for a second, he felt himself swaying while the world stayed still—like he was trapped in a cage that was gently swinging from side to side.

꩜ CHAPTER SEVEN ꩜

NOWHERE TO HIDE

When the bell finally rang, Charlie didn't budge. He was too exhausted to move.

"Hey—you all right?" Paige whispered, her brow creased with worry.

He wasn't all right. Far from it, in fact. But Charlie still managed to nod.

"Then get up," Paige urged, "or we'll both be late for PE."

Alfie and Rocco were waiting in the hall. All around them, chattering seventh and eighth graders vanished into classrooms. Then the last blue locker was slammed shut, and the four friends were alone.

"Geez, Charlie," Rocco said as they rushed for the gym. "You look like a zombie."

"You need to get more rest," Alfie said. "Do you know what sleep deprivation can do to you? There was a study conducted at Harvard last year, and they discovered that chimpanzees that stay up all night watching television—"

"Do I *look* like a monkey to you?" Charlie snapped, and everyone's eyes went wide.

"Oookay, Charlie Laird!" Paige snatched the back of Charlie's shirt, bringing him to an abrupt halt. Charlie tried to wriggle away, but Paige had him firmly in her grip.

"You guys run ahead," she ordered Alfie and Rocco. "I need to have a chat with our grumpy little friend here."

"Make sure to tell him that chimps aren't *monkeys,*" Alfie muttered. "They're *apes.*"

Alfie could be such a nerd. "Yeah, and you know what *apes* do to people who mess with them? They fling a big pile of their—"

Paige clamped a hand over Charlie's mouth before he could finish. "Whoa, whoa, whoa," she repeated as Rocco and Alfie disappeared down the hall. "Take it easy, there, Charlie. And don't even *think* about saying anything mean to *me.*"

Charlie knew he wouldn't. No matter how bad things

got—or how horrible he felt. Paige could be bossy and annoying, but he owed her too much to ever be mean to her. For months after his mom died, Paige showed up at Charlie's door every day after school. She didn't want him to talk or expect him to go outside. She just kept him company. And having her there had made all the difference.

"We good?" she asked.

Charlie nodded mutely.

"Alfie's right, you know. This is getting serious. Why aren't you sleeping at night?"

Paige slid her hand away from his mouth, but Charlie had already forgotten the question. The route to the gym had led them past the library. The door was wide open, and a group of third graders were sitting on a rainbow-colored rug in the middle of the cluttered room. The boys and girls were all perfectly still. Even Hans and Franz, the librarian's two white rabbits, seemed to be listening from their cage.

Charlie followed the sound of his brother's voice and spotted Jack nestled at the center of the group, reading loudly from a piece of paper. On the other side was the picture that Charlotte had drawn and Jack had stolen. No one—not even Mrs. Russell, the strict head librarian—seemed to care that Charlie's eight-year-old brother was dressed up like Captain America.

"At night," Jack read . . .

*". . . the tower room was never completely dark.
Instead, it was perfect for shadows, which need
a little light to live. Every evening, the moon
and the stars shone through the window and
drew shapes on the wall. Lottie had been with
her grandmother for less than a week when she
thought she saw one of the shadows move."*

Paige stood on her tiptoes and peered over Charlie's shoulder. Her shampoo always made her hair smell like strawberries. The fragrance had never affected Charlie before, but now it left him feeling a little light-headed. "What's he reading?"

"Who knows," Charlie said, annoyed once more. It had to be part of Charlotte's story. Did the stepmonster have to follow him *everywhere* he went?

In the background, Jack was still reading.

*". . . when our nights become battles and our days
    become dreary,
When our eyes grow all saggy and droopy and
    teary,
The time then has come to stand up to our fears.
Come, nightmares, we dare you to fight us RIGHT
    HERE!!!"*

"Well, everyone seems to be into it," Paige said. "And look at Jack—he's the star of the show. Love the costume too."

Charlie grunted, but he had to admit that Jack did look pretty thrilled. And somewhere, deep down inside, he was glad to see that his little brother had recovered from their morning argument.

The Swiss Army watch on Paige's wrist started to beep. "We have exactly twenty-nine seconds to get to class," Paige announced. "But don't think you're off the hook, Charlie Laird. After PE, you to have to explain what's going on with you these days."

"Must have something to do with the weather," Charlie muttered as they headed off toward the gym.

"Wouldn't be surprised," Paige sighed. "Every morning, the weatherman swears it's going to be bright and sunny, but then it's nothing but drizzle for the rest of the day."

It was almost too dark to see the dirty soccer ball, and a light rain had turned the field to mud, but Coach Kim believed that bad weather built character. His PE classes were held outside most days of the year, rain or shine.

Paige, Alfie, Rocco, and Charlie stood shivering on the sidelines of the soccer field while a bunch of their classmates positioned the portable goalposts.

"Okay, here's the plan, Laird," Rocco said as soon as he was sure the coach wasn't looking. "I'll distract Coach Kim while you run across to the little-kid playground. That tunnel in the obstacle course should be long enough for you to lie down inside. Get a good nap. You definitely need one. And the rest of us need you to have one too."

Charlie couldn't fight sleep any longer, and a quick nap couldn't do that much harm. His stomach might have churned at the thought, but the rest of him was willing to take the risk.

"You guys are the best," he said.

"Just make sure you set your alarm," Paige reminded Charlie as Rocco jogged out onto the field. "Five minutes before class ends—or you'll get left behind."

"If anyone heads in your direction, I'll warn you by shouting *en garde*!" Alfie offered, and everyone groaned. Fencing was the only contact sport Alfie's parents allowed him to play. For years, he'd been trying to make it seem cool.

"I think *goal* might work better at a soccer match," Paige suggested, trying to keep a straight face. "Looks like Rocco's got the ball—you're good to go, Charlie."

Rocco was dribbling the ball across the field, with all eyes glued to him. Even the kids who usually showed no interest in sports were always eager to witness one of Rocco's spectacular goals. Coach Kim was in charge of the Cypress Creek soccer team, so he paid more attention than even most of the kids. While the teacher's eyes followed the school's star athlete, Charlie took off toward the little kids' side of the schoolyard. The playground equipment hadn't been used since the weather turned bad. The brown plastic tunnel designed to look like a log was in the center of a child-sized obstacle course, between the monkey bars and the balance beam. It might not have been the warmest, softest, or cleanest place for a nap, but desperate times called for desperate measures. And if Coach Kim couldn't find him there, then maybe the witch couldn't either.

Yet Charlie had barely laid his head down when the walls of the tunnel melted away and a cackle made him leap to his feet.

"Charlie Laird! How kind of you to drop by for an afternoon visit!"

Charlie spun around. He was back at the belfry—this time in a parlor. He couldn't bring himself to call it a *living* room, since almost all of the creatures in it were dead. There were rats wrapped in blankets of spiderwebs and insect carcasses littering the floor. The witch stood by the room's only window, where she'd been watering a box filled with Venus flytraps. One of the meat-eating plants was struggling to consume something quite large. Something that appeared to be *wriggling*.

"Excuse me while I finish my gardening," the witch

said, returning to her plants. "I thought it was best to feed them before I set off on my trip."

"Your trip?" Charlie asked, though he knew he didn't want to hear the answer.

"You've forgotten already?" the witch snapped. "I'm paying you a visit at home tonight!"

He was so tired. As much as Charlie hated the witch, he didn't have the strength to fight anymore. He slumped down into a tattered armchair. A cloud of dust swirled around him as he put his head in his hands. "Why can't you just leave me alone?" he groaned.

The witch set down her watering can and stuck her lower lip out to mock him. "That's exactly where I plan to leave you. *All alone* in your cage."

"But *why*?" Charlie asked. "What did I ever do to you?"

"I'm afraid you're in the way."

"In the way of *what*?" Charlie demanded.

"Everyone! Can't you see how much better off they'd all be without you?" the witch lectured him. "That's why you have to bring your body back to the Netherworld with me. It's your home now, Charlie. It's where you belong."

"I'm not going to live in a cage in your house," Charlie told her, wishing his voice were less squeaky. He sounded like a little kid. He could see his reflection in the witch's mirrored eyes, and he looked like a little kid too.

"You think I live here in a *belfry*?" the witch cackled. "This isn't my house. You built this whole place, from the dungeon up. You even gave yourself that cage with a *lovely* view of the forest. You wanted a place where you could sit and sulk and be perfectly safe. Because you know that as long as you stay in the cage, your worst nightmare can't find you."

Charlie shuddered. There was truth to what the witch said. He'd choose to suffer in the cage before he'd face the other nightmare—the one that was out there, searching the woods for him.

"That doesn't make any sense. I don't want to be here!" he insisted. "Why would I dream up a cage for myself?"

The witch shrugged. "Believe what you want, boy. All this arguing is starting to bore me. If you won't bring your body back tonight, that's fine by me. I've got my eye on a little human who won't be so hard to convince. And he'll make a delicious stew. The cat has already called dibs on the bones. She'll probably gnaw on them for days."

"Who are you going to eat?" Charlie demanded. He was starting to feel a bit nauseous. It was his fault that some other kid was about to be the witch's dinner.

"Awww, isn't that *sweet*!" the witch mocked him. "Charlie Laird, you almost sound *jealous*! Now, off you go!"

The witch's parlor began to fade.

"No, wait!" Charlie called out. Maybe if he could just figure out who . . .

"Charlie!" Someone was shaking him.

"Charlie!" whispered a second voice.

"MR. LAIRD!" a third person bellowed.

Charlie forced his eyes open. Alfie and Rocco were on their hands and knees inside the playground tunnel, and a pair of perfectly pressed pants was blocking the exit.

Principal Stearns's face appeared. Even though his head was upside down, his gelled hair was a perfect helmet. "Mr. Laird. Were you *sleeping* in there?"

"Uhhhh, yes?" There was no point in denying it. After

all, he had leaves in his hair and drool trickling down his chin. But Charlie knew it was best to say as little as possible.

The principal's lip curled into a nasty sneer. "Mr. Laird, what grade are you in?"

Charlie wiped the drool away with his sleeve. "Seventh."

"Naps ended in preschool, Mr. Laird. PE is for *exercise*. Just as science class is for *science*."

Mrs. Webber must have ratted him out, Charlie thought. Was *everyone* in Cypress Creek out to get him?

"Now climb out of the tunnel," Principal Stearns ordered, "and get to class immediately. And please—take your friends with you. If any of you is so much as five seconds late for next period, you'll be the lucky winner of a full week of detention."

"We won't be late, sir. We have lunch now," Alfie offered. "Our next class is almost an hour away."

Charlie winced. Sometimes Alfie didn't know when to stay quiet.

"Almost an hour—are you certain you can make it?" the principal inquired, a sinister smile on his lips. "I just had the honor of watching you play soccer, Mr. Bluenthal, and as slow as you are, I'm surprised you manage to arrive *anywhere* on time. Did your mother happen to marry a turtle?"

Charlie felt his jaw drop. Two years earlier, a group of

older kids had started calling Alfie "Turtle" after he had made the mistake of wearing a green turtleneck and brown backpack to school. Rocco and Charlie put an end to the teasing, but not before the damage was done. Alfie could barely stand to *look* at a turtle anymore.

Now Charlie knew he should come to his friend's defense, but as usual, Rocco got there first.

"Excuse me? You're an *adult*. You can't say stuff like . . . ," Rocco began.

The principal turned on Rocco. It had to be a trick of the light, but his eyes seemed to flash red for a moment. "I'm sorry, Mr. Marquez. Were you trying to tell me there's something I can't do?"

Just say no, Charlie pleaded silently.

Rocco wisely backed down. "No, sir."

"I'm glad. Because last time I checked, I could do anything I pleased. I can discipline my pupils however I see fit. I can even hold a child back a year. How much have you been enjoying the seventh grade, Mr. Marquez? Enough to go back for seconds next September?"

"No!" Rocco almost screamed.

"Then I suggest you shape up. All three of you. It's time you started taking school more seriously. Things are going to get a lot stricter around here very soon."

Charlie and his friends waited until the principal was

stomping off across the schoolyard. Only then did they slide out of the tunnel.

"Is it my imagination or does he just keep getting meaner?" Rocco asked.

"I'm not qualified to make psychiatric diagnoses, but I'd say he certainly displays symptoms of Sadistic Personality Disorder," Alfie noted. "I'll consult the DSM-IV when I get home."

"I have no clue what that means," Rocco said. "All I know is that Old Man Stearns is definitely out to make my life miserable. Looks like he might have his eye on Charlie now too."

As usual, everything was all Charlie's fault. "Sorry for getting you guys in trouble," he said, and sighed. Then he glanced up at the sky. It was almost dark enough to be night. "I must have forgotten to set my alarm."

"We figured," Rocco said. "Coach Kim noticed you weren't in the locker room with the rest of us, so he called the principal."

"We're sorry we didn't get to you quicker. Soon as the bell rang, we ran out to warn you," Alfie said.

"You wouldn't wake up, though," Rocco added. "I gotta say, it was getting a little weird."

"Yeah," Alfie agreed. "You kept muttering something about a witch. Were you having a nightmare?"

Charlie could feel his face flushing. "Something like that, I guess. . . ." He would rather have been caught picking his nose than whimpering in his sleep.

Rocco put his hand on Charlie's shoulder. "You're not the only person who has nightmares, you know," he said.

"I've had the same one for the past three nights," Alfie confessed, his voice almost a whisper. "I keep dreaming that I'm taking the physical fitness exam and I—"

The darkness rose so quickly that it took even Charlie by surprise. "Hold on. You dream about *fitness exams*?" he interrupted. He wanted to laugh at how easy that sounded. "I *wish* I had nightmares like that."

"Hey!" Alfie yelped. "You have no idea how scary those exams can be!"

"Scarier than a witch who wants to eat you?" Charlie countered.

"Charlie," Rocco butted in, "are these nightmares the reason you're always so tired?"

"And cantankerous?" Alfie added.

"What difference does it make?" Charlie realized with a jolt that he'd already said too much. "Why is everyone ganging up on me all of a sudden?"

"Ganging up on you?" scoffed Alfie. "Charlie, we almost got detention for you!"

Charlie bit his lip and tried to keep the darkness inside. "Sorry," he said.

"Look—you don't have to tell us what your dreams are about," Rocco said. "But you better think up a good excuse for napping on the playground. 'Cause if I know Principal Stearns, he'll be phoning your mom this afternoon."

"Charlotte is *not* my mom," Charlie almost yelled. The mention of the stepmonster only made his mood worse.

Rocco cracked a smile. "Then why does it bug you so much when I say she's hot?"

"Because it means that you're crazy," Charlie grumbled. "Charlotte DeChant is a witch."

CHAPTER EIGHT

MIDNIGHT SNACK

Nightmares aren't real. They can't come to get you. Charlie had spent the whole afternoon trying to convince himself. Soon he'd find out. It was only dinnertime, and Charlie was so tired that he was in danger of falling face-first into his soup. If it had been anything other than split pea, he might not have minded. He *hated* split pea soup. But Charlotte was a vegetarian, of course, and whenever she cooked dinner, the rest of them were too.

Charlie was lifting a spoonful of green mush to his mouth when the phone rang. It had to be Principal Stearns calling. Charlie groaned inwardly. He and his dad were already barely speaking; the last thing he needed was a lecture about falling asleep in school.

"Hello?" his father answered. Then his voice deepened, and his spine straightened. "Oh, good evening, Mrs. Russell."

Charlie sighed with relief. Mrs. Russell was the head librarian, and as far as he knew, he'd done nothing to offend her.

"*Really?*" Andrew Laird broke into a grin. "Is that right? Well, I believe it must have been my wife. . . . Yes . . . Yes . . . Yes . . . Well, I'm not sure she's ready for that, but I'll certainly pass along the compliment. Thank you so much for taking the time to call!"

Charlie's dad returned to the table, Aggie the cat weaving between his legs as he walked. He looked happier than he had all day.

"What was that all about?" Charlotte asked, looking oddly nervous.

Andrew Laird laughed and mussed the hair of his younger son. "Seems you've got an excellent publicist. Jack shared one of your pictures with his classmates in the library today."

"Jack?" Charlotte yelped, dropping her spoon in her bowl with a splash. "Why did you take my drawings to school?"

Why does it bother her so much? Charlie thought. *What is she trying to hide?*

Jack's cheeks blushed red. "I only took *one*," he admitted, pulling the piece of paper out of his back pocket and handing it to Charlotte. "I'm really sorry. It's just so good! I wanted to show everyone what my mom—I mean, stepmom—can do."

Mom. Charlie bit down on his spoon so hard that his teeth hurt. The word had the opposite effect on Charlotte. She still looked annoyed, but she leaned over and gave the small boy a squeeze.

"Don't do that again," Charlie heard her whisper in Jack's ear. "A little bit of knowledge can be a dangerous thing."

"Apparently, there was a story written on the back of the picture. Mrs. Russell said the kids all went crazy for it," Andrew Laird continued. "She says she might be able to hook you up with a publisher when you're ready."

"Wow. That's really, really *great*," Charlotte mumbled absentmindedly, wiping her soup splatter off the tablecloth.

Charlie kept his eyes trained on her face. Something was going on. He couldn't tell if she was upset or happy, but he knew how *he* felt.

"Aren't you thrilled?" Charlie's father asked, finally noticing his wife's discomfort.

"We're all *delighted*," Charlie snarled sarcastically under his breath, but just loud enough to reach his dad's ears.

"I'm glad to hear that." Andrew Laird swiveled in Charlie's direction. He wasn't smiling anymore. "By the way, that reminds me. Mrs. Russell's call wasn't the only one I received today. Principal Stearns phoned me at work to inform me that my elder son has been taking naps at school. Care to explain, Charles?"

The principal hadn't even waited until the end of the school day to get Charlie in trouble. The ogre really seemed to enjoy his job. Charlie would have liked nothing better than to give him a swift kick in the shins.

"I just took a nap during PE," Charlie told his father.

"And in science class too, apparently. Is there a reason you can't pay attention?"

Charlie's morning chat with his dad was still fresh in his mind. He didn't expect much sympathy. "I don't want to talk about it right now, okay?"

"Well, you better start talking soon. Principal Stearns wants you to see the school psychologist. He thinks if you aren't able to focus on your schoolwork, there's a chance you might have ADD."

Charlie's mouth fell open.

"What's a *dee dee*?" Jack asked.

Out of the corner of his eye, Charlie saw Charlotte's lips twitch.

The darkness erupted. "Don't you dare laugh at that!"

Charlie shouted. He could not keep it down. It spewed from his mouth like soda from a shaken can.

"I wasn't—" Charlotte started to say.

"Do *not* raise your voice to her!" Andrew Laird ordered.

"She's not my mother!" Unlike his dad's voice, which deepened with anger, Charlie's just got squeaky. He sounded like a little kid again. "I don't even like her!"

"*I* like her!" Jack jumped up and wrapped his arms around Charlotte.

"Shut up, Jack!" He wished he could drag them apart—then wipe the smirk off Charlotte's face.

"That's it, Charles Montgomery Laird." Charlie's father stood up from the table and pointed to the stairs. He'd finally cracked. "You will not behave like this anymore. What's wrong with you? What has turned you into such a monster?"

"It's this house," Charlie answered, looking directly at his stepmother. "It's all *her* fault. She's—"

His dad shook his head sadly and put his hand up, stopping Charlie before he could finish. "I think you need to go to your room," he said. He'd already chosen sides.

Just before he rushed upstairs, Charlie saw Charlotte's eyes turn upward. She seemed to be looking straight through the ceiling and into the tower above them.

An hour after sunset, Charlie was lying on his bed in the dark when there was a knock at the door. Instead of answering, he rolled over to face the wall.

The door cracked open and light from the hallway lit the room. "Where are all of your boxes?" It was Jack.

"They won't do any good," Charlie replied. There was no way to beat the witch. Even the school playground wasn't safe for sleeping.

"What do you mean?" Jack asked.

Charlie remembered that no one knew about the battle he waged every night. He was all alone. "It doesn't matter," he muttered.

He heard his brother cross the bedroom floor. Then the boy took a seat on the side of Charlie's bed.

"Have you been having bad dreams?" Jack asked quietly.

Charlie rolled over and crossed his arms. "Get out, Jack."

"Okay, but if you get too scared tonight, you should come sleep in my room."

In an instant, the darkness had disappeared, leaving behind only misery. Charlie remembered how things used to be when he didn't have to share his brother and father. Before Charlotte had come along, they'd been a team. Charlie had always believed that nothing could possibly come between them. Now he could see he'd been wrong.

Charlie felt the bed rise as the little boy got up.

"Jack?" he said softly.

"Yeah?"

"I'm sorry if I'm mean to you sometimes."

"It's all right," Jack told him. "Charlotte says it's because you're still sad."

Charlie buried his face in the pillow.

"She's really nice, you know," Jack said. "Here. I brought this for you to look at. Maybe it will help."

Charlie looked up to see what had been left on the pillow. It was a page from Charlotte's binder.

"You stole another drawing?" Charlie asked. "You're going to get in big trouble, Jack."

Jack shrugged. "That's okay. It's not a picture, anyway. It's some kind of poem. I don't know what it means. I thought it might help you. Maybe it's some kind of spell to keep bad things away. Want to hear it?"

Charlie nodded silently.

Jack picked up the page again. "Okay," he said, clearing his throat. "Here's how it goes. . . ."

"Monsters, witches, snakes, and demons
Who've come here for some terrible reason—
Whatever it is, I'll figure it out.
So I won't be scared. Instead, I'll shout:
Witches, monsters, demons, and snakes,
I'll fight you all for as long as it takes!

"Want me to say it again for you?"

"No thanks," Charlie said, and rolled back to face the wall. "I'm way too old for nursery rhymes."

"I know it sounds silly, but maybe it will help," Jack pleaded.

"Maybe," Charlie told him. "Thanks for trying."

Jack sighed, and a few seconds later, Charlie heard him leave the room.

As soon as his brother was gone, Charlie did the only thing he could do. If the boxes weren't able to keep the witch out of his room, he'd just have to hide. So he emptied one of his thirty-eight boxes and curled up inside. Then he closed his eyes. He'd lost the will to fight. He just waited for the nightmares to begin. But for the first night in ages, sleep simply refused to come. Charlie listened in the dark as his brother brushed his teeth and was tucked into bed by Charlotte. He heard his dad make his nightly rounds, locking doors and turning off lights. Afterward, the house was silent. Then the faint creaking of hinges reached Charlie's ears. He pulled his knees to his chest and held his breath, waiting to see what would happen next.

A floorboard groaned. A stair squeaked. Someone—or something—was creeping down the second-floor hall.

Charlie pinched himself hard. He wasn't asleep. For a moment, he was too terrified to move. As the footsteps drew closer, he realized there had to be more than one person outside.

"This is so exciting!" It was the witch's cat. "We're on the other side!"

Charlie pinched himself again—this time hard enough to leave no doubt. The witch had come while he was still one hundred percent awake. He heard his bedroom door open.

"Hmph! Well, where *is* he?" the cat asked. "Shall I check the closet?"

"There's no time for a scavenger hunt," the witch answered. "Come along, Agatha. Let's go ahead with plan B."

Agatha? The cat's name was Agatha? The intruders' steps grew quieter as they retreated; then Charlie heard the sound of whispering in the hallway. He climbed out of his box and tiptoed to the door, pressing his ear against it.

"I'm so glad it's plan B. I'm absolutely famished!" purred the cat. "Should we see if the neighbors have any pets? A poodle would make a *wonderful* appetizer."

Something worse than fear made Charlie rush to the hall. He found the witch with her hand on Jack's doorknob.

"What are you doing?" he asked. Then the horror crept over him like a million millipedes. The other kid—the one the witch said would be easy to catch—was Charlie's little brother.

"Look who it is," the witch said as she opened Jack's door. "It's Mr. All I Want Is to Be Left Alone."

"Wait!" Charlie whispered.

The witch pulled the door closed. "What?" she demanded.

Charlie could see himself in her eyes, looking small and frightened. He stood up straight and stuck out his chin. "You can't eat Jack."

"What do *you* care if we eat the boy?" the witch asked. "You don't like him much. He's always taking your stuff and embarrassing you in front of your friends. And what kind of dork wears a Captain America costume to school anyway?"

Charlie took a step toward the witch. As bad as the situation was, he wouldn't let anyone else call Jack a dork. "He's not a dork. He's just a kid. He may be a little weird, but he's still my brother."

"You say *brother*," the cat said, baring her fangs. "I say *delicious*."

Suddenly an idea popped into Charlie's head. "If I go with you now, will you promise to leave Jack alone?"

The witch regarded him through narrowed eyes. "You'll get in the cage?" she asked skeptically.

"Yes," Charlie said.

"You're ready to leave the Waking World forever?"

"Yes." Hearing his answer chilled Charlie to the bone. He could feel goose bumps breaking out all over his body.

Agatha stood on her hind legs and whispered in the witch's ear.

"Agatha doesn't want to go hungry tonight," the witch said. "After we put you in the cage, will you give her a few of your toes?"

Charlie gulped. He had a plan, but he was taking a *very* big risk. "Do I really have a choice?"

"No," the witch answered. "Don't worry, we'll start with the pinkie toe. Such a strange-looking thing! And such a stupid name."

"Fine," Charlie said, guiding them toward the bathroom. "Then let me grab my toothbrush and we can go."

"Toothbrush!" The witch cackled. "What are you going to do with a *toothbrush*?"

"Shhh!" Charlie froze outside the bathroom. He cupped a hand to his ear as if listening. "I think you just woke someone up! Quick, get inside!"

Charlie held the bathroom door open for the witch and her cat—and hoped they didn't spot the skeleton key sticking out of the antique door. Six months earlier, Jack had locked himself inside and shaved the stepmonster's cat. That was when Charlotte had moved the key to the *outside* lock.

With his nightmares inside, Charlie prepared to slam the door shut. He just needed to trap the witch in the bathroom long enough to get his dad out of bed. He went for the key, but it was no longer there.

"Thought you were going to trick me?" the witch asked with a nasty grin. She reached deep into her mouth and pulled a slimy skeleton key from her throat.

How had she known what Charlie was planning? His brain was too panicked to figure it out. Who'd told the witch about the key?

"No more deals, Charlie Laird," she told him. "We're taking the boy. And when he's nothing but bones, we'll come back to get you. Let's go, Agatha. I've had enough fun and games for one night."

"No!" Charlie hurled himself at the witch and threw his arms around her neck. "You can't have him!"

"Let go of me!" the witch screeched, spinning around while Charlie desperately clung to her robe. In the struggle, Charlie latched on to the witch's head, and her hat came off in his hand.

Bright red curls bounced around the witch's horrible green face.

"You're going to pay for that, Charlie," she sneered, picking him up and tossing him into the bathroom. The door closed and he heard the key turn in the lock.

"Let me out!" Charlie banged on the door. His little

brother's life depended on someone hearing him. "Dad! Dad! Wake up! Don't let them take Jack!"

"Charlie! What on earth is going on?"

He was still banging on the door when it suddenly swung open. Standing in the hall was Charlotte with Aggie the cat by her side.

"Charlie, it's okay!" she tried to calm him. "It's just me."

"Where's Jack? Did they kidnap him?"

"Jack's asleep, Charlie." A strange look came over Charlotte's face. "You were having a nightmare just now—weren't you?"

"No!" Charlie exclaimed with a vigorous shake of his head. He hadn't been asleep. That was the most horrible part—Charlie knew he'd been awake the whole time. His heart was pounding so hard that every beat seemed to shake his whole body.

"Then what are you doing . . ."

"The witch locked me in the bathroom. She said she was going to eat Jack!"

"A *witch*? Listen to me, Charlie." Charlotte reached out for him and her curly red hair fell into her face. "You have to tell me *exactly* what happened."

That was when Charlie realized that the witch had the same hair as Charlotte. And the same pointy nose. Aside from the green skin and mirrored eyes, the resemblance was uncanny. They looked enough alike to be sisters. Charlie retreated to the far corner of the linen closet, just out of his stepmother's reach.

It all made sense now. He'd never dreamed about witches until he moved to the mansion. Charlotte wanted Charlie out of the way—and the witch from his nightmares wanted him locked up in a cage. And the witch knew things—about Charlie's boxes and the key in the bathroom door—that she couldn't have known unless someone had told her. Then there were the secret potions the stepmonster kept hidden—and the bizarre pictures she drew in her lair. It confirmed what Charlie had known in his heart all along: Charlotte DeChant wasn't who she claimed to be. She looked like a witch. She acted like a witch. And now Charlie knew for sure. Charlotte DeChant *was* a witch.

"Get away from me!" Charlie gasped. He pushed her back, scrambled out of the closet, and sprinted down the hall.

When he reached Jack's door, he paused to check over his shoulder. The stepmonster was still standing in the dimly lit corridor.

"That's not your room, Charlie!" Charlotte whispered. She was a great actress, he thought. She actually looked worried.

"I won't let you have Jack," Charlie told her. Never in

his life had he felt so certain of anything. "I know what you are, and I'm going to prove it." Then he stepped inside and locked the door. He stood there with his back against it until he heard his stepmonster climb the steps to her lair. Then Charlie Laird, more terrified than he'd ever been, crawled into the bed with his little brother.

CHAPTER NINE

CARRIED AWAY

The stepmonster is a witch. Charlie's eyes followed Charlotte as she cooked breakfast for the second day in a row. He had so many questions, and he was dying for answers. Was she from this world or the Netherworld? Why would a witch want to marry his dad? Was that her real face or was it just a disguise? Did she ride a broomstick? Did she like to eat kids?

Charlotte spun around with two plates in her hands. For a moment their eyes met, and Charlie saw it. Charlotte's skin was a little paler than usual, and her hair still hadn't been tamed. It looked like she hadn't slept a wink. Charlotte DeChant was worried.

She should be, Charlie thought. He hadn't whispered a word to anyone. Not yet. Without solid proof, no one would ever believe Charlotte was a witch. Charlie didn't have the evidence he needed to kick her out of his family forever. But he'd get it.

"We really need to talk," Charlotte whispered in Charlie's ear as she bent over to serve him a beet-red waffle.

"No." Charlie shoved the plate to the center of the breakfast table, hopped out of his chair, and grabbed a banana instead.

Andrew Laird drove past the family's old house—just as he did every weekday morning. But this time Charlie didn't look—he was too busy devising a plan to keep Jack safe. He had considered running away, but there was nowhere to go. He'd called the police, only to have a cop hang up on him when he accidentally mentioned that a witch was involved. So for the time being, Charlie had no choice but to keep his own eyes on his little brother. Even if it meant watching him twenty-four hours a day.

"Come on, Charlie! Give me some room!" Jack

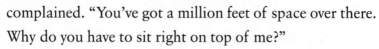

complained. "You've got a million feet of space over there. Why do you have to sit right on top of me?"

Charlie scooted one inch to the side. He didn't care if he was being annoying—there were lives at stake.

"Charlie? What's going on?" asked Andrew Laird, peering at the two boys in the rearview mirror.

Charlie reluctantly slid all the way across the car's backseat.

"You should let me carry that for you," he said, pointing at the book sitting in Jack's lap. One of Charlotte's drawings was tucked between its pages.

"No!" Jack yelped, clutching the book to his chest. "Leave me alone, Charlie! Dad!"

"Charles!" his dad warned from the driver's seat. "What on earth are you doing? I've gotten used to you being cranky—but I have to say, this is just *weird*."

Charlie looked out the window. He'd spent most of the night in his brother's room. At first, Jack had been happy to see him. But then Charlie had insisted on taking the chair next to Jack at breakfast. Later, he had guarded his brother's door while Jack got dressed. For a while, Jack had thought it was all a big joke, but by the time the two brothers set off for school, he was starting to seem a little scared.

"I'm going to be stuck at work until late," Charlie's father announced as the Laird family Jeep approached Cypress Creek Elementary. "Charlotte will pick you up after school today."

"Are you kidding?" Charlie started to argue. "I'm not going anywhere with that—"

"I was talking to *Jack*," their dad interrupted impatiently. "*You're* old enough to be home by yourself."

Charlie felt his fear building. "Jack has plans with me," he insisted. He couldn't allow the stepmonster to get Jack alone.

Andrew Laird was watching the fight in the mirror. "Whatever plans you two may have, consider them canceled," he said. "Jack is only allowed to leave school with *Charlotte*."

The car stopped in front of the school and Jack's hand instantly shot out for the door handle.

"Hold on and I'll walk you to class!" Charlie offered cheerfully.

"No!" Jack shouted, jumping out of the car and sprinting for the front entrance.

Charlie was halfway out of the Jeep when his dad turned to face him. "Stop right there!" Andrew Laird ordered, and Charlie reluctantly slid back inside. "Why on earth are you torturing your brother like this?"

"I'm not torturing him! I'm protecting him!" Charlie insisted, trying to keep his eyes on Jack as the boy made his way through the mob of kids.

"From *what*?" demanded his dad.

For a second, Charlie considered confessing, but he decided to keep his mouth shut. His dad was already on the stepmonster's side.

"*Fine*. Don't tell me," Andrew Laird said. "But listen up, Charles. There better be no funny business this afternoon when your stepmother comes to pick him up. You understand?"

"Perfectly," Charlie replied through clenched teeth.

Charlie ran toward the school, desperate to catch up

with his brother. Just through the doors, he spotted him. The little boy's back was pressed against a wall, and Principal Stearns was hovering over him. The ogre's face was stretched into a hideous smile, which meant something terrible was about to take place.

"Mrs. Russell informed me that you read your classmates a story yesterday," he heard the principal say to Jack. Charlie stopped short and instinctively dropped to one knee to eavesdrop. Kids of all sizes weaved around him as he pretended to tie his shoelace. As far as Charlie could tell, neither the principal nor his brother had spotted him.

"Sorry," Jack whispered, his voice trembling with terror.

"Don't be!" The principal's laugh was loud as thunder—and just as alarming. "I've heard the story was a big success. Your stepmother wrote it, is that correct?"

Charlie raised his head. He couldn't resist sneaking a peek. He'd never heard the principal be so pleasant to anyone.

"Yes," Jack said, and Charlie could hear the boy's confidence growing. "She can draw really well too."

"How wonderful," the principal replied. "Did you happen to bring any more of her stories with you to school today? Do you think I could take a look?"

"Charlotte says she's not ready to share," Jack told the man.

"Ah." Principal Stearns nodded. "And where do you suppose she might keep her work? Perhaps in a desk drawer—or on one of the shelves in the library downstairs?"

Charlie leaned to one side for a quick glimpse of his brother's face. Jack looked almost as confused as Charlie felt. "No idea," the little boy said with a shrug.

"That's all right," the principal said. "Can you tell me what she's been writing about?"

The principal was being way too nosy. It was time for the conversation to come to an end, Charlie decided. Whatever the man was up to, no good could come from it. Charlie should never have let the ogre get so close to his brother. He stood up and pushed his way through the crowd. "Her story's about a princess with horrible body odor," he said before Jack could answer. "She can't find anyone to marry her because she smells so bad. Then her fairy godmother finally tells her to take a bath. So she does. But it doesn't work. She still stinks. Really bad. And then she marries a guy with no nose."

"Mr. Laird." The principal scowled. "Were you eavesdropping?"

It took every bit of courage Charlie could muster to continue. "I'm just trying to save you from our stepmother's terrible writing."

"It's not terrible!" Jack argued. "And it's not about some stinky princess!"

Charlie rolled his eyes. "Have you read the whole thing? 'Cause *I* have. And let me tell you, it's offensive. Both to the stinky and to the noseless."

"Such a shame," said the principal. Then, in an instant, his smile vanished. He clearly had no more use for the two of them. "Excuse me, gentlemen, I have a school to run."

It worked! Charlie thought, giving himself an imaginary high five. As soon as the principal's back was turned, Charlie felt a sharp pain in his leg. Jack had kicked him.

"Oww!" Charlie yelped. He was trying his best to protect his brother, and he'd been kicked in the shin for his trouble.

"That was for being a jerk, Charlie," Jack growled. "I don't care if you're having bad dreams. It's no reason to be so mean. I don't want a brother like you anymore."

The words hurt more than the bruise growing on Charlie's leg. Charlie stared at his little brother. Jack didn't say things like that. No matter how mean Charlie was to him, Jack never fought ugly.

"Jack," Charlie started to explain, but the boy had disappeared into the stampede of kids heading for their classrooms.

Charlie didn't hear a word Mrs. Webber said during science. He was too busy trying to figure out how to save Jack.

"Pssst!"

Charlie looked over at his lab partner. Paige tapped a sheet of paper. *What's wrong with you?* it said.

Charlie grabbed the paper. Just as he started to write out his answer, the sheet was ripped out from under his pencil.

"No passing notes!" Mrs. Webber said. "Charlie Laird, see me after class."

And so it went for the rest of the day. Every time Charlie tried to tell his friends what was going on, someone seemed to be lurking nearby. Coach Kim stood beside Charlie throughout all of PE. Principal Stearns sat right behind their table at lunch.

It wasn't until two o'clock that Charlie managed to grab Paige as she brushed shoulders with him in the hall.

"When the last bell rings, get the others and meet me outside."

"Why?" Paige looked worried. "Are you in some kind of trouble?"

The principal was making his way toward the two of them. "There's no time to explain," Charlie said before sprinting away.

Throughout his last class, Charlie felt sick to his stomach. He couldn't do anything but stare at the minute hand on the clock above the teacher's desk. The moment the end-of-school bell finally rang, he was out of his seat. Two minutes later, Paige, Alfie, and Rocco burst through the front doors of the school and formed a circle around Charlie.

Charlie had just opened his mouth when Alfie pointed at a figure making its way toward the school.

"Is that your stepmom?"

"Hey, guys!" Charlotte waved to the group.

The stepmonster looked more normal than Charlie had ever seen her. She wasn't wearing anything black—just a white button-down shirt and a pair of jeans. There were no weird amulets around her neck, and her crazy red hair had been pulled back in a perfectly normal ponytail. She almost looked like she could have been one of his classmates' parents.

Charlie heard Rocco let loose a low whistle. "That's right. Come to Papa, Big Red," he said softly.

"You're revolting," Charlie told him. "And so is she."

Out of the corner of his eye, he saw Jack rush out of the school. His brother ran past him and his friends and straight into Charlotte's arms.

"Jack doesn't seem to think she's revolting," Rocco said under his breath. "Lucky kid."

"That's why he needs our help," Charlie said, hurrying in his brother's direction with his confused friends trailing behind him.

"Let's go," Jack said when he saw them all coming. Then he took the stepmonster's hand and tried to tug her toward the sidewalk.

"Come on, don't be like that," the stepmonster said. "Hey, Charlie, I'm taking Jack for ice cream. You and your friends want to come? It's on me, and everyone's invited—the more the merrier!"

"Don't tempt me with ice cream, Mrs. Laird," Alfie groaned, patting his ample belly. "I'm trying to get into shape. It's almost fencing season."

The darkness found its way to Charlie's heart, which pounded in protest. The sound grew so loud that it almost drowned everything out.

"We don't have time for ice cream," he told his friends. "We've got that *thing* to do, remember?"

"What *thing*?" Paige asked. Charlie shot her a warning look, and she caught on fast. "Oh, *that* thing. *Riiiiight*. I can't believe I almost forgot."

"Sorry, Mrs. Laird," Rocco said in his suavest voice. "We've got a *thing*. But maybe another time?"

"Sure! Whenever you like!" Charlotte responded with forced jolliness.

"Come on, guys," Charlie said. He grabbed his brother's arm. "You too, Jack."

"No," Jack said, pulling away. "I'm only supposed to leave with Charlotte."

The sky rumbled ominously, and a thick black cloud swallowed the dim afternoon sun.

"That's okay, Jack," Charlotte assured him. "I won't be upset if you walk home with your brother."

"No," Jack insisted, looking frightened. "I don't want to go with them. I want to go with *you*."

Charlie turned on Charlotte. She raised an eyebrow, as if warning him not to push it any further. "Well, that settles it, then!" the stepmonster announced. "Jack and I will get ice cream and we'll bring a carton home for you, Charlie. What flavor would you like?"

"I don't take ice cream from witches," Charlie snarled.

Jack's eyes nearly popped out of his head. "I heard that!" he yelled. "I'm going to call Dad right now and tell him what you just said to our stepmom!"

"Oh no, you *aren't*!" Charlotte said with one of her irritating cackles. She stooped down and hoisted the boy over her shoulder fireman-style. "We're not calling anyone. We're getting ice cream, remember? See you later, kids!"

"Jack!" Charlie shouted as Charlotte headed toward the sidewalk. "Don't go! We're supposed to stick together!" He tried to rush after them, but Rocco and Paige held him back.

"Stop, Charlie!" Paige hushed him. "You're in enough trouble already!"

Bouncing against Charlotte's back, Jack was laughing

too hard to respond. Charlie saw Charlotte turn right at the sidewalk. Then Alfie stepped in front of Charlie and blocked his view.

"What in the heck was all *that* about?" Alfie asked. But Charlie just shook his head in reply. He couldn't figure out where to begin.

"Okay, grab your books, guys," Paige ordered. "We're heading to the bunker!"

"There's not enough time!" Charlie insisted.

"We're going to the bunker," Rocco said. "You've gotta tell us what's going on, Charlie. How else are we going to help you?"

CHAPTER TEN

THE BUNKER

In the middle of the lawn that stretched out in front of the Cypress Creek library stood a gigantic pine. It was so tall that the previous December, when the tree was decorated with lights, Charlie had been able to see it from the mansion on DeChant Hill. The sight had been one of the few things that had given him comfort during the first Christmas he and his brother had been forced to spend with the stepmonster.

"Let's go," Paige ordered. She checked the sidewalk for passersby and then pulled one of the pine's low-hanging branches to the side. Charlie ducked and waddled toward the open space at the center by the trunk. The others followed until all four of them were sitting with their legs crossed, hidden from the world beneath the pine's broad branches.

This was the bunker. Whenever there was a problem that needed to be solved—or gossip that had to be shared—this was where the four would meet. It was secret, convenient, and close enough to the town library that they could tell their parents they were heading there and not actually be lying. To enter the bunker, you had to agree to two rules: You could speak nothing but the truth when you were under those branches. And nothing that was said there could ever be repeated. This was where the four friends had devised the plan that defeated Alfie's bullies. It was the place they had visited every afternoon for weeks after Paige's mom got so sad that she had to stay in a hospital. And it was where they'd come to study with Rocco when his dad threatened to take him off the basketball team unless his grades improved.

"Okay, spill it," Paige told Charlie. "What's going on?"

"I'll tell you, but you won't believe me," Charlie grumbled. The darkness now filled him from the tips of his toes to the top of his head. Things couldn't possibly get any worse. He'd just watched his little brother be carried away.

"How do you know?" Alfie challenged.

"I think Charlotte DeChant might be a witch," Charlie said.

His three friends traded glances.

"All right then, I'm *sure* she is!" Charlie insisted, his frustration growing. The longer Charlie waited to save Jack, the more likely his little brother would end up on a spit. "Look—ever since I moved into the purple house, I've been having horrible nightmares about a witch who wants to lock me up in a cage. I kept telling myself she isn't real.

But she *is*. And last night I found out that she and Charlotte are working together."

"You're having nightmares about your stepmother being a witch." Alfie looked relieved. "That seems perfectly normal to me."

"Except that Charlotte actually *is* a witch!" Charlie cried. "Think about it. She cooks up all sorts of weird potions that she won't sell in her shop—she keeps them in the tower. And she has a binder filled with horrible pictures she's drawn of monsters and freaks. And you've heard Charlotte laugh! A real human being can't make sounds that awful!"

No one said a word. Charlie knew what he said must have sounded insane. But these were his best friends in the world. Shouldn't they see he was telling the truth?

"I figured you wouldn't believe me." Charlie pulled his legs up to his chest and rested his head on his knees.

"It's not that I don't *believe* you," Alfie said diplomatically. "It's just that I don't know if I believe in witches. Do you really think your *stepmom* is a—"

"I believe you," Rocco declared.

Charlie lifted his head and saw Paige and Alfie staring at Rocco in surprise.

Rocco's glossy black hair hid much of his face as he used a twig to draw stick figures in the dirt. Art had never been Rocco's strong suit, and the doodles all looked like ogres with glaring eyes and a pointy haircut. "I've been having nightmares too," he said. "They started a few nights ago, and they're getting really bad. I haven't seen any witches, but the same guy is in all of my dreams. He wants to keep me in the seventh grade forever. In my dreams he's got a different name, but I'm pretty sure it's—"

"Principal Stearns!" Alfie gasped. "I keep dreaming about him too! He's the one who makes me take the physical fitness exam over and over again, and no matter how hard I try, I never pass!"

"Stearns is proof that monsters exist," Rocco said. "So why wouldn't I believe in Charlie's witches too?"

Shadows danced across the dirt floor of the bunker, and the air was heavy with the fragrance of pine.

"Okay, so we've all been having bad dreams," Alfie finally said. "But nightmares can't be *real*. According to the laws of physics—"

"I don't know a thing about physics. But I'm pretty sure nightmares are real," Charlie said. "The witch from my dreams told me that when you go to sleep, your spirit travels to a nightmare land. And if you're scared enough, your body can pass over to the other side too."

"The other side?" Paige asked.

"It's called the Netherworld," Charlie explained. "I don't know where it is—or how you get there. But the witch has figured out how to pass between the two worlds.

Last night she came to my house and tried to steal Jack. She wants to eat him. I think the stepmonster may be helping her."

"What?" Paige gasped.

"Whoa." Rocco looked stunned. "I'll buy that Charlotte might be a witch—but are you trying to say that that hot redhead likes to eat kids?"

"Who knows?" Charlie said. "Maybe that's why she moved to Cypress Creek in the first place. Maybe she ate up all the kids in her old town and came here looking for fresh meat."

His friends stared at him in silence.

"And now Charlotte's got to act fast 'cause I know what she is!" Charlie added. "That's why we have to find Jack right away."

Alfie whimpered and hugged himself tighter. "It makes no scientific sense whatsoever. But this is all getting really creepy."

"Your brother is alone with Charlotte right now?" Rocco asked. Charlie could see his friend was worried.

Paige frowned and twisted a strand of her hair the way she always did when she was trying to figure things out. "Let's not panic yet. Jack's probably fine," she said—though she didn't look completely convinced.

"Maybe," Charlie said. "But what if he's not?"

"There's a way to find out if Jack's in trouble," Rocco

said. He rose to his knees and brushed the pine needles from his pants and coat. "Surveillance mission."

"Good idea," Alfie said. "Charlotte said she was taking Jack for ice cream."

"There's only one place to buy ice cream in Cypress Creek," Paige pointed out.

"Yeah," Rocco said, "and it's two blocks from here."

The ice cream parlor next door to Hazel's Herbarium was a brightly lit vision in pink and light blue. Painted on its front window, pastel-colored teddy bears danced with double-scoop cones in their hands. The herb store beside it was decorated in black and several shades of green. Its window was filled with bizarre plants collecting the dim Cypress Creek sunlight. One shop was a little kid's fantasy. The other was straight out of a nightmare.

Charlie checked the line of cars parked along the street. Charlotte's old Range Rover wasn't among them.

"Her car isn't here. She must have taken Jack to the purple mansion. We need to go!" Charlie urged his friends.

"Just hang on for a second," Paige said. "We walked here. Maybe Jack and Charlotte did too."

Charlie almost stomped away. "We're wasting valuable time!" he argued. "She could be cooking my brother!"

"You guys hang tight. I swear I'll be fast," Rocco said.

Then he took off across the parking lot at maximum speed. He'd watched a million action movies, and he'd memorized all the moves. When he reached the ice cream parlor, Rocco flattened himself against the wall commando-style, then inched over to the glass window and peeked inside. After a moment he turned toward his friends and shook his head. Jack wasn't inside.

"Come back!" Charlie called, just as Rocco dropped to all fours and began to crawl toward the store next door.

"Shhhh!" Paige ordered.

"He's taking a look inside the herbarium," Alfie said.

Rocco cupped his hands together and peered between the plants in the herb shop's window. Then he frantically waved his friends over.

"I think I'm going to throw up," Charlie said.

When they reached the window, he peered through a tangle of creeping thyme. Charlotte was at the store's counter, slurping something out of a black bowl.

Charlie's heart dropped. They were too late. His little brother had been turned into stew.

"Look!" Alfie said. Jack had just hopped up on a stool on the other side of the counter. He too had a black bowl in his hands.

"She must be trying to poison him!" Charlie said.

"I don't think so," Paige told him. "Looks like they're eating ice cream."

Inside the store, Charlotte said something they couldn't hear, but it must have been funny, because Jack laughed so hard that he fell off his seat. And when he got back onto it, Charlotte was waiting with her spoon poised like a catapult. She sent a glob of ice cream sailing toward Jack's nose. It hit with a splatter. And as Jack wiped the mess from his cheeks, he couldn't have looked happier.

"I'm sorry, Charlie," Paige said sympathetically. "But that doesn't look like a witch to me."

Charlie said nothing. As much as he hated to, he had to agree.

"Jack's in serious danger, all right," Rocco noted. "He's about to eat *waaaay* too much ice cream."

"Maybe we should go get some too," Alfie said. "You know, like an undercover mission? Maybe Charlotte left some clues in the ice cream parlor."

Charlie shook his head in disbelief.

"Sorry, it's just all this talk about witches and night-mares. . . . Stress makes me hungry."

"Yeah, I know what you mean," Rocco said. "I'm dying for a cone right now."

"Do you mind?" Paige asked Charlie. "I mean, now that we know Jack's safe and all, is it okay if we get some ice cream?"

"Do whatever you want," Charlie grumbled. "I'm head-ing home."

CHAPTER ELEVEN

THE INTRUDER

Charlie marched toward the mansion with his jaw clamped tight, his head down, and his arms crossed. He felt like an idiot. He'd dragged his friends all the way across town to watch his little brother pig out on ice cream. She'd planned it all, he thought. The stepmonster must have known he'd tell his friends about her. They'd almost believed him. Now he was back where he'd started—alone.

But Charlie had one last chance. If he could get into Charlotte's lair, he might find something that would prove she was dangerous. When he reached the purple house, he charged upstairs toward the tower, racing past the portrait of Silas DeChant. Right before he got to the second floor, Charlie came to a stop. Even when the rest of his family was home, the second-floor hallway gave him the creeps. The pictures on the wall always seemed to be watching him. The people in the frames were all Charlotte's ancestors. Not only did many of them share the same curly hair, but in most of the portraits, the purple house could be seen somewhere in the background, as if it were a proud part of the clan.

Charlie took a cautious step toward the door that led to the tower stairs. The house was quiet. His dad was still at work. Charlotte and Jack were in town. Charlie hadn't set foot in the stepmonster's lair in over a year. He didn't really want to now, but evidence of Charlotte's true identity might be hidden inside—and with his family gone, he had a rare chance to do some snooping.

Charlie reached out and twisted the knob. The door in front of him opened with a creak. He heard chair legs scrape against the floorboards—followed by a loud crash. He counted six heavy footsteps and then . . . nothing.

Charlie almost dashed downstairs to call 911. His knees felt weak. He was breathing too fast. But Cypress Creek wasn't home to burglars or bad guys, he reminded himself. Most people never even locked their doors. So Charlie gripped the doorknob and tried to stay standing. There had to be another explanation. "Hello?" he called out. "Dad?" There was no response.

Charlie held his breath and listened for signs of movement. Minutes ticked by and nothing happened. He began to wonder if it might have been Aggie. It wouldn't have been the first time the beast had raised a racket while chasing down the mice that lived in the mansion's walls.

He put a foot on the first stair. Then he forced his legs to lift him up to the second. He tried not to think about what might be waiting in the room at the top. With Jack's life at stake, he couldn't run away.

When he reached the last stair, Charlie craned his neck and peeked into the room. Lit by a silvery afternoon light, the tower was empty. He searched for Aggie, but the cat wasn't there. Whatever had made the commotion was gone—though it hadn't left by the stairs. But there had been an intruder, that much was certain. One of Charlotte's desk drawers had been broken into, and the floor was strewn with drawings. Charlie recognized a handful of the illustrations Jack had shown him at breakfast. He spotted a familiar picture of two young girls—and a few drawings of monsters that he'd probably never forget. Some of the illustrations were so lifelike it was hard to believe the creatures hadn't posed for their portraits.

Charlie bent down for a closer look. He was surprised

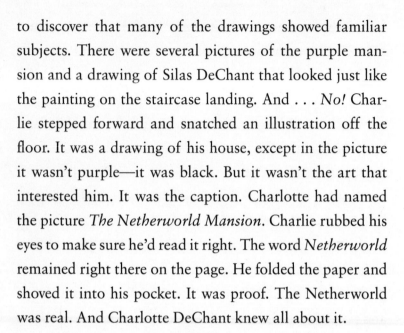

to discover that many of the drawings showed familiar subjects. There were several pictures of the purple mansion and a drawing of Silas DeChant that looked just like the painting on the staircase landing. And . . . *No!* Charlie stepped forward and snatched an illustration off the floor. It was a drawing of his house, except in the picture it wasn't purple—it was black. But it wasn't the art that interested him. It was the caption. Charlotte had named the picture *The Netherworld Mansion.* Charlie rubbed his eyes to make sure he'd read it right. The word *Netherworld* remained right there on the page. He folded the paper and shoved it into his pocket. It was proof. The Netherworld was real. And Charlotte DeChant knew all about it.

Grinning in triumph, Charlie turned his attention to the top of Charlotte's desk. The binder that had once held her drawings was spread open. Beside it sat a screwdriver that had been used to break the lock on the drawer in which the binder was kept. The desk chair was lying on its side. Whoever had ransacked the office must have been sitting in it when Charlie surprised him. Charlie looked around the room. There was only one door, and the windows were shut. How had the intruder managed to leave without Charlie seeing him?

Spooked once more, Charlie picked up the overturned chair and took a seat. He began to thumb through the pages still left in the binder, not sure what he wanted to find. Then his eyes landed on an image that stopped him cold—a picture of a small blond girl. Dressed in an ordinary T-shirt and jeans, she was glaring up at a horrible, leering clown. The girl's teeth were gritted and her fists clenched. She looked ready to take on every monster in the world. Charlie knew the look well. And he knew it had belonged to his mother.

On the back of the drawing was a strange poem.

When creatures are shrieking and howling like
  jackals,
Monsters with sharp claws and ghouls wearing
  shackles,
Demons of darkness that are by your fears made,
My lessons will teach you to be not afraid!
The first thing to do is to know that you're
  dreaming
When nightmares come sneaking and snarling and
  creeping.
Those creatures are just your worst fears in disguise.
What truly scares you might be a surprise.

The front door all the way downstairs creaked open and slammed shut. Charlie froze, paralyzed with fear.

"Hey!" he heard Jack shout from the foyer. "Charlie! You here?"

Charlie leapt into action, gathering up the remaining pages from the stepmonster's binder. If she found him, she'd think he was responsible for the broken desk lock and the mess. He shoved the illustrations back into the binder and dropped the book into the desk drawer. He started to tiptoe toward the door, but before he could reach it, he heard Jack bounding up the stairs to the second floor. There was no escape.

"Hey, Charlie! We brought you some ice cream! It's your favorite, cookie dough! Hey, Charlie! Paige said you'd be home. Where are you?"

Doors were being thrown open in the hallway below. Charlie slipped back to Charlotte's big wooden desk and ducked into the space beneath it. He'd just pulled the chair into position when the tower door flew open. He held his breath while his brother looked around the room.

"He's not up here either!" Jack shouted down to Charlotte.

It was dark, warm, and surprisingly cozy beneath his stepmonster's desk. Even with his legs curled up beneath him and his head resting against the wood, Charlie's eyelids began to grow heavy. It was no time for a nap, but he couldn't resist.

And suddenly he was inside the witch's dungeon. The

cauldron in the center of the room was bubbling. Rats raced around the rubbish pile, and the cat snacked on the slowest. The witch was seated in a chair by the fire. She appeared to be fixing her hair, using the side of a shiny meat cleaver as a mirror. When she looked up, she didn't seem happy to see him.

"Oh, it's you," she said, returning to her primping. "It's not a good time. Agatha and I are about to leave. We have a big night planned."

"What are you going to do?" Charlie demanded.

"My, my," the witch chided him, "what terrible manners. The answer is *none of your business*."

"We're going to eat your brother!" Agatha howled.

"*Really?*" The witch shot the cat a dirty look. "Was that necessary?"

"You're not going to eat anybody tonight," Charlie declared, wishing he felt as brave as he sounded.

"Is that right?" the witch asked, putting down the cleaver. "And just who do you suppose is going to stop us?"

"Me," Charlie said. He rushed at the cauldron, which was as big as a bathtub and filled to the brim with a foul-smelling brew. He hit the side of the pot with all his weight, and to his surprise it fell over, letting loose a wave of bubbling brown liquid that washed over the witch.

"You nasty little brat!" the witch screeched, plucking what looked like chicken claws and frog guts off her dress.

"Did you think I was going to dissolve? Now you've destroyed my dress and ruined the broth."

"This isn't a movie," Agatha said with a roll of her eyes. "Witches don't *melt*."

"Get him!" the witch yelled. "We'll tie him up and make him watch us eat."

The cat pounced, knocking Charlie onto his back and holding him there as the witch got the rope. Soon Charlie was bound to the dungeon's cot—and the witch and her cat were gone.

"Noooooooo!" he screamed. "Wake up!" he told himself. "Wake up, wake up, *wake up*!"

Then, to his amazement, he was wide-awake. And under Charlotte's desk.

Charlie slid out and realized that night had fallen. But the tower was far from dark. Outside, the moon was shining, and light flooded the room.

Charlie scrambled down from the tower. When he got to the second-floor hallway, he could hear his father talking on the phone. He crept down to the landing between the first and second floors to listen.

". . . around four p.m. by the ice cream parlor. He told his friends he was walking home. . . . My wife is out looking for him right now. . . . He was wearing jeans and a hoodie. Blue sneakers with green stripes . . . No, Officer, he's been a bit difficult lately, but he's never done anything like this before. . . ."

It was then that Charlie heard a familiar creak. He spun around just in time to catch sight of the door to the tower stairs swinging shut. He could hear footsteps climbing to the top, and he wasted no time charging up behind them. When he reached the tower, he came to a halt at the door. The octagonal room no longer had eight solid walls. One side had vanished, and where there had once been plaster and wood, Charlie now saw the forest from his nightmares. He rushed toward the opening before it could close. There in the distance was the witch with a little boy thrown over her shoulder.

CHAPTER TWELVE

CLOWN DOWN

"Jack!" Charlie shouted, but the boy didn't budge. His body appeared to be bound in a blanket, wrapped like an insect in a spider's web.

The witch turned around and raised a crooked finger to her lips. "Shhh!" she hissed. "You'll wake the baby!" The cackle that followed seemed to ricochet off every tree in the forest.

"Bring him back!" Charlie ordered, stepping off of the tower's firm wooden floorboards and onto moss-covered ground.

"My world, my rules," the witch sneered. "Come and get him, you sniveling brat."

The last thing Charlie saw before the witch vanished behind a tree was his brother's body bouncing against the hag's hunched back. That was when Charlie started to run.

A narrow path snaked through the woods, but it was impossible to stay on the trail. Only a few weak beams of moonlight reached the forest floor. The darkest shadows were pitch-black, and Charlie rushed through them blindly, guided by the fading sound of the witch's laughter. He waded through a foul-smelling mire that sucked both sneakers off his feet. Thorn-covered brambles ripped his clothing and tore at his skin. Barefoot and bleeding, Charlie kept running until the witch's cackle grew too faint to hear—and the path he'd been following was nowhere to be seen.

His lungs burning, Charlie stumbled to a stop. He doubled over to catch his breath and massage the painful stitch in his side. When he looked

up, he realized how lost he was. The trees hovering over him were taller than any he had ever seen. Scabs of lichen clung to their trunks, and limp gray moss dangled from the branches like a hag's hair. One of his feet was slowly sinking into a murky black pool. The other foot was dripping with sludge. But what scared Charlie the most was the thing he sensed lurking between the trees. He listened but heard nothing. Nothing at all. No chirping birds or buzzing insects. No rustling of leaves or croaking of frogs. The woods were utterly silent.

But he wasn't alone. The witch might have been gone, but he knew that his very worst nightmare was near. And he knew it would be coming for him.

Ahead stood hundreds of trees. Hundreds more grew to the left and right. A surge of fear spun Charlie around. The view behind him was exactly the same. This was the forest he'd tried so hard to avoid. Charlie frantically hunted for his footprints in the mud, hoping he could follow them back to the tower. But then he stopped. He'd promised his mom he would take care of his brother. She hadn't asked Charlie for anything else. And that meant he couldn't leave the Netherworld without Jack. Until he rescued his brother, he couldn't go home. And so Charlie kept moving, though he knew the worst nightmare of all could be waiting behind any tree.

He would not let the witch win, Charlie swore to himself. He'd find Jack, whatever it took. But he had to act fast. Even if the thing in the woods didn't find him, he had a feeling he wouldn't survive in the Netherworld more than a couple of days. It appeared to be one big forest. The water he'd seen was too nasty to drink. And there was nothing to eat but lichen, moss, and the strange red mushrooms that sprouted out of the ground. Charlie remembered little of what his mom had taught him about mushrooms, but he was pretty sure that these weren't the kind of fungi you'd put in an omelet. Each specimen had five red tentacles that oozed globs of green slime, and a black hole in the center like a gaping mouth. Charlie bent to inspect one of the mushrooms more closely and caught his breath. As he watched, its squidlike tentacles began to writhe. Then something horrible poked its head out of the hole in the center.

It was shiny and black with two twitching antennae. Just above the bug's wings was a dull yellow segment with a black spot in the middle. Charlie recognized the creature at once. It was a carrion beetle—and its food of choice was rotten flesh. Two years earlier, a kid in Charlie's class had brought three of the insects to show-and-tell, and for weeks after, they'd crawled through Charlie's bad dreams. The real bugs had been horrible, but at least they'd been small. In the Netherworld, they seemed to grow as big as rats.

Charlie felt something tickle his foot and glanced down to find a monstrous beetle creeping across his toes. He kicked, flinging the bug against a tree. It bounced off the bark, hit the ground, and kept walking, and to Charlie's horror, it was no longer alone. While he'd been investigating the mushroom, an army of carrion beetles had appeared. Thousands blanketed the forest floor, and they marched over his feet as if he wasn't even there.

Everywhere Charlie looked there were bugs. There seemed to be no end to the swarm, which left him faced with three terrible choices: He could stand still, hoping

the bugs would pass. He could try to escape, which would mean crushing the creatures and feeling their guts ooze between his toes. Or he could shuffle his feet along the ground and do his best to move with the beetles.

Charlie slid one foot forward, and thousands of beetles flapped their wings, as though they were sending him a sign of approval. They appeared to be leading him somewhere. Charlie knew it might not be a place he wanted to go, but he had no other options. He was stuck in a nightmare. If there was any chance of saving his brother, he had to find out where the bugs wanted to take him.

Charlie shuffled along for what felt like forever, without seeing anything other than trees. Just as he was about to give up, he caught the faint scent of food wafting through the air. It reminded him of the concoctions Charlotte always left bubbling on the kitchen stove at the mansion. As he raised his nose to sniff, his eyes turned skyward. High up in the forest's canopy, nestled between two skinny trees, sat a cottage. Despite its location, it was an ordinary-looking structure. The walls were made of logs, and the pitched roof was thatched with brown straw. A warm, golden light illuminated four little windows. It looked perfectly cozy— and yet the sight of the house was unsettling. Charlie knew he'd seen it somewhere before.

The army of bugs that had delivered him to the cottage began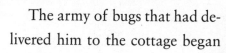

to scatter. Some dug back into the earth. Others climbed trees. Most simply slipped into the darkness. Charlie fought the urge to run. Along with the beetles, the cottage was one of the few signs of life he'd enountered. He knew he couldn't just turn away. He searched for a ladder or a set of stairs, but there appeared to be no way to reach it. Finally he stood back and shouted.

"Hello!"

The wooden floorboards high above his head began creaking. The figure of an enormous feline appeared on the porch. It reached out a paw and swatted down a beetle that was flying past. A loud crunching followed.

Charlie cringed when he saw the cat standing on her hind legs and peering down at him from the balcony. Her whiskers were wet with something green. Bug guts, Charlie realized, and almost gagged with disgust.

"How kind of you to bring some hors d'oeuvres!" the cat purred. "I'm so pleased you could make it for dinner."

"Agatha," Charlie breathed. As much as he despised the cat, it was a relief to have found her.

"Hello, *dinner,*" Agatha replied.

"Where's the witch?" Charlie demanded. "And where's Jack? If you've touched so much as—"

"Oh, *relax,*" the cat said with a yawn. "We have to fatten him up before we feast. The little piggy is probably eating a gallon of ice cream as we speak. Now climb on up and come inside. It's time for my dinner. I'm absolutely *ravenous*."

The whole situation was so strange that Charlie almost laughed. "Do I look stupid?"

"You'll be safe," the cat purred. "That thing in the forest can't reach you up here."

Charlie's heart skipped a beat, but he didn't budge. "I'm not climbing up there so you can eat me."

"I won't eat *all* of you," Agatha said. "Just a few little pieces you don't really need. A *very* important gentleman has been waiting for you to arrive. I can nibble on those *delectable* toes, but he wants to meet the rest of you later."

"I didn't come here to meet anyone. I'm here to get Jack, and as soon as I do, I'll find a way to wake up."

"Wake up?" Agatha snickered. "You can't *wake up*, Charlie Laird. You're not asleep! You came through the portal of your own free will. Your body's here too, which means you're stuck in the Netherworld. That was all part of the plan."

Charlie couldn't have been more confused. "What *plan*?" he yelled.

Agatha yawned again. "I'm not allowed to say."

"Then I guess we have nothing to talk about." Charlie turned away.

"Do you really believe I'd let you escape that easily?" Agatha called. "Surely you recognized this lovely cottage?

I borrowed it from an old woman you read about once. She and her house gave you nightmares for weeks. Another little fear you never quite dealt with."

"How would *you* know?" Charlie scoffed without glancing back. But he was getting more nervous by the second. The Netherworld seemed to be home to all of his childhood nightmares, and he wasn't eager to see which one would be showing up next.

He set off through the forest. But he hadn't gone very far before the earth began to tremble beneath his feet. He froze, and after a pause, there was another quake. Then he realized what it was: footsteps. Whatever was following him was enormous—and getting closer and closer.

Charlie peeked back and nearly fell to his knees. The two trees on which the house was perched were not trees at all. They were legs—enormous, scaly legs that ended in birdlike feet. The long talons at the tips of the toes dug into the soil with every step the house took. Suddenly Charlie remembered the book that had frightened him when he was younger. It was a collection of folk tales. In it was the story of a child-eating crone whose hut walked about on two giant chicken legs. Reading about the house might have given him nightmares, but *seeing* it was a million times more terrifying.

Charlie ran faster than he'd ever run before. But even with a head start, he couldn't beat the house. His lead lessened with every step it took. He expected to be squashed at any moment. Then, over the pounding of his heart against his ribs and over the earthshaking thuds and crashing of trees, Charlie's ears picked up another sound.

Ahhhhbleeeewgah! Ahhhhbleeeewgah! Ahhhhbleeeewgah!

Like everything else he'd encountered in the Netherworld so far, it was oddly familiar. It reminded him of the horn on a toy car Jack had played with when he was little. Charlie risked another glance over his shoulder. A rusted, banged-up yellow convertible was zipping through the trees. At the wheel was a clown who appeared to be at least twice the size of the vehicle. His knees were up against his chest and his two patches of bright red hair were flattened by the wind.

Ahhhhbleeeewgah! Ahhhhbleeeewgah! Ahhhhbleeeewgah! the car honked as the clown steered it around the legs of the house. There appeared to be something trailing from the car's back bumper. A rope, Charlie realized, just as his toes jammed beneath a tree root and he fell face-first into the muck. In a flash, he rolled onto his back, expecting the house to attack. But it had been stopped in its tracks by the rope that was now twisted around its legs.

Up on the porch, the cat looked enraged. "What do you think you're doing?" she screeched at the car's driver. "He's *ours,* you stupid clown!"

The yellow car pulled up beside Charlie. A grotesquely

proportioned clown unfolded himself from behind the wheel.

"You'll pay for this, Dabney!" Agatha howled.

The clown ignored the angry feline and held out a gloved hand to Charlie. His face was grayish white. Painted blue diamonds framed two bloodshot eyes, and a leering red smile stretched from ear to ear. It was the clown from Charlotte's illustrations.

Charlie scrambled back, away from the gloved hand the clown held out to him.

"Hey!" the clown urged. His voice was high and squeaky—and he sounded like he might break into giggles at any moment. "Hop up and get in the car!"

"Wh-wh-what?" Charlie sputtered.

"The ropes around the house's legs won't hold for long! Get behind the wheel and get out of here! I'm trying to save you!"

Charlie grabbed the clown's hand and was yanked to his feet. "But I don't know how to drive," he said.

"It's easy," the clown insisted. "Just step on the pedal, turn the wheel, and try not to kill anyone. Now go!"

Charlie slid into the driver's seat. "Where am I supposed to go?" he asked.

"It doesn't matter," the clown told him. "Wherever you end up, someone will find you."

Somehow that didn't make Charlie feel any better. He

gently pressed the pedal with his foot and the car lurched forward. He took his foot off and the car came to a sudden stop.

"Go!" the clown shouted. Charlie heard a loud snap as the ropes binding the house's legs finally broke. The house took a giant step forward, and one of its chicken claws reached out and curled around the clown.

"I can't leave you!" Charlie shouted back.

"Go!" the clown yelled. "I'll be fine! Nightmares like me never die!"

Charlie found the gas pedal again and slammed it all the way down to the floor of the car. The vehicle careened through the woods. Whichever direction he turned, there seemed to be a tree blocking the way. It was almost as if the forest was trying to stop him. By the time a road miraculously appeared, Charlie had lost count of the number of trees he'd sideswiped. His nerves were so frazzled that he didn't even care where the road led him. Charlie took a left when he hit the pavement—and drove right out of his nightmare.

❧ CHAPTER THIRTEEN ❧

MEDUSO

To Charlie's surprise, the Netherworld was far more than
a forest. As the little yellow car raced through it, he traveled from one horrible dream to the next. Some of the nightmares were as small as a single haunted house. Others were
the size of an entire cursed kingdom. Charlie cruised past
a stone castle with live gargoyles perched like pigeons on
its battlements. The creatures dive-bombed him as he drove
by, trying to snatch him out of the car with their beaks and
claws. In the hills beyond the castle, a pack of ravenous
wolves chased him down a stretch of winding road. They
vanished at the edge of a tropical realm where a smoking

volcano reached toward the sky behind herds of dinosaurs. Charlie didn't dare stop driving. Even when velociraptors weren't barreling after him, there didn't seem to be a single safe place to pull over. Everywhere he went, the terrors kept coming. They weren't part of *his* bad dreams. Charlie had always *liked* dinosaurs. Somehow he'd gotten lost in the nightmares of strangers.

Worst of all, there was no sign of Jack. Charlie saw graveyards, asylums, swamps, and subdivisions, but he never spotted the witch's bell tower. The farther he traveled, the more desperate he felt. With every wrong turn, he imagined Jack being fattened for the witch's feast, and he banged his head against the wheel in frustration.

He was speeding through an abandoned town when his car finally sputtered to a stop. The shops on the left side of the road had broken windows and fire-blackened walls. The stores on the right side were barricaded with boards. Abandoned vehicles littered the street, their doors wide open, as if the people inside had leaped out and run. The town was clearly not the best place for a breakdown.

Charlie saw no option but to step out of the car. The wind whistled ominously as he looked around. It wasn't his nightmare, that much was for sure, but he felt as though he must have been there before. Then, in the dusty window of a ruined shop, he saw it—a teddy bear with an ice cream cone in its hand. The burned-out village was Cypress

Creek. Charlie looked around, overcome by a mixture of horror and relief. As terrible as it was to see his hometown destroyed, Charlie realized it meant that Jack might not be too far away. He wanted to set out in search of his brother. But who knew what creatures were on the prowl in this part of the Netherworld? And without a car, Charlie was aware that there was a pretty good chance he might not make it as far as the end of the block.

Charlie popped open the car's hood the way he'd seen his father do and shook his head at what he saw. Instead of an engine, there was only an enormous brass key. The car was nothing but a windup toy. Charlie tried to turn the key, but it barely budged. He was starting to sweat.

"There he issss."

Charlie spun around. A breeze blew dead leaves across the road. Curtains fluttered in the window of an empty café. A broken traffic light blinking red swung on a line above. But there was no one there.

"Now issss our chance," hissed a second voice. "Act fasssst."

"Who's there?" Charlie called out, trying his best to sound tough. "What's going on?"

"I'm afraid you don't have time to fix that car," said a third voice. This one was smooth and so refined that it sounded as if the owner's throat were lined with silk. "They're sure to spot you any moment now."

"Who?" Charlie flinched and the car's hood fell with a deafening crash.

"Oh dear. Must you make such a racket? They heard you for certain that time." The voice seemed to be coming from a metal grate set into the curb. Someone was in the sewer.

"Who are you?" Charlie demanded anxiously. "And why are you down there?" He knew there were no good answers to that question. Only alligators, escaped criminals, and homicidal cartoon characters ever spent time in the sewers.

"I'm not the one you should be worried about," replied the mysterious voice. "Have a look around."

In the distance, a crowd was gathering in the street. For a moment, Charlie felt a flicker of hope. They were the first of his kind that he'd seen since he'd arrived in the Netherworld. Then, as they began to shuffle toward him, he realized that they weren't *quite* human. Not anymore.

"Zombies?" Charlie groaned and kicked a tire on the car that had just betrayed him. "Someone's turned Cypress Creek into a zombie nightmare?" He'd never been particularly scared of the undead, but according to Rocco, who was a connoisseur of zombie movies, they could be quite a nuisance.

"You needn't worry about zombies either," the voice replied. "Those fellows are falling apart. Even the ones who still have legs couldn't outrun a toddler. These days, it's the bunnies that will get you in this part of town."

"*Bunnies?*" The word burst from Charlie's lips, followed by an incredulous laugh.

"That's right," said the voice. "Whoever dreamed them up has *quite* the imagination. Take another look and you'll see what I mean."

Charlie was still smirking as he glanced over his shoulder. Sure enough, there were a dozen fluffy white bunnies hopping down the street in his direction. He could tell they were rabbits by the large pink ears, but there was something horribly wrong with their faces. They had no eyes. No noses. No whiskers. Their heads held nothing but gaping mouths loaded with razor-sharp teeth. And judging by the bright red stains on their fur, they'd eaten something quite recently. Something *large*.

Without the teeth, they would have lookèd a lot like Hans and Franz, the bunnies in his school's library. They'd been kidnapped once by an eighth-grade bully and hidden inside a younger girl's locker. They both sprang out the second she opened the door, scaring

the girl so badly that she'd stayed home from school for the rest of the week.

Charlie turned back toward the

sewer grate and dropped to his knees. "They're coming right at me! Let me in!" There was no way that anything awaiting him beneath the street could compare to being torn apart by bloodthirsty bunnies.

"I thought you'd never ask," the voice replied. "Simply pull off the grate and slide on down. The rabbits won't follow you. The sewer system doesn't belong to their nightmare."

It only took a few seconds for Charlie to remove the grate and drop down into a wide concrete pipe. He landed with a splash at the feet of a surprisingly ordinary-looking man. His gray three-piece suit was nicely pressed—and buttoned up over a belly that appeared rather soft. On top of the man's head was an old-fashioned hat with a wide gray band. His eyes were hidden behind sunglasses with black lenses.

Charlie was relieved beyond belief to discover that his benefactor was human. He stood up and brushed himself off. "Thanks for the help," he said, holding out a hand. "My name is Charlie." When the man grimaced at the sight of Charlie's filth-covered palm, he wiped his hand on his trousers and held it out again, feeling a little offended. The man was awfully fastidious for someone standing ankle-deep in a sewer. "Who are *you*?"

"I'm a friend of a friend," the man replied. "You might say I work with Dabney. I'm supposed to help you get out of here." The way he said it made it clear that it wasn't a duty he was eager to perform.

Charlie gave up and dropped his hand. "Who's *Dabney*?" He recognized the name, but he couldn't quite place it.

"You've been driving his car all over the Netherworld and you can't even remember his name?" The man with the sunglasses sounded annoyed.

"Oh, right!" The pieces fell together. "The clown." The truth was, Charlie had almost forgotten. It felt like ages since the clown had saved him. "Is Dabney going to be okay?"

The man sighed and rubbed his eyes without removing his glasses. "I suppose that depends on what you did to him."

"I didn't do *anything* to him. He told me to take the car, so I did. But I'm pretty sure the witch's cat and that walking house captured him before I drove away."

The man sighed even louder. "Which witch? Which cat? Both species are a dime a dozen around here."

"The cat's name is Agatha. I don't know the witch's name, but I do know she has a friend named Charlotte."

The man's spine stiffened. "You must be mistaken. There are no witches named *Charlotte*. I've never even *heard* of a witch with that name. I'd wager your witch is Brunhilde," the man declared. "Which means she'll demand a ransom to set Dabney free. I'll probably spend the next few days

gathering eye of newt just to pay her. All because one meddling child—"

"Excuse me?" Charlie said, interrupting the man's one-
sided conversation. He was making Charlie feel like a nuisance, which didn't seem fair, since Charlie hadn't actually
asked for his help. "You never answered me. Who are you
exactly, and why are you here?"

This time the man reluctantly offered his hand. "The
name's Meduso," he replied with a sniff. "And I'm here because of you. I usually do my best to avoid such odiferous
conditions."

He was rude, Charlie thought. But Charlie was in no position to turn away someone who'd been sent to help him.

"So where are your friends?" Charlie asked as they
shook hands.

"What friends?" Meduso asked in return.

Charlie kicked himself for letting his guard down. "I
heard three voices coming from the sewer," he said. "Only
one of them was yours."

"Oh, *those* voices." Meduso fidgeted in discomfort.
"I'm afraid that was just me."

"Really?" Charlie stood his ground. Why did everyone
in this world seem to think he was stupid? "Where are the
other guys, Meduso? Are you planning an ambush?"

"That's ridiculous!" Meduso snapped. "I just saved your
behind—what happened to *thank you*? I swear, children

these days! I'm a well-dressed man standing in a sewer. What's not to trust?" Then he took a deep breath. "Fine. You want to meet the 'other guys'? I'll introduce you. Just remember—we don't have time for idle chitchat. We need to get out of this pipe before the next sewer nightmare begins."

Meduso lifted his hat with one hand and three serpents uncoiled from beneath it. Charlie hopped back in horror but managed not to scream. He'd already faced gargoyles, zombies, and bloodthirsty bunnies. He should have known better than to think the Netherworld sewers were safe.

The first snake was dark red. Its muscular body swayed from side to side like a hypnotist's pocket watch. The one next to it was a dusty, washed-out brown. It flicked at the air with a pink forked tongue. The third snake, an emerald-green beauty with beady red eyes, immediately bared its fangs.

"Meet Larry, Barry, and Fernando," Meduso said. That was when Charlie realized that all three snakes were

growing directly out of the man's head. "The green one is Barry. He hasn't spoken since that whole 'forbidden apple' misunderstanding. The other two never shut up."

"It'ss a pleassure," hissed the red serpent in a thick Spanish accent. "My name iss Fernando."

"The boy'ss barefoot in a ssewer," said the brown one. He didn't bother to introduce himself, but if Barry never spoke, Charlie figured it had to be Larry. "That'ss just not ssanitary."

"You can talk!" Charlie gasped.

"Sso can you. Don't ssound sso ssurprissed."

"Ssettle down. Ssnakess can't talk where he comess from," said Fernando. "Don't you remember? She ssaid the ssame thing."

"She?" Charlie asked, preparing to take a step forward.

Meduso clapped his hat back on his head and the three snakes disappeared beneath it. "I wouldn't get too close. Barry's a biter."

"And what are *you*?" Charlie asked, still keeping his distance.

"I'm a gorgon," Meduso replied haughtily, as if it should have been obvious.

"What's a gorgon?"

Meduso snorted at Charlie's ignorance. "Surely you've heard of Medusa—the monster from the myths? The lady with snakes for hair and eyes that can turn men to stone?"

"Yeah?" Charlie said. "So?"

"So?" Meduso repeated, outraged. "So she's one of the most famous nightmares that ever lived—and she's a gorgon just like me. Over two thousand years old and as fearsome as ever."

"Medusa's still alive?" Charlie asked in astonishment. "I thought some guy cut off her head a long time ago."

Meduso sniffed. "That was just a story. You shouldn't believe everything you read. Besides, you're talking about a legend. Show some respect or I'll turn you into one of those cute little cherub statues that pee into fountains. All I need to do is take off my sunglasses and give you a peek at my baby blues."

"You can't turn me to stone if someone sent you to help me," Charlie pointed out. "Who was it?"

Meduso answered the question by marching past Charlie. "I have to *help* you, not humor you. If you want to leave this world, I suggest you follow me," he called. "It's a long trip to the portal, and I haven't got—"

"Portal?" Charlie interrupted.

"The only door between the Netherworld and the Waking World. It's inside that mansion you live in. We need to get you back there before—"

"No." Charlie's voice echoed through the tunnel. For once he almost sounded grown up. "I can't leave the Netherworld until I find my little brother."

"Pardon me?" Meduso stopped and spun around. "No one mentioned a word about a little brother."

"The witch stole my brother," Charlie said. "She's planning to eat him."

Meduso slapped his forehead with his palm. "Don't be a fool. Look, boy, I know you've visited the Netherworld a few times in your dreams. But you have no idea how much trouble you're in this time around. When you came through the portal, your body and spirit both passed to this side. That means you're stuck in this world until you find your way back to the place you came in. And if something happens to you while you're here, it happens for real, buster. You could get stomped by a mammoth or swallowed by a sarlacc. Do you understand what I'm trying to say? I'm telling you that you could *die*."

"It doesn't matter," Charlie said. "I'm not leaving this place until I find my brother." He might have sounded brave, but he didn't feel it. Charlie was as scared as he'd ever been. But there was no point in going back if he didn't have Jack.

Meduso lifted his hat an inch. "Did you hear that?" he asked his snakes. "The child is clearly insane. This is the last time I do any favors—"

"Assk him what happened to his brother," Fernando interrupted.

Meduso sighed. "Fine. What happened—"

"I heard the question," Charlie butted in. "The witch took my brother out of his bed and carried him up to the tower at the top of our house. When I got there, one of the tower walls was gone, and there was a forest behind it. I saw the witch run into the woods with Jack over her shoulder. I tried to follow but I ended up getting lost."

Suddenly Meduso looked terribly serious. "You say there was a witch *inside* your house? Your house in the Waking World?" the gorgon demanded. "Are you absolutely certain?"

Charlie nodded. "I followed her through the portal. The witch's cat told me it was all a big trap. They lured me here because some VIP guy in the Netherworld wants to meet me."

Meduso's face turned even paler. "Did the cat say who it was?"

"No," Charlie replied. "She just said he was very important."

"Will you excuse me for a moment?" Meduso asked politely.

Meduso walked a few yards into the darkness. He took off his hat and his snakes slithered down to face him.

"SSomeone'ss found the portal?" Charlie heard Larry hiss.

"A witch," Fernando replied. "And if she brought the boy back to the Netherworld to meet *him*, that meanss *he* knowss about the portal too."

"Are you ssure *he'ss* the one who wantss to meet the boy?" Larry asked.

Charlie shivered as his skin broke out in goose bumps. Who was *he*? And why would anyone in the Netherworld want to meet a twelve-year-old kid from Cypress Creek? Whatever the answer was, Charlie figured it couldn't be very good.

"It has to be him," Meduso insisted. "Who else would it be?"

"Do you think the boy'ss brother might be here on thiss sside?"

"It's possible," said Meduso. "The ability to pass to this side seems to run in families."

"We're in sseriouss trouble," Larry moaned. "I told you we should sstay out of thiss!"

"What are you talking about?" Charlie shouted. "Who is this guy who wants to meet me?"

Before anyone could answer, an almighty roar rushed through the sewer pipe, followed by a hot wind perfumed by the stench of rotting meat.

Meduso stomped back to Charlie, his hat still in his hand. "Time to go," he announced. "A new nightmare is about to start. And if you thought those bunnies were bad, you certainly don't want to cross paths with the reptiles that live down here."

"But where are we going?" Charlie asked.

"To resscue your brother," Fernando said.

"What?" Larry complained. "Wait jusst a ssecond! Don't I get a ssay in thiss?"

"I'm sorry, are you the one here with feet?" Meduso snapped.

"Of coursse not!" the snake replied.

Meduso grabbed Charlie's arm and dragged the boy behind him as he charged through the sewer. "Then say what you like, Larry. You're still coming along for the ride."

Trudging through the sewer was the most disgusting experience of Charlie's life, and he almost wished his friends had been there to share it. The insects that scuttled along the sewer's brick walls would have fascinated Alfie. Six inches long and shaped like centipedes, the creatures were nearly transparent. Charlie could see their organs, and judging by the contents of their stomachs, they appeared to enjoy eating each other. Rocco would have marveled at the enormous piles of dung the sewer gators left behind. The first one Charlie encountered was so large that he mistook it for a coiled anaconda. But most of all, he wondered what clear-headed Paige would have said if she'd seen Charlie wading through sewage behind a mysterious gorgon.

Meduso claimed he'd been sent to help, but he didn't seem like a natural choice for a rescue mission. Charlie

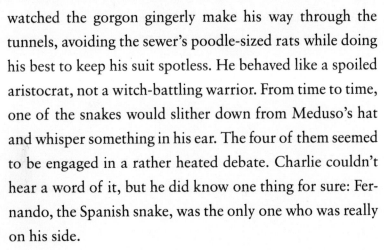

watched the gorgon gingerly make his way through the tunnels, avoiding the sewer's poodle-sized rats while doing his best to keep his suit spotless. He behaved like a spoiled aristocrat, not a witch-battling warrior. From time to time, one of the snakes would slither down from Meduso's hat and whisper something in his ear. The four of them seemed to be engaged in a rather heated debate. Charlie couldn't hear a word of it, but he did know one thing for sure: Fernando, the Spanish snake, was the only one who was really on his side.

Finally, after what seemed like hours, they emerged from a manhole at the side of a road that cut through a dense forest.

Charlie was elated. "This is it!"

It was hard to believe that he was so happy to be back inside his bad dream. But as horrible as the woods were, with their witches and beetles and walking houses, Charlie knew the forest was where he stood the best chance of rescuing Jack. "How did you know where to find my nightmare?" he asked Meduso.

"It was easy. You've got your own plot, boy," Meduso said. "Around here, we call it a *terror-tory*. And every time you visit, you add a bit more. Most people only come to the Netherworld a few times a year, so they don't need a permanent plot. Their terror-tories are more like timeshares. Vacation rentals. But you've been showing up every single night. You've got serious real estate. And every time you visit, it all gets a little more real."

Charlie surveyed the forest. "So this is all mine?"

"You built the belfry and planted every tree," Meduso confirmed.

"What will happen to it if I stop having bad dreams?"

"It will get recycled and become a part of someone else's nightmare. Cypress Creek is a pretty popular setting these days. Every kid in your town seems to be having bad dreams. I blame cable television."

Charlie heard the faint hum of an engine, and two specks of light appeared in the distance. A large black car was barreling toward them through the darkness.

"Quick, get off the road," Meduso hissed, pushing Charlie into the bushes. "We can't let anyone see you."

"Yeah, but why are *you* hiding?" Charlie asked when he saw Meduso pulling his jacket over his head. "Don't you belong here?"

"Do you always ask so many questions?" Meduso snapped.

"Yeah, sstop being sso nossey," spat Larry.

The speeding vehicle was getting closer, and soon what looked at first like a long black hearse appeared. The sight reminded Charlie of the second-worst day of his life. "Is there a funeral?" he asked.

"There's *always* a funeral around here," Meduso said,

peeking out from beneath his jacket. "But *that* is a Netherworld limousine. I've heard they're quite spacious in back."

"Who's in it?" Somehow Charlie knew he needed an answer. The limousine was driving through his forest. It couldn't be there by accident.

"It'ss the man the witch wantss you to meet," lisped Fernando.

"Fernando!" Meduso barked, shoving his hat down onto his head. "You meddling fink!"

Charlie saw the limousine slowing to make the sharp turn.

"I'm going to try to get a look at him." Charlie stood and stepped out of the hiding place before Meduso could stop him. Something big was going on, but Charlie didn't care. The man in the limo had sent the witch to steal Jack. And that meant he knew where Jack was.

"You're making a *terrible* mistake," Meduso warned. "That man is dangerous—and you're not the only one he's after."

"If you're scared, you don't have to come." Charlie walked out into the road. Without his brother, he had nothing left to lose.

"How 'bout that! The kid has losst it," one of the snakes hissed. "He didn't even bother to look both wayss!"

CHAPTER FOURTEEN

THE GLADIATOR

Charlie jogged down the road after the limo. He knew he was heading toward danger, but he just didn't care. His own safety hardly mattered anymore. Finding his brother was his top priority. And somehow that made being brave a million times easier.

The road came to a dead end at the edge of the woods and the limousine stopped. When the driver turned off the engine, Charlie ducked behind a tree and watched in amazement as the earth shook and a small stadium rose out of the ground a few yards from the limo. He was desperate to see what was inside the arena, but his gut told him not to get too close. He looked around and found the perfect solution: if he could reach the top of one of the trees, he'd have a bird's-eye view. So he grabbed a branch above his head and began to climb.

The sound of huffing and puffing drew closer as Meduso finally caught up with him. "Get . . . down . . . here . . . now!" the gorgon gasped from below.

When Charlie ignored the command, Meduso began to come after him. Charlie didn't stop—he climbed until he couldn't climb anymore, and then he looked down. Inside the unlit arena was a grassy field ringed by a running track and metal bleachers.

"What's going on?" Charlie asked when Meduso joined him at the top of the tree.

"I haven't a clue," the gorgon replied. He was struggling to catch his breath as he scratched at a splotch of pine sap that had stained his suit sleeve. "It's much too dark. I can't see a thing."

Charlie snorted at that. Meduso had been able to see perfectly well in the sewer. "Maybe you should take off the sunglasses," he suggested.

"Or perhaps we should pay a visit to the last human who joked about my glasses," Meduso answered. "He's feeling a bit stiff these days. And last I heard, he was standing in a park wearing three or four inches of pigeon poop."

In the stadium below, floodlights suddenly lit the grass

oval in the center of the track. Charlie was surprised to find himself staring down at the Cypress Creek athletic center, where the town's sports teams held their games.

"Looks like a nightmare is about to begin," Meduso remarked.

Compared to the Netherworld's swamps and sewers, the brightly lit stadium seemed downright pleasant to Charlie. "Wait—someone's nightmare is going to happen down *there*?" He laughed. "What's so scary about a running track?"

"Your guess is as good as mine," Meduso replied. "But then again, I don't know what's so scary about witches either. Some of my best friends happen to be witches. Look, boy, everyone's got their own fears to deal with. The same guy who will wrestle a sewer alligator might faint at the sight of a giant squirrel. If I were you, I wouldn't make fun of someone's nightmares until you've slept a night in his pajamas."

Charlie barely heard what Meduso was saying. His attention had been captured by the sight of a hunchbacked creature in a navy chauffeur's jacket that had hopped out of the driver's seat of the limousine and scampered to open one of the back doors. Charlie gaped in wonder at the figure that emerged. The man had to be at least nine feet tall. He wore a black suit in the style of Frankenstein's monster, and his buzz cut looked sharp to the touch. Charlie couldn't recall seeing the brute in any bad dreams—and yet he knew him from somewhere. Charlie shivered, and for a brief moment he almost wished he'd taken Meduso's advice and not followed the limo.

"Who's the big guy?" he asked.

It seemed like a perfectly simple question. Charlie was surprised when he had to wait for the answer.

"The boy should know." It was Fernando, his head emerging from beneath the gorgon's hat.

"*Fine*," Meduso said with one of his signature sighs. "They call him President Fear. He's the self-appointed leader of the Netherworld. And in case you're wondering, he didn't get to the top by being nice."

Another chill trickled down Charlie's spine. "He's the one the witch wants me to meet?"

"Perhaps," Meduso admitted reluctantly.

"Yess," Fernando corrected.

A million questions popped into Charlie's head, but they'd all have to wait. The limo's hunchbacked chauffeur was opening the trunk of the vehicle. President Fear reached inside and hauled out a body bound in ropes. It wasn't large enough to be a full-grown human—and it looked still enough to be lifeless.

The surprise hit Charlie like a bowling ball to the gut. "That kid's not . . ." He couldn't finish the thought.

"Dead?" Meduso offered. His expression was somber.

"No, but in a few minutes he'll probably wish he was. The president is one of the best in the business. And he doesn't make personal appearances in everyone's nightmares. That boy down there must be someone special if he's getting *this* kind of attention."

Charlie wrapped an arm around the tree's trunk, anchoring himself in place more firmly. He was feeling a little light-headed. It could have been him down there, thrown over the giant's shoulder. "So I guess if the president wants to meet me, that must mean I'm special too."

"Oh no, not *at all*." Meduso's voice was thick with sarcasm. "If President Fear went out of his way to have your body brought here by the witch, you're *much* more important than *that* poor child. I can't even imagine what terrible fate he might have in mind for you. Aren't you glad you decided to stick around?"

Charlie didn't argue. He knew he was pushing his luck by staying to watch the other kid's nightmare. And yet he couldn't bring himself to shinny down the tree. He followed President Fear's progress to the center of the stadium and watched closely as the man dropped the kid onto the grass. A group of creatures armed with pruning shears rushed in to cut the ropes that bound the boy.

"What are they going to do to him?" Charlie asked.

"Do I look like a mind reader?" Meduso tapped his head with an index finger, and the snakes beneath his hat hissed loudly. "It's that boy's nightmare, not mine. The more creative he is, the more interesting his torment might be. But bad dreams aren't meant to be a spectator sport. They're supposed to be scary for the dreamer—not entertaining for *us*."

The moment the words left Meduso's mouth, the little stadium began to grow bigger. Enormous blocks of beige stone appeared out of nowhere, stacking one on top of another. Stone by stone, a tall, curved wall was being built around the athletic field. Concrete filled in the gaps, and paint decorated even the tiniest details. When the construction was complete, Charlie counted three tall stories of arcades and columns. Statues of ancient gods and goddesses appeared in the upper windows. Charlie could hardly believe it. In front of him stood Rome's famous Colosseum.

"Did you see that?" Charlie marveled.

"I'm not blind," Meduso snapped. "Looks like the twerp's nightmare just got a lot more interesting."

Inside the Colosseum, the roar of a crowd erupted, but Charlie couldn't see past the wall. He could sense that the danger had grown, but his curiosity was too much to bear. "I'm going in," he announced, sliding off his branch and dropping to the one below.

"You can't be serious!" Meduso yelped.

"Your president might know where my brother is. I have to go inside," Charlie told him.

Meduso's hand shot out for Charlie's arm, but he grabbed only a fistful of air. "Young man, get back here this instant!"

Charlie was already at the base of the tree. "Are you coming or not?" he called up to the gorgon.

"Jusst let him go," Charlie heard Larry the snake say. "He'ss more trouble than he'ss worth."

"We can't leave him!" Fernando argued. "We promissed!"

"Fine," Meduso barked. "I'll escort the loathsome little human. But you three better stay hidden. If I hear one word out of any of you, I'll be paying a visit to the barber first thing in the morning."

Charlie entered the Colosseum with Meduso following reluctantly. They walked through a short, dark passage and emerged in the open amphitheater with the Roman sun suddenly shining down on them. Charlie's jaw dropped. The Colosseum's stands were packed with thousands of spectators. The entire population of Cypress Creek could have fit inside and there still would have been seats to spare. The noise was deafening; the crowd shouted and catcalled. As Charlie and Meduso squeezed down an aisle toward two of the few empty seats, Charlie passed several people he recognized.

He called out to a girl from his school, but she showed no sign that she'd even heard him. Charlie tapped her shoulder, but she didn't turn around.

"What's going on?" he asked. He examined the front and back of his hand to make sure it was solid.

"She's just a prop," Meduso explained. "The people you see are products of the dreamer's imagination. He created them, just like he built this arena. But look—see the goblins? Those are all too real. They arrived with the president."

Charlie scanned the crowd. "Goblins? How can you tell which ones are goblins?" he asked, just as his eyes landed on a remarkably ugly creature with wiry black hair sprouting from its ears—and a long, crooked finger crammed up its nose. "Never mind," he said. "I see them now." Once he knew what to look for, he realized they were everywhere.

"Yes, they're hard to miss. That's their one good quality," Meduso said as he and Charlie slid into their seats. "Otherwise, they're the vermin of the Netherworld. Most are too stupid to star in nightmares. The few smart goblins are far too cruel. That's why they were banned from our land before President Fear came to power. Then he found them lurking in the shadows outside our borders and brought them back here to be his own little army. These days, he never leaves home without a few dozen of the nose pickers. They pounce on anyone who looks like he might

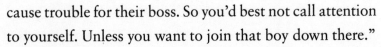

cause trouble for their boss. So you'd best not call attention to yourself. Unless you want to join that boy down there."

Meduso pointed to the center of the arena, and Charlie dragged his attention away from the goblins.

Below, the president of the Netherworld stood with his hand on the shoulder of a short boy with chunky black glasses. The kid's blue pajamas were decorated with brightly colored planets and stars. Charlie was too far away to get a good look at the kid's face, but he would have recognized those pajamas anywhere. He rose out of his seat. His heart was thumping so loudly that it nearly drowned out the crowd.

"Alfie?"

He felt someone grab his shirt and pull him back down. Charlie spun to his right to face Meduso. "That's not some regular kid down there. That's one of my best friends! We've got to do something!"

"Keep your voice down!" Meduso ordered, peering around Charlie to see if anyone else had heard. "We're staying right here. *Doing something* was never part of the deal."

"I don't understand," Charlie said, his frustration building. He was tired of all the secrets. "What *deal*?"

Meduso leaned closer. "The deal is, I'm supposed to smuggle your little butt out of the Netherworld. I'll even help you rescue your brother, since you refuse to leave without him. But there isn't *anything* I can do for that kid down there."

Charlie glanced back at Alfie. He looked so tiny and helpless standing beside President Fear in the middle of the enormous arena. "But there might be something *I* can do," he said.

"Oh really? You're going to help him? Well, guess what, Charlie?" Meduso tapped Charlie's chest with one perfectly manicured fingernail. "You're probably the reason that boy's here in the first place."

"Me?" Charlie almost choked on the word.

Meduso smiled like a man who'd decided to get a few things off his chest. "I heard you've been having bad dreams for a while now. Is that right?"

"Yes," Charlie admitted.

"You haven't figured out how to stop them, and you won't listen to anyone who tries to help you."

"Who are you talking about? And how would *you* know if anyone's tried to help me?" Charlie argued.

Meduso replied with sealed lips and a maddening shrug.

"Besides—so what if I've been having bad dreams?" Charlie added.

"Don't you see?" Meduso asked. "If you don't get rid of them, they rub off on others. Fear is like tar. It sticks to everything and swallows it all up. Your friend probably got the nightmares from *you*."

It makes perfect sense, Charlie thought. Back in the bunker, Alfie, Rocco, and Paige had all confessed to having bad dreams. Charlie must have been the one who'd passed the nightmares along.

"So it's *my* fault Alfie's here?" The wave of guilt that hit Charlie left him reeling.

"Don't bother worrying about him," Meduso replied. "He'll still wake up in the morning. His spirit may be here, but his body is back on the other side. So as unpleasant as his nightmare may be, he can't really get hurt. But you *can,* Charlie. And that's not even the worst thing that could happen. If we're caught in this stadium, that man down there could keep you trapped here in the Netherworld forever. Goodness only knows what he'd do to *me.*"

"LADIES, GENTLEMEN, AND GOBLINS! MAY I HAVE YOUR ATTENTION!" A booming voice broke through the din, and the stadium fell silent. Down in the arena, the president was addressing the crowd.

"His voice," Charlie whispered to Mr. Meduso. "I swear I've heard it before."

"Thank you for coming!" President Fear called. "We've got quite a show planned for you this afternoon. Now please give a warm Netherworld welcome to Alfie Bluenthal!"

The crowd hissed and booed. A goblin two rows down

from Charlie threw a glob of rancid hamburger into the arena. It splattered just to Alfie's left and was quickly followed by a maggot-ridden steak that sailed out of the stands and passed within an inch of Alfie's right ear.

"That's meat!" Charlie exclaimed, completely disgusted. "The goblins are throwing rotten meat!"

"Indeed," Meduso confirmed. "I assume they have a good reason. And I assume the reason has something to do with the show we're about to see. My guess is that the smell of the food is meant to whet something's appetite. I believe your friend is about to get eaten."

That thought, combined with the hot Roman sun and the stench of putrid meat filling the stands, made Charlie's stomach turn.

"Pull yourself together," Meduso hissed. "If you throw up, our cover is blown. Then we'll both be down there dodging rotten steaks."

Charlie swallowed and sat up straight.

"I've invited Mr. Bluenthal here today to show us what he's made of," the president announced, and knowing laughter rocked the stadium. "You see, Alfie *claims* to be a genius. But he's been hiding a nasty little secret. Our friend here is failing *gym*."

"Gym!" A goblin screeched with laughter, setting off the rest of the crowd. Shrieks of glee echoed across the Colosseum while Alfie buried his face in his hands.

"Look! He's crying!" shouted someone.

"Alfie's failing gym?" Charlie didn't even know that was possible. "Who fails *gym*?"

"And here I was thinking you were his friend," Meduso said, putting Charlie in his place. "No wonder Alfie never told you."

Charlie felt terrible. He'd always felt he could trust Alfie with anything. But for some reason, Alfie hadn't been so sure about *him*.

President Fear raised a hand and the Colosseum went quiet once more.

"What would you like to see first, ladies and goblins?" he asked the crowd. "Push-ups? Pull-ups? Some calisthenics? Or shall we see Alfie run the forty-yard dash? There's a reason he's called *Turtle*, you know."

"Turtle?" Charlie repeated. Why was the man's voice so familiar? The answer came to him in a flash. "I know that guy!" he whispered to Meduso. "He looks different over here, but that's Principal Stearns! The president of the Netherworld is the principal of my school. I always *knew* he was some kind of monster!"

"Don't be ridiculous," Meduso replied. "He's not the principal of your school. Do I need to explain how nightmares work? You people come *here* to our world. We don't go to yours. Even if we wanted to, there's only one way to get there—and until you came along, the portal stayed *closed*."

"I'm telling you, it's the same guy!" Charlie's voice was as close to a shout as a whisper can be. "He came to our school a few months ago. He's been horrible to all of us, but he's really nasty to Alfie and Rocco. Our principal is President Fear in disguise!"

"It's simply not possible," Meduso insisted, dismissing the idea with an imperious shake of his head.

"Of course it's possible! The witch got into my house, remember? And President Fear was the one who sent her to get me! So why is it so hard to believe that he's been to the Waking World too?"

Behind his sunglasses, the gorgon's plump face paled. He couldn't argue with Charlie's logic.

Charlie could hear the snakes whispering to each other beneath the gorgon's hat. "We should go," Meduso announced as he edged to the front of his seat. "If you're right about all of this, we're in far more trouble than I thought."

"No way," Charlie responded. He wasn't going to let Alfie down. He had to prove to his friend that he could really be trusted. Alfie had always been there for Charlie—even lately, when Charlie hadn't deserved it. Leaving him behind wasn't an option. "I've got to rescue my friend."

"The forty-yard dash it is!" President Fear's bellow rose from the center of the ancient battleground. "But before we begin, there's one little mistake I'd like to correct. I don't think I've ever seen a Turtle wearing glasses, have you?" He snatched the glasses off his captive's face.

"I need those!" Alfie cried meekly.

" 'I *need* those!' " President Fear mocked the boy. "Only losers *need* glasses." He threw the spectacles on the ground. "Now. On your mark!" President Fear held a starter pistol in the air. "Get set! Go!"

Alfie stumbled forward, his arms waving in front of him. Charlie's heart sank for his friend. He knew Alfie was practically blind without his glasses.

"RUN, CHUBBY! RUN, CHUBBY! RUN, CHUBBY!" chanted the crowd. But after a few minutes, the goblins had grown bored with watching the boy flounder.

"Now, *that's* entertainment!" President Fear had made his way to the opulent emperor's box on the north side of the stadium. "But why don't we make this a little more interesting?" A cloud of dust rose from the Colosseum floor. When it settled, Charlie saw that a bear had appeared at the far end of the stadium. A tiger was pacing in the middle. And a lion was crouched in the dirt right in front of their seats. "Place your bets, ladies and gentlemen! Which of these magnificent beasts is about to have *Turtle* for dinner?"

The hungry animals were all tethered to the Colosseum floor. Without his glasses, Alfie was bound to stumble into one of them. Charlie knew it was only a matter of time before his friend was torn to shreds.

"I'm going to get him," Charlie told Meduso. He couldn't wait any longer. "I don't care if this is only a dream. It's my fault he's down there. I'm not going to stay here and let Alfie suffer."

"Sit down!" Meduso demanded, more alarmed than ever. "Your friend will wake up when he's ready. He can't run away from his fears. If that boy leaves his nightmare now, he'll just be back tomorrow night. And next time, his fear will be worse. Every time you run away from a nightmare, it gives your fear strength. Is that what you want for Alfie?"

"It's better than being bear food," Charlie said.

Meduso grabbed Charlie's arm and held him back. "We can't reach the arena without a hundred goblins dragging us both away," he whispered. Then he stopped, smiled, and nodded cordially at a nose-picking goblin who'd happened to glance in their direction. The creature sucked snot off its finger and looked the other way.

"Yes there is," Charlie insisted once the danger had passed. "We can get to the arena the same way those animals got there."

Meduso shook his head, exasperated. "This is a dream. Your friend imagined those animals. He brought them to life and made them appear. It's the magic of how dreams work."

"This is *Alfie* we're talking about," Charlie said. "I've known him since kindergarten, and Alfie Bluenthal doesn't just *imagine* anything. He does his research first. I know *exactly* how those animals got into the arena, and it didn't have anything to do with magic."

CHAPTER FIFTEEN

ALFIE'S SECRET POWER

The previous year, Cypress Creek Elementary's sixth-grade history class had studied the Roman Empire. When it was time to write about what they'd learned, Charlie turned in a short, gruesome paper on the murder of Julius Caesar—and received a respectable B. Alfie, on the other hand, had produced a ten-page essay on gladiators, complete with hand-drawn illustrations and a model of the Roman Colosseum that he'd constructed out of balsa wood. During his presentation, he'd captivated his classmates with a tour of the ancient stadium—from the arena, where gladiators and wild animals fought to the death, to the hypogeum, the labyrinth of tunnels hidden beneath the Colosseum's wooden floor.

Charlie remembered very little about Julius Caesar. But thanks to Alfie, he knew more about ancient Rome's most famous stadium than most people four times his age.

Charlie guided Meduso out of the seating area and back inside the main structure. After a little searching, he found what he was looking for: a set of stairs that led to the hypogeum. It was exactly where it had been on Alfie's model.

Far below the stands where goblins cheered, Charlie led Meduso through a series of deserted passages. He had to give Alfie credit—his Colosseum was remarkably detailed. It was hot, dusty, and one hundred percent authentic. The floor was littered with fragrant piles of animal droppings. There was even graffiti on the walls that showed exactly what happened to inexperienced gladiators.

Charlie was scared, but his mission was clear: he had to save Alfie. That was all there was to it—and he knew what he had to do. With his mind off his own fears, Charlie could feel the darkness draining away. Soon he'd have a friend by his side. If he and Alfie put their heads together, they'd stand a good chance of finding Jack. Charlie remembered what his mother had said: *Two will always be stronger than one.* He wished he'd been quicker to understand. As always, his mom had been right.

The gorgon trailed a few paces behind Charlie, a silk handkerchief held over his nose and mouth.

"Did you hear what the kid ssaid?" Larry the snake whispered.

"Yess," Fernando answered. "It sseemss President Fear hass been vissiting the Waking World."

"What iss the president up to?" Larry asked. "Why doess he want to meet ssome wimpy kid?"

"This boy iss no coward," Fernando replied. "Just look where he'ss led uss."

Charlie smiled. He was really starting to like Fernando.

"You alwayss make excuses for humanss," Larry sneered. "Esspecially the sstupid oness."

"What can I ssay? I'm a people persson," Fernando hissed.

"Just because I can't see you guys doesn't mean I can't *hear* you," Charlie informed them.

"Ssee? The boy'ss not asss dumb asss you think," Fernando remarked.

"The jury's still out on that one," Meduso said, his voice muffled by his handkerchief. Then he lowered the cloth from his face and called out to Charlie. "So would you like to tell us what we're looking for down here?"

"An elevator," Charlie replied.

"And you ssaid he wassn't sstupid," Larry snickered.

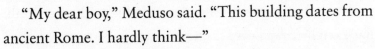

"My dear boy," Meduso said. "This building dates from ancient Rome. I hardly think—"

"Found one!" Charlie announced. He pointed to a thin square of light on the ceiling high above. It was a trapdoor. On the floor below it was a wooden platform. It was attached to a system of ropes and pulleys that could lift the platform up to the ceiling.

Meduso examined the platform skeptically. "That crude contraption is an *elevator*?"

"Yes, and up there is a trapdoor that leads to the floor of the Colosseum," Charlie said, directing Meduso's attention to the ceiling. "Alfie taught us in class that the Romans used elevators and trapdoors to make things appear in the arena. It looked like magic to the people who were watching, but it was all just smart engineering."

Charlie hopped onto the wooden platform and pointed to a rope hanging from the ceiling. "Pull on the rope and the elevator will take me all the way up."

"I wasn't told I'd be performing manual labor," the gorgon grumbled, removing his suit jacket. He folded it carefully, put it down, and rolled up his shirtsleeves. "I didn't endure eight years of gorgon finishing school to end up an elevator man."

Eventually Meduso got to work and the platform slowly began to rise. When he reached the top, Charlie pushed up on the trapdoor just enough for a peek inside the arena. Sand poured through the crack, and he coughed as thick yellow dust filled his lungs. A lion's roar rattled his eardrums. The beast was so close that he could smell the rotten hamburger on its breath. When the dust cleared, Charlie could see that it was straining to sink its teeth into something just out of its reach. With a little more rope, it could have attacked. Charlie pivoted and saw Alfie shaking in his pj's only a few yards away. His friend's legs were crossed, and his hands were clenched into fists. Charlie knew that Alfie's bladder shrank three sizes whenever he got scared.

"PEE YOUR PANTS!" chanted the delighted crowd. "PEE YOUR PANTS!"

"Alfie!" Charlie called, but the shouting was so loud that his friend couldn't hear.

"PEE YOUR PANTS!" shouted the crowd. "PEE YOUR PANTS!"

"ALFIE!" Charlie yelled as loudly as he could, the word grating his throat on its way out.

Alfie stood up straight, an expression of sheer surprise on his face. Charlie read his own name on Alfie's lips.

"I FOUND ONE OF THE TRAPDOORS! I'M THREE YARDS TO YOUR RIGHT!" Charlie yelled.

Alfie didn't need to be told twice. He started inching in

Charlie's direction but froze when the lion nearby issued another powerful roar. The boy stood perfectly still, one leg poised in midair. As Charlie waited for the foot to drop, he noticed something sparkling in the dirt. Alfie's glasses were lying on the ground halfway between the boy and the lion.

"STOP!" Charlie shouted. "GET DOWN ON YOUR HANDS AND KNEES. YOU HAVE TO CRAWL TOWARD THE ROAR!"

"What?" Alfie said. The confusion, fear, and hopelessness on his face were hard for Charlie to bear.

"TRUST ME!" Charlie called. "I'LL GUIDE YOU TO YOUR GLASSES."

Alfie looked like he was about to cry. He closed his eyes, took a deep breath, and dropped to his knees. Then he began to creep toward the lion.

The spectators went wild with excitement. Then a hush fell when they saw Alfie locate something in the dirt. After a quick cleaning, the glasses were on Alfie's face. Once he could see, he let loose a scream. A massive lion stood less than two feet from him. Alfie turned tail and began crawling full speed toward the open trapdoor.

"EAT THE TURTLE!" the crowd demanded. The goblins among them were on their feet. They were furious that Alfie might make it to safety. "EAT THE TURTLE!"

"Don't fret, ladies and goblins!" President Fear called

from the emperor's box. "I promised a show, and I intend to deliver!"

The president clapped his hands and the ropes holding the beasts disappeared. The lion launched itself at Alfie, with the bear and the tiger close on its heels. The lion would have the first bite, but the others were determined to get the leftovers.

"QUICK! KICK UP SOME DUST!" Charlie shouted.

Alfie followed Charlie's order, and for a moment, the creatures disappeared beneath a cloud of yellow dust. In the confusion, Charlie felt a warm body brush against his arm. Thinking it was Alfie, he made a grab for it and his fingers wrapped around a fur-covered leg. The roar that followed left him temporarily deaf in one ear. A claw grazed Charlie's forearm, leaving a trail of fire from his wrist to his elbow. He let go of the lion's leg and the beast spun around, knocking a body flat on the ground. Charlie reached out and located Alfie's arm.
He dragged

his friend through the opening. Alfie's feet had just left the arena when the trapdoor slammed shut. They could hear a furious beast stomping on the wooden boards above their heads.

"Charlie?" Alfie panted. "Is that really you?"

"In the flesh," Charlie confirmed, bending over to catch his breath as Meduso began to lower the platform back down to the tunnel. A little blood had seeped from the scratch on Charlie's forearm and stained the side of his jeans. The wound was still burning. On all his trips to the Netherworld, he'd never actually been hurt before.

"You saved me!" Alfie cried, throwing his arms around Charlie. Such displays of affection always embarrassed Charlie, but Alfie came from a family of huggers.

"You saved yourself," Charlie corrected, pushing Alfie back a bit. The boy's pajamas were soaking wet with a substance that had to be either flop sweat or lion spit. "I wouldn't have known about the elevators if it hadn't been for your presentation in history class."

Alfie looked astonished. "You mean you were actually listening?"

Charlie grinned. He always listened to Alfie—even when he couldn't understand what his friend was saying. "Yeah, and it's a good thing I was," he said. "That's how I knew how to get to you. Even though this is a dream, I figured you'd probably built a perfect copy of the Colosseum."

Alfie looked stunned. "I did, didn't I?" he said as the platform beneath their feet finally hit the ground with a thud.

"I hate to interrupt this touching reunion," Meduso drawled. "But we're about to be up to our butts in goblins. Do either of you fellows feel like running?"

Alfie looked at Charlie. "Who is *that*?"

"Meduso, meet Alfie Bluenthal. Alfie, Meduso."

"It's a pleasure to make your acquaintance, sir," Alfie said, holding out a hand. It dropped to his side before Meduso could shake it. A mob of goblins had just turned a corner and was heading straight for them.

"It's too late to run," Meduso observed. Then he slipped behind a column. "Stay where you are."

"While you get away?" Charlie demanded. "What kind of coward—"

"Shush!" ordered one of the snakes.

"When I shout *FREEZE,* you two close your eyes," Meduso commanded from his hiding spot. "I thought I'd given up sculpting, but it's time to make a little art."

He was going to turn the goblins to stone, Charlie realized, wishing he could watch.

"What's he talking about?" Alfie moaned.

"I'll explain later. Just do what he says," Charlie instructed. "Close your eyes the instant you hear *FREEZE* or you'll never use those eyes again."

A split second later, the goblins were upon them. They were all wearing filthy blue uniforms. Or rather, the top half of the uniforms. They didn't appear to be wearing any pants. Charlie had never seen such ugly creatures in the flesh. Their heads were mostly hair-free, and their noses were long, pointy, and brimming with snot. Up close, the goblins' skin was a pale, mottled green, with scaly patches that looked as though they might be moving. The creatures were spindly legged and had prominent potbellies. Most were only a few inches taller than Charlie, and none of them looked terribly strong, but there were dozens of them. There was no point fighting.

"Go ahead and take me." Alfie stepped forward bravely. "But please leave my friend alone. He doesn't belong in this nightmare."

Charlie reached out and pulled Alfie back while the goblins snickered. One in the front dug around his nose and wiped a trail of snot down the side of his uniform.

"Who says we're here for *you*?" it squeaked in a shrill voice.

"*You're* not the fugitive," another goblin sneered.

"Let me see what we've got." A third goblin stepped forward and smiled, flashing a set of broken black teeth. He was taller than the others and wore a pair of pin-striped pants. There was no doubt about it—he was one of the smart ones Meduso had mentioned, and he seemed to be in charge of the others. The goblin grabbed Charlie's arm and sniffed at the bloody scratch that the lion had left. Then a smile spread across his face. "Real blood," he announced to the crowd. "We've been looking all over the Netherworld for you, Charlie Laird."

Charlie shivered at the sound of his name. The goblin's voice was cruel and its smile sinister. This was no henchman. This was a creature that hurt others for fun—and enjoyed it all the more when his victims were helpless. The nightmares in the Netherworld might have been scary. But the goblin that stood before him was evil.

"But this is *my* dream," he heard Alfie say. "Why are you looking for *Charlie*?"

"Don't worry." The head goblin playfully pinched Alfie's cheek. "You'll be getting your share of attention soon. Once the president has Charlie Laird, he'll let us do whatever we want to *you*."

"I know! I know! Let's feed the Turtle to the tiger!" a smaller goblin shouted.

"Not all at once," another added. "Just a little bit at a time."

"We'll decide how to dispose of the Turtle later," said the head goblin, putting an end to the discussion. "First we deliver the fugitive." He grabbed Charlie's arm and twisted it. "You escaped from the witch, boy, but you won't get away from us."

"There's no clown to help you now, is there?" a small goblin taunted.

"He's all locked up," another chimed in.

"And his trial is tomorrow."

The goblins were talking so fast that Charlie could barely keep up with them. The dumber ones seemed to think with a single brain.

"When the clown is found guilty, we get to punish him."

"Then no more Dabney!" Two dozen goblins snorted with laughter.

"Come with us," the head goblin ordered Charlie. "The president wants to see you."

"He doesn't like to wait," one of the lesser goblins added.

"And you should see what he does to anyone who makes him." The head goblin leered at the boys as he spoke, and the mob howled with laughter.

Charlie was beginning to wonder if Meduso had abandoned them to a terrible fate when he heard the magic words: "FREEZE, VERMIN!"

Charlie squeezed his eyes shut and clapped a hand over Alfie's just in case.

"'Vermin'?" sneered one of the goblins. A chorus of shrill squeals followed. There were several loud crashes, as if large rocks had collided. And then there was perfect silence.

Charlie opened his eyes. The hideous mob was still crowded before them, but the creatures were stone from head to foot. Meduso was adjusting his sunglasses. But there was no time for celebrating.

"Goblins down! Goblins down!" came a voice from behind the mound of statues. The smart goblin must have figured out what was happening and closed his eyes just in time. He was crouched behind his frozen comrades, screeching into a walkie-talkie. "A gorgon is here! Alert the president and bring out the gorgon shields!"

"You're a gorgon?" Alfie gazed up at Meduso in awe.

"What did you think I was?" Meduso shouted at the boy. "Stop gawking at me and go!"

"Right!" Alfie agreed. "I suppose we can get acquainted later."

The fugitives tore off down the tunnel, only to come to a sudden halt at a fork in the passage. There were three routes to choose from, and they looked identical to Charlie.

"What do we do now?" he groaned. They'd come too close to escaping to get lost in an underground maze.

"I don't suppose it matters which passage we take," Meduso said, out of breath. "All routes will eventually lead us out of the building. And the president must have the entire stadium surrounded by now. You gentlemen should prepare yourselves to face a few goblins."

"That won't be necessary," Alfie answered. "Follow me. I know the secret way out."

Charlie looked at his friend with a whole new respect. Without Alfie, they'd be trapped. Charlie might have saved Alfie—but now Alfie was going to save him right back.

"*You* know a secret way out?" Meduso scoffed.

"Yep," Alfie replied as he calmly led them down the right side of the fork. "You see," he began happily, "this passage was built by the Emperor Commodus in the second century AD. Commodus was a terrible ruler, and no matter how many games or gladiator tournaments he held, he never won the hearts of the citizens of Rome. In fact, he was so reviled that he was forced to construct a secret tunnel beneath the Colosseum so he could enter and exit the stadium without going through the crowds. Then, in the year 182—"

Meduso grabbed Charlie's arm, and they both paused while Alfie charged on ahead, still lecturing to the walls.

"Is this kid for real?" Meduso asked Charlie.

Charlie smiled. "I don't think anyone could dream up someone like Alfie."

⚬ CHAPTER SIXTEEN ⚬

THE STONE GARDEN

Just when Charlie was beginning to think the underground passage might go on forever, it abruptly stopped. He, Alfie, and Meduso found themselves facing a brick wall with a rickety wooden ladder propped against it.

Charlie looked up, but he couldn't see where the ladder went. The top disappeared into a round hole in the ceiling. "Where does it go?" he asked Alfie, figuring the boy genius would know.

Alfie shook his head. "Beats the heck out of me."

"We've reached the end of his nightmare. I'm surprised it went this far," Meduso answered. He gazed up at the hole. "I suppose I'll have to take a look," he said with a huff, as if Charlie and Alfie had both refused the job.

The rungs of the ladder creaked as the gorgon climbed. A few seconds after he disappeared into the hole, Charlie heard a loud thump.

"Hey!" cried Larry. "Watch where you're going!" Charlie figured Meduso must have hit his head.

"My apologies," the gorgon said. "It seems we've found an exit," he called down to Charlie and his friend.

Hinges squeaked, and suddenly the hole was lit. Charlie looked up to see Meduso's butt blocking out the Netherworld sun.

"Of all the places to end up," the gorgon grumbled. Then he peered down at the boys in the tunnel. "You'll be fine. Follow me."

Alfie looked at Charlie nervously. "Should we?"

Charlie shrugged and began to climb the ladder. It wasn't as if they had much of a choice.

Back in the Waking World, a curious site lay at the foot of a mountain just to the west of Cypress Creek. There were no roads that led to the spot. To reach it, you had to hike for an hour or more, through waist-high grass and blackberry barbs. Just when you thought you were hopelessly lost, you would find it: a little patch of garden in the middle of nowhere, guarded by a giant oak and filled with wildflowers of every imaginable color. Five remarkably lifelike stone statues stood or sat among the blooms: A deer appeared ready to bolt. A stone dog growled ferociously. A lady with a walking stick always looked surprised. A skunk lifted its tail to spray. And an elderly man in tattered clothing sat cross-legged on the ground, gazing upward in sheer astonishment.

When Charlie's mom was alive, she had hiked to the strange little sculpture garden a few times every year. And when Charlie was five, she began to take him along. His mom never talked much during their visits. She plucked weeds away from the statues while Charlie piled leaves or scattered wildflower seeds. Before they hiked back, Charlie's mom would always leave a bone for the stone dog. She said it reminded her of a pet she'd loved when she was a girl.

Charlie hadn't returned to the spot in the three years since his mother died. Back when he was eight and the whole world felt enchanted, the sculpture garden hadn't seemed so unusual. Now that he was older, he suspected his imagination made it eerier than it really was. Still, Charlie had never expected to come across another place like it. Then he climbed up the ladder at the end of Alfie's nightmare.

Meduso had thrown open the plain wooden door that

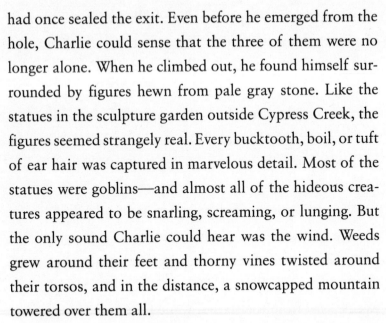

had once sealed the exit. Even before he emerged from the hole, Charlie could sense that the three of them were no longer alone. When he climbed out, he found himself surrounded by figures hewn from pale gray stone. Like the statues in the sculpture garden outside Cypress Creek, the figures seemed strangely real. Every bucktooth, boil, or tuft of ear hair was captured in marvelous detail. Most of the statues were goblins—and almost all of the hideous creatures appeared to be snarling, screaming, or lunging. But the only sound Charlie could hear was the wind. Weeds grew around their feet and thorny vines twisted around their torsos, and in the distance, a snowcapped mountain towered over them all.

"Where are we?" Charlie asked. He knew the figures were stone, but it was still unnerving to be so outnumbered. He reached out a finger and flicked the nearest goblin—a skinny specimen with its tongue stuck out. Sure enough, the goblin was hard as rock.

"It's the Netherworld dump," Meduso answered. "A new batch of goblins should be arriving from the Colosseum shortly."

Charlie's eyes darted nervously in Meduso's direction. "Did you turn all these creatures to stone?" he asked, suddenly overwhelmed. There were far too many to count.

Meduso didn't utter a word, and that was all the answer Charlie needed. He knew the goblins had probably deserved what they got, but that didn't make Meduso any less terrifying.

"They're not dead." Meduso seemed to have read his mind.

"But they're—" Charlie started to argue.

"They're *NOT DEAD!*" Meduso shouted at the top of his lungs, and Charlie sealed his lips.

Fernando slid out from beneath the gorgon's hat. "They're jusst frozen for now." He wrapped himself around Meduso's neck for a moment as if to give him a hug. Then he disappeared back under the hat.

"Hey, what's going . . . *Whoa.*" Alfie had pulled himself up onto solid ground. Charlie spun around to see his friend blinking furiously as his eyes adjusted to the bright sunshine. Charlie had spent the trip through the tunnels bringing Alfie up to date on the situation. But nothing he'd said had prepared either of them for the sight of thousands upon thousands of frozen goblins.

"Are we safe here?" Alfie whispered to Charlie.

Meduso overheard. "This is the Netherworld," he snapped at the boy. "You're not safe anywhere." He jabbed a finger in Charlie's direction. "And *this one* was stupid enough to bring his body along. So unless you want to see him barbequed by a dragon or smothered by a giant slug, we need to keep moving."

"But where are you taking us?" Charlie asked nervously.

If Meduso had disliked him before, he seemed to absolutely loathe him now. "You'll see" was his unsatisfying answer.

Under ordinary circumstances, Charlie would have refused to go anywhere, but the circumstances were far from ordinary. He nudged Alfie and they trailed behind Meduso as the gorgon headed off through the petrified crowd. Not all the statues were goblins, Charlie quickly noticed. There were other creatures mixed in among them. He spotted a Minotaur, a giant chipmunk, a blob that appeared to be made out of cheese, even a man in a business suit who looked almost human. Charlie wondered what they'd all done to earn the gorgon's wrath.

Alfie stuck close to Charlie's side. "Thanks again for rescuing me," he said, interrupting Charlie's dark thoughts. "This may be scary, but it's a million times better than my usual nightmares."

"I'm delighted to hear that *you're* both having fun," Meduso called back.

"Why are you thanking *me*?" Charlie asked Alfie, ignoring the gorgon. "You're the one who saved our butts in the end. That secret passage idea was brilliant."

Meduso suddenly spun around to face the boys. "Don't you think it's a *little* too early to be patting each other on the back? Do you have any idea how much trouble you're in? Or how much trouble you've gotten *me* into?" Charlie could see Alfie's startled face reflected in the gorgon's glasses when Meduso made a move toward him. "I suppose your friend Charlie forgot to give you the *bad* news, Alfie Bluenthal. You just ran away from your nightmare. That means you broke one of the Netherworld's biggest rules. You didn't face your fear. You'll have to go back— and next time it's bound to be worse."

Alfie met the announcement with a shrug. "At least I won't have to go by myself," he told the gorgon. Then he looked at Charlie and rolled his eyes. "Is he always this grumpy?"

"He'ss jusst upsset," came a lisping voice from beneath Meduso's hat.

"Who said that?" Alfie spun around in confusion. Charlie took his friend's arm and pointed at Meduso's hat. A red snake head was peeking out from beneath the brim.

"Wow!" Alfie exclaimed, hopping up and down like an agitated toad. "You really *are* a gorgon! Can I see your snakes? Can I see? Can I see?"

Meduso reluctantly lifted his fedora. Charlie took a step back as the three serpents unwound to get a good look at Alfie. Barry's forked tongue flicked over the boy's face.

"That's Barry," Charlie said, pointing to the green snake. "He bites. The brown one is Larry, and the red one is Fernando."

Charlie expected Fernando to offer a pleasant hello,

but apparently the snake wasn't in the mood for introductions.

"Our friend iss in danger," Fernando hissed. "There'ss no time to wasste."

"What friend?" Charlie asked, confused once again.

"Dabney the clown!" Meduso snapped. "Don't you ever pay attention? The goblins said Dabney's on trial for saving your rump from the witch. He'll be found guilty—there's no doubt about that. And you can't begin to imagine what those goblins could do to a rebel clown."

Charlie saw Alfie's eyes following Barry as the snake swayed from side to side—and he snapped his fingers in front of Alfie's face before his friend ended up hypnotized.

Alfie emerged from his trance with an idea for Meduso. "Why don't you go to the trial and turn them to stone?" he suggested. "That worked pretty well back at the Colosseum."

"It only worked because I was able to surprise them," the gorgon said. "President Fear and his goblins will be expecting me to show up at the trial—and believe me, they'll be prepared. Besides, freezing goblins is one thing. I can't just go around turning other hardworking nightmares to stone."

Charlie glanced at a statue of an ogre that towered over the goblins around it. Meduso hadn't had any problem turning *him* to stone.

"That's the first thing you two need to learn while you're on this side," Meduso said, sighing miserably. "You can't skip the hard stuff. Try to solve a problem the easy way and it will only get worse. There are no shortcuts in the Netherworld. If I'm going to rescue Dabney, I'll have to do it the hard way."

"We'll help you save the clown," Charlie announced. "Just as soon as we've found Jack."

"Yep!" Alfie agreed wholeheartedly. The adventure at the Colosseum seemed to have done wonders for his confidence.

Meduso slammed his hat back on his head and marched off, leaving the two boys in the dust. "Oh yeah?" he asked. "How are two Waking World twerps supposed to help *me*?"

Charlie raced to catch up with the gorgon, nearly stumbling over a leprechaun carrying a pot of stone coins. He had a hunch that Dabney's capture wasn't the only thing responsible for Meduso's foul mood. Something was telling him that Dabney was just part of a much bigger story— one that involved the nightmare giant Alfie and Charlie had known as Principal Stearns.

"What's going on?" Charlie pressed the gorgon. "This isn't just about two kids trapped in the Netherworld, is it? Alfie and I are special in some way, aren't we?"

"Oh, you're *special*, all right," Meduso grumbled. "But I wouldn't take that as a compliment."

"Why not?" Alfie demanded.

Charlie pushed past the gorgon so he could stand face to face with him. "Spill it, Meduso. Tell us everything you know. We're not going anywhere until you do."

"You want to talk *here*?" Meduso gestured to the crowd around them. A few feet away, two winged imps stared up at them from the weeds. Despite their stone eyes, they appeared to be eavesdropping. Charlie could tell that the portly gorgon was itching to move on. Being surrounded by his own victims made him squirm with discomfort. "Right now?"

"Yep," Charlie said, standing his ground. "Let's start with this: why were you looking for me when I got here?"

Meduso crossed his arms like a petulant child. "Must I repeat myself? I was told that a human boy had entered the Netherworld of his own free will. I promised to return you to the Waking World. That is all."

"Who did you promise?" Charlie asked.

"I'm afraid that's privileged information," Meduso replied stiffly. He wasn't going to reveal the name of Charlie's mysterious benefactor.

"Do you know why President Fear is trying to find me?"

"No clue," the gorgon said.

"That'ss a lie," Fernando hissed from under the gorgon's hat.

"Traitor," Meduso grumbled. "Why can't you mind your own business?"

Charlie arched an eyebrow and tried to look tough.

"Okay, fine!" Meduso said with a huff. "I have a few ideas. If President Fear is the principal of your school, he's clearly been going through the portal—"

"The portal in the purple mansion? President Fear has been in *my* house?" Charlie couldn't believe it—until he realized it made perfect sense. He remembered the footsteps he often heard in the early-morning hours. Charlie had assumed it was the witch, but it could have been the president instead. Maybe that was why Principal Stearns was always at school before everyone else and why he left before the last bell of the day rang. He could have been coming through the portal when the Laird family was still asleep and returning to the Netherworld before they all got home.

"Wait a second." Alfie jumped in. "He's been going through the same portal that Charlie came through?"

"Of course," Meduso said. "There's only one door between the Waking World and the Netherworld. Very few creatures on this side know it exists because it almost always stays shut. But if it's opened, nightmares can pass through it."

"How does it open?" Alfie asked.

Meduso looked at Charlie and frowned. "There are people in the Waking World who can unlock the portal and visit the Netherworld while they're still awake. But they never realize they have the ability until it's too late."

"Too late?" Charlie asked.

"They end up opening the portal by accident. It always happens the same way. Someone living in the mansion lets his life become as dark as the Netherworld. The portal unlocks and the person begins traveling between the two realms."

"It—it's happened before?" Charlie sputtered.

"Oh yes. The man who built the purple mansion was the first to visit this side. When he finally mastered his fears, the portal was sealed. Since then, it's been opened twice by humans who allowed fear to take over their lives."

"I still don't understand—who opened the portal this time?" Alfie asked.

Charlie felt his face burning. "I did." The shame was so heavy he thought it might crush him.

"You?" Alfie sputtered.

"Yes," the gorgon confirmed. "Charlie is terrified of something. Whatever it is, he must still be scared of it. If he weren't, the portal would have closed by now." Meduso took a step toward Charlie. "That is why President Fear is looking for you. He wants the portal to stay open for some reason, and that means he needs to make sure you stay scared."

"Why is he doing this?" Charlie asked. "Why does he want the portal to stay open?"

"That I don't know," Meduso said. "But I do know that you're not the only one who has problems now. Nightmares have been crossing over to the other side. Thanks to you, Charlie Laird, your entire town is in danger."

Charlie's arms fell to his sides. He had no more questions. Meduso stepped around him and began to wind among the statues toward the edge of the crowd. He seemed to be heading toward a dirt road that led up the side of the nearby mountain. Charlie and Alfie followed silently for a while, though Charlie could sense that Alfie was itching to speak.

"I just don't understand, Charlie," Alfie whispered at last. "Why are you so afraid?"

Immediately the darkness was back again, bubbling inside him. "Because my stepmother is a *witch*!" Charlie lashed out. He couldn't bring himself to admit that there was something that terrified him far more than Charlotte. He couldn't tell Alfie about the thing in the woods. "At least I'm not afraid of the forty-yard dash!"

"Excuse me? I think tigers and lions are a *lot* scarier than some old stepmom."

"Gentlemen!" Meduso spun around to face them. "Don't make me take off these glasses. If you start fighting, the danger will double. For better or worse, you two are in this together. Now apologize this instant."

"Sorry, Charlie," Alfie said, staring down at his feet.

"Me too," Charlie told his friend as the darkness drained away and turned to shame. "And I'm sorry for getting you guys into this mess."

"Thank you," Meduso replied haughtily. "I'll let you know when I'm ready to forgive you."

Charlie was about to roll his eyes when he realized he still had a question for the gorgon. "Wait—how do *you* know so much about the portal, anyway?" he asked.

Meduso stopped and let the question linger for a moment. "Because I was around the last time it opened—twenty-five years ago," he said at last. "That's the only thing I'll say on the matter because we're running out of time. We have a town, a clown, and a kid to rescue. And if you two are going to make it out of the Netherworld in one piece, the three of us need some expert assistance. The only person who can give it lives way up there."

He pointed to the side of the mountain that towered over them, and for the first time, Charlie noticed a tiny dot near the top that looked like it might be a cave.

∿ CHAPTER SEVENTEEN ∿

THE CAVE DWELLER

Charlie couldn't imagine how things could get much worse. He was trapped in the Netherworld. His little brother might get eaten by a witch. He'd put his whole town in terrible danger. And he was following a mass murderer up a mountain. No one would have blamed him if he'd burst into tears. The situation was as bad as situations can get. And yet, Charlie found that thought almost comforting. He'd heard that when life can't get any worse, it can only get better. Charlie was about to find out if that was true.

One thing was certain, though: he was still scared. Just

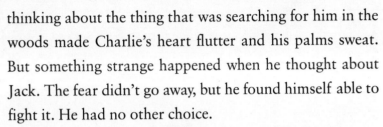

thinking about the thing that was searching for him in the woods made Charlie's heart flutter and his palms sweat. But something strange happened when he thought about Jack. The fear didn't go away, but he found himself able to fight it. He had no other choice.

Without that extra bit of courage, Charlie would never have been able to scale the mountain. The road to the top was lined with figures frozen in stone. These weren't like the goblins and nightmares from below. Here were heroes dressed in the dazzling armor of ancient Greece. A battalion of Amazon warriors. Two UPS deliverymen. Mongol scouts on horseback, arrows aimed and swords raised. And a flock of sheep that must have crossed the wrong path at the wrong time. The only thing the statues all shared was the look of sheer terror that had been preserved on their faces.

"Are you sure we should be following this guy?" Alfie asked Charlie softly. "Look at all the people he's frozen!"

Meduso must have heard him. "I'm getting rather tired of being insulted by you two puny humans," the gorgon called back. "I'll take credit for the goblins, but I had nothing to do with any of *this*."

The last stretch of road was blocked by a Roman legion. Hundreds of soldiers armed with shields, swords, and javelins were frozen in midaction. It took ages for Charlie, Alfie, and Meduso to squeeze between them. Then at last, the group arrived at the cave on the mountainside. It might have been carved into the hard rock face, but it wasn't the dank, gloomy den Charlie had been expecting. The door was ten feet high and decorated with inlaid gold. Beside the entrance were wide picture windows trimmed with scarlet drapes, and above, a stretch of french doors opened onto a sweeping balcony.

"This is the fanciest cave I've ever seen," Charlie observed. He was impressed, though he knew living in luxury didn't make the creature inside any less dangerous.

"Hey, look at this!" Alfie called to Charlie. He was standing off to the side of the cave's entrance, admiring the view.

The entire Netherworld was spread out below them. Charlie could see a patchwork of swamps, deserts, abandoned cities, and haunted woods in the distance. But that wasn't where Alfie was pointing. At the base of the mountain lay a nightmare version of Cypress Creek. The downtown shops were now a bunny-infested zombie town. The town's athletic field had been replaced by the Colosseum. He even spotted a strange black version of the purple mansion that reminded him of the picture Charlotte had drawn. And right at the edge of town stood Charlie's forest, the witch's belfry sticking out from among the trees. The sight made Charlie's stomach twist with nervousness. That was where he needed to be.

"Listen up!" Meduso called out. "You two better be on your best behavior. Our hostess is one of the Netherworld's biggest celebrities. And if you both enjoy being able to move, I suggest you treat her with the respect she deserves."

Meduso rang the doorbell and took a quick step back. Charlie tried to guess who might call the cave home. Maleficent? The Red Queen? Cruella de Vil?

The door to the cave flew open. "Darling!" cried the creature on the other side. "My sweet, dear little Basil. Give your mumsie a kiss!"

Charlie was awestruck. He'd seen more than his share of monsters, but nothing compared to the one in the doorway. Medusa had the face and torso of a beautiful older woman, the body of a giant serpent, and a hundred snakes growing out of her head. Fortunately a pair of oversized sunglasses protected her guests from her deadly eyes.

When she bent down to kiss her son, her serpents wrapped themselves around his head.

"Ouch!" Meduso cried. "Can't you teach your snakes not to bite? They're scaring Larry, Barry, and Fernando."

"Oh, darling, you know that's how they show their affection. When are you going to stop being so *sensitive*?" Medusa chided. Then she peered around her son at the two boys standing on her doorstep. Charlie tried to smile, but his lips wouldn't obey. "And what's this you've brought me?" She sighed dramatically. "You should be

turning children to stone, darling, not dragging them home to meet your mother."

"They're not ordinary children," Meduso argued. "They're—"

His mother held a hand up to stop him.

"I was only joking, darling. I know exactly what they are. I was just on the phone with our *dreadful* president. He seems to think my renegade son might show up here with two young fugitives in tow. I've been ordered to alert the authorities the moment I see you."

Charlie found his voice. "Will you?" he blurted out.

"Certainly not, child! *No one* tells Medusa what to do."

"Thank you, ma'am." Alfie sounded genuinely starstruck.

"Ma'am?" Medusa pouted girlishly. "Do I look old enough to be a *ma'am*?"

"He's a little boy, Mother. He calls everyone ma'am," Meduso assured her. "You're still just as gorgeous as ever."

Charlie saw her give Meduso a playful pinch on the cheek. "Thank you, darling. That's why you've always been my favorite son."

"I'm your *only* son," Meduso pointed out.

"And I do wish you would learn how to take a compliment. Come inside, boys. Let's not be seen dawdling outdoors."

The cave certainly looked like the home of a rich villainess. The floors were a slick white marble. Every doorknob was gilded, and each chandelier was made from a cavern's worth of crystal. Charlie was surprised to see mirrors on every wall. It seemed a bit dangerous to have so many around. If the legends were true, looking at her own reflection would turn Medusa to stone just as fast as anyone else. She must have worn her sunglasses twenty-four hours a day.

Charlie and Alfie followed Medusa as she slithered over to a seating area, her green scales shimmering in the light. Twice, Charlie had to leap over the rattle on the end of her tail as it whipped across the floor.

"Now, what can I do for you gentlemen?" Medusa asked once she was stretched out on an antique chaise longue. "Basil never visits unless there's a reason. Let me guess. You three are in need of some costumes?"

"Yes, Mother," Meduso confirmed. "And they'll have to be your finest work. I need to get these two humans back to the Waking World, which will mean smuggling one of them to the portal. It would be a challenge even if President Fear didn't have his goblins on the hunt for us."

"Oh, Basil," said Medusa, her voice dripping with disappointment. "Is *that* why you need my help? This is just a lowly *smuggling* operation?"

"What's your point, Mother?" Meduso snapped. "What do *you* think I should be doing?"

Medusa casually examined her nails. Charlie noticed they were painted scarlet and were as sharp as daggers. "I simply thought the three of you might be on your way to the courthouse. Your friend Dabney is on trial today. Shouldn't you be attempting to rescue him?"

Meduso sneered. Charlie was shocked to see the grown-up gorgon behaving like a spoiled teenager. At least Meduso *had* a mother to annoy him. Charlie would have given his left arm for a little mom nagging.

"You're worried about *Dabney*?" Meduso asked. "When I was a boy, you told me to stay away from clowns. You said they didn't know how to be frightening."

Medusa waved away the criticism with a dainty hand. "Sweetheart, we *all* say things we don't mean sometimes."

"Oh, you meant it," Meduso said. "I just wonder what made you change your mind."

"I've been keeping up with the news. The clown may not be frightening, but he's certainly courageous," Medusa replied dreamily. "And I have always *adored* a hero."

"Even the ones you turned to stone?" Meduso quipped.

Medusa pursed her ruby-red lips, and Charlie knew her son was in for a lecture. "Are you referring to my lawn or-naments?" she responded. "You and I both know that most of those statues are nothing but props. Besides, Dabney is a *real* hero. He only acts for the good of his fellow night-mares. If it weren't for him and his fellow rebels, President

Fear and those vile goblins would have complete control. So do you understand why you have to save Dabney—or do I need to have a word with Fernando? I know *he* realizes what's at stake."

Charlie saw something stir beneath Meduso's fedora. The gorgon yanked his hat down firmly before any snakes could pop out.

"No," Meduso said sullenly.

When Medusa smiled and reached out to pat her son's knee, Charlie could see that the scolding was over. "So, darling, will you save the clown? Before you do anything else?"

The question nearly jolted Charlie out of his seat. "Excuse me," he cut in before Meduso could answer. "I know we need to help Dabney, but what about my little brother? Shouldn't we rescue *him* first?"

"A witch kidnapped the boy's brother, and she's threatening to eat him," Meduso explained. "I hate to side with a human, but his problem may be a little more pressing than Dabney's. The kid brother's body may be here in the Netherworld. The boy could really get eaten."

"Oh, Basil." Medusa's theatrical sigh sounded exactly like one of her son's. "You've stopped thinking like a nightmare." She leaned over and clutched one of Charlie's hands. It took every ounce of restraint he could muster to keep from pulling it away. "The witch won't eat your brother, no matter how tasty he looks."

"How can you be sure?" Charlie asked.

"Because if she ate him, you'd no longer be so afraid that she would. Do you understand? Your fear is the only power the witch has over you. She's not going to trade that power for anything."

It took Charlie a moment to realize that the gorgon was right. Then his whole body seemed to relax. The witch had taken Jack so Charlie would come after him. If his brother got eaten, the witch would have nothing to use as bait. Of course, Jack would still need to be rescued. Wherever he was, odds were it wasn't too comfortable. But at least he was alive. That bought Charlie a little more time.

"Now come along, children," Medusa said. "If you're going to the courthouse, we'll have to ensure that you're properly dressed."

Medusa's wardrobe room was bigger than Charlie's old house. She slithered down the aisles, past countless costumes—most designed to fit a creature that was half woman, half snake. When she wasn't scaring humans senseless, Medusa was an actress, her son had explained. She owned the most popular theater in the Netherworld.

The voluptuous gorgon stopped at a rack stuffed with kid-sized disguises. "Aha!" cried Medusa, shoving a group of hangers to one side. "This might just work!"

Hanging from the bar were two furry gray costumes with long pink tails. The heads had mouths filled with sharp, pointy teeth.

"Rats?" Charlie rubbed the fur between his fingers. It felt a little too real. "Do you have anything scarier?"

Two of Medusa's snakes bared their fangs.

"But these are giant, *man-eating* rats, darling! One of the very worst nightmares of all! They've been starring in terrible nightmares for thousands of years. They're a classic!"

Meduso sighed. "Mother, if the boy—"

"No, no, it's perfectly fine," Medusa said, already examining more costumes. She stopped at a ruffled pink pinafore that was splattered with blood. "What about killer dolls?"

"No dolls!" Alfie blurted out.

"All right, then," Medusa replied. "Not to worry. Let's see what else we have here." She flipped through the costumes hanging in front of her. "Disease-carrying mosquitoes? Too many legs. Little gray aliens, complete with probes? Too adorable. Ah, here's one! Perfection at last!" The last costume was nothing but a dirty, dusty ball of tightly wound fabric.

Alfie began bouncing with excitement. "Can I be Tutankhamen? Please, please?"

"Certainly, darling!" Medusa exclaimed. "That's an *excellent* choice. You two share the same lovely complexion.

Though his nose isn't quite what it used to be. It got a bit mangled while he was trapped in that sarcophagus."

Charlie pointed at the ball of fabric. "How is *that* a King Tut costume? Where's the headdress and fake beard?"

"You're thinking of the mask Tut was wearing," Alfie said. "I'm going to be what they found *behind* the mask."

"A dead teenage boy?" Charlie joked.

"Good one," Alfie admitted. "No, I'm going to be a mummy!"

"Isn't that a bit lame?" Charlie argued. "Is anyone really scared of mummies?"

"They're *terrified* of the mummies *I* create," Medusa said with a sniff.

"And what about me?" Charlie asked.

Medusa held up a white sheet and black wig. "I'm afraid the only thing left in your size is a *yurei*."

"A what?" Charlie asked.

"It's a type of ghost," Alfie chimed in. "They're very big in Japan."

Charlie groaned. He'd never even heard of a yurei. But it would just have to do.

Within an hour Alfie was wrapped in rags and seated at Medusa's vanity, painting the skin around his eyes a raw, meaty red. With his rags ripped to reveal gaping holes in his flesh, Alfie was suitably terrifying. A few feet away, Charlie let Medusa help him into the sheet and stood still as she adjusted the wig. She hummed to herself as she worked, just like Charlie's mother had when she'd made her boys costumes for Halloween. It had been a long time since anyone had tended to Charlie so gently. He liked feeling Medusa's fingers fixing his hair and tugging his sheet into place. It was wonderful to be cared for. It was only when he closed his eyes and tried to pretend his own mother was there that the happiness began to turn painful.

"May I ask you a question, ma'am?" Charlie ventured.

"Not if you call me ma'am" was the reply.

"Okay, miss . . . ah . . . Medusa. I was just wondering . . . do most nightmares have children?"

"No, I'm one of the few lucky ones. Two thousand years ago, a little boy had a nightmare about a terrible gorgon baby and my son was born. I was so thrilled that I didn't even mind that the child had given my baby human legs instead of a tail. Or that his snakes never stopped talking. I loved my little Basil just the way he was."

For a moment, Charlie missed his own mother so much he could barely speak, but he did his best to keep up his side of the small talk. "You're two *thousand* years old?"

"No, darling, *Basil* is two thousand years old. I'm thirty-nine."

Medusa smiled at the confusion written on Charlie's face. Behind her painted lips were two perfect rows of sharp white teeth. "You'll get that when you're older. Anyway, there's always work out there for a gorgon. Every year hundreds of nightmares are forced to become new creatures, but snake hair never seems to go out of style."

The idea took him by surprise. "Other nightmares change?" Charlie asked.

"Oh yes," Medusa said. "They must evolve in order to keep up with the times. For instance, in the Middle Ages, Europeans were terrified of taking baths. Their fear kept some creatures busy for centuries. But no one's frightened of soap anymore. Not even the French. Same thing happened with the Black Death. The doctors who treated it wore terrible masks with long, birdlike beaks. The Netherworld used to be packed with them. Now everyone's wearing hockey masks and carrying chain saws. You see, when a nightmare stops being scary, it's given a choice to become something else. I try to help whenever I can. Nightmares often come here to my costume room to try out new identities."

"But what if a nightmare creature doesn't want to change?"

"Then it retires and disappears," Medusa replied.

The air around Charlie seemed suddenly icy. "I don't understand," he said. "How can a nightmare just disappear? Where does it go?"

Medusa sat back. "That's an excellent question. Some say that when nightmares retire, they turn into dreams. But none of us has ever laid eyes on the Dream Realm, so no one here can be sure it exists. I'm afraid most nightmares have come to believe that we have only two options: either we keep scaring people forever—or we die."

"Die?" Charlie remembered what Dabney the clown had shouted to him in the forest—that nightmares never die. Dabney had saved Charlie's behind, so he hoped for the clown's sake it was true. "What do you think?" he asked Medusa.

"I think I'll discover the truth soon enough," Medusa said. "I don't really mind. Death doesn't scare me. After a few thousand years, scaring children gets to be a bit of a bore. It's Basil I worry about. He doesn't want to be a nightmare, yet he refuses to retire. He does just enough work to stay in the Netherworld. But his attitude has gotten him into a great deal of trouble. The president thinks he sets a bad example."

"Why doesn't Meduso want to be a nightmare anymore?" Charlie asked.

When Medusa sighed, several of her snakes sighed with her. "There was a time when my son was the most terrifying nightmare of all. He'd turn any creature he encountered to stone. Then one day Basil found a way into the Waking World. He brought me that." She pointed to a stone chipmunk sitting on her work desk nearby. "It's a horrid little beast," Medusa said appreciatively. "Are there many more like it in your land?"

Charlie struggled to hide his amusement. "The woods are full of them," he told her.

Medusa shivered and continued her tale. "Basil was very ambitious back then. When he took a second trip to the other side, I worried he might try to conquer the Waking World. But he didn't. And when he returned to the Netherworld, my son wasn't the same."

"How was he different?" Charlie asked softly.

"He wasn't interested in frightening humans anymore. He told me he'd met some children on the other side, and he'd come to admire them."

Human children, Charlie thought. "Who were they?"

"I have no idea, dear," Medusa replied. "I've never fraternized with your kind."

"If he doesn't want to be a nightmare, why won't he retire?" Charlie asked.

"Because he's scared," Medusa said simply.

"Nightmares get scared?" The thought had never occurred to Charlie.

"Certainly," Medusa replied. "And Basil isn't the only one who's frightened these days. President Fear is determined to make all of us question whether the Dream World is real. Before the president came to power, our lives were simple. If you enjoyed being a nightmare, you kept scaring humans. If you got tired of it all, you could retire and become a dream. Now, thanks to our president, everything's changed. Today most nightmares don't believe in the Dream Realm—and no one retires because they're scared it means dying."

"But Dabney said nightmares don't die."

Medusa smiled at the mention of the clown's name. "Dabney is convinced that the Dream Realm exists. That's why he's such a thorn in the president's side. Dabney says our job isn't to keep humans scared. Our job is to help humans face their fears. And if we do our jobs well, we deserve to retire. The Dream Realm is our reward."

"No one believes that?" Charlie asked. "Not even Meduso?"

"Fear can be hard to fight," said Medusa. "But I know Basil *wants* to believe. That's why I give him a nudge now and then. He's braver than he realizes. He just needs to find his courage."

She finished fixing Charlie's costume, pulling the long black hair of his wig down over his eyes and helping him step into a pair of Japanese-style flip-flops with wooden soles.

"Now turn around and have a look in the mirror," Medusa ordered. "Keep your hair in your face at all times."

Charlie faced himself in the floor-length mirror. There before him was the scariest ghost he'd ever seen. But there was something odd about the costume, Charlie noticed. Now that it was on, the sheet looked more like a kimono.

"Wait a second," Charlie said. "Am I wearing a *dress*? Did you just turn me into a *girl* ghost?"

"Yurei are traditionally female," Medusa replied with a rattle of her snake's tail. "But I'll have you know girls can be every bit as scary as boys. Besides, who's going to make fun of you here? No one in the Netherworld gives a hoot about such things."

Charlie frowned at his reflection. He doubted anyone could stand to look at him long enough to realize he was dressed as a girl. "Okay," he finally said. "I'll wear it."

"Thank you, darling," Medusa said. Then she added softly so that only Charlie could hear, "I'm glad you and your friend will be there to help Basil."

"I'm doing it for Dabney," Charlie admitted. "I don't think your son likes me that much."

"You're wrong about that," Medusa confided. "I know Basil can be grumpy at times. And we've all heard him say nasty things about your kind. But you must understand, he's only trying to keep his horrible secret from getting out."

"What secret?" Charlie asked.

Medusa bent down and whispered in Charlie's ear. "Basil *enjoys* helping humans."

∽ CHAPTER EIGHTEEN ∽

THE GUINEA PIG

The Netherworld courthouse was a dismal-looking structure. It was built in the same style as the Cypress Creek courthouse, but several varieties of mold made it look like it was covered in furry vomit. Most of the building's windows were broken, and shards of glass littered the sidewalk outside. A long line of creatures stretched down the front steps, all waiting to be granted admission to the trial inside. There were millipedes, wraiths, yeti, and three almost-normal-looking humans wearing shorts, sneakers, and baseball hats.

"What are *they*?" Charlie wondered out loud.

"Gym teachers," Alfie responded with the air of an expert. "The first two are mean types. The third is the kind who's always saying you just have to try harder. Those are the *worst*."

In the square in front of the courthouse, a thuggish gangster was hawking mirrored sunglasses in all shapes, styles, and sizes.

"Rebel gorgon on the loose!" he shouted. "Get your gorgon shields today! Or risk ending up a piece of art!"

"Do those things really work?" Charlie whispered to Meduso, who was dressed as the Grim Reaper. He wore a black cloak, his face hidden under an enormous hood, and he carried a scythe in his hand. Charlie was impressed by how convincing he looked. Even the other nightmare creatures were careful to keep their distance.

"The shields work quite well, I'm afraid," Meduso responded. "If I were to see my reflection in the mirrored lenses, it would turn me to stone. Mirrors are a serious occupational hazard for gorgons. Why do you suppose there are only two left?"

"But your mom's house is filled with mirrors," Alfie pointed out.

"Yes, she loves mirrors," Meduso replied. "She may be a gorgon, but she's also a diva. One is a terrifying creature that can turn men to stone, and the other is a gorgon."

Meduso guided Charlie and Alfie to the end of a long

line that led into the courthouse. At first, Charlie was entertained by the parade of monsters. Then he realized that they'd been standing still for quite a while.

"Why is this taking so long?" Alfie whined.

Charlie stood on his tiptoes for a peek inside the building. He was starting to get a bit nervous.

"The guards are inspecting everyone," Meduso explained. "It's a good thing your costumes are top-notch. You make a truly terrifying young mummy. And, Charlie, you make a lovely lady ghost."

Charlie scowled. He was far too anxious to joke.

"President Fear has all the goblins and guards looking for us, doesn't he?" Charlie asked.

Meduso sighed. "There you go, feeling *special* again. For your information, they're looking for me too."

The line kept inching forward, and Charlie finally entered the courthouse. Ahead, he saw each nightmare creature being stopped and examined at a checkpoint manned by a giant grub. Its glossy white body was at least six feet long and four feet in circumference. A tiny brown head with enormous pincers sat on top. Beneath it were six wiggling legs so small that they barely seemed useful. The guard's beady black eyes watched as a man dressed as a dentist pulled an obscenely long needle out of his doctor's bag. Next up was an otherwise jolly-looking garden gnome who unhinged his jaw to reveal a set of flesh-ripping teeth.

"What's the grub making them do?" Charlie asked Meduso.

"She's administering a scare check," said the gorgon. "It's the best way to tell a real nightmare from a fake."

Charlie felt sweat begin to bead along the edge of his wig.

"Look!" Alfie pointed at an elderly human woman who'd made it to the front of the line. "Let's see what happens to her."

The old lady gestured for the grub to bend down. As soon as its cheeks were within reach, the woman pinched one as hard as she could—and planted an icky wet kiss on the other. The grub squirmed free and shook her head. She wasn't satisfied. Then the old lady opened her mouth. Six tentacles shot out, wrapped around the grub, and hoisted it into the air.

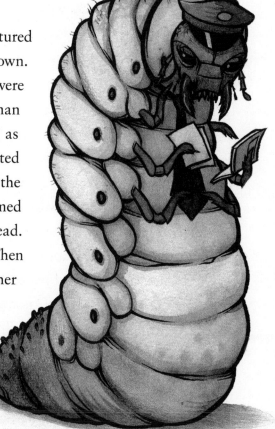

"Impressive," Meduso admitted. "I wouldn't have guessed she had it in her."

"Alfie and I are never going to pass that test!" Charlie's palms were perspiring now. "We've got to get out of this line. We need to come up with another plan."

"Nonsense," said Meduso. "Mother always thinks of everything." He put his hand on the back of Charlie's neck and felt around under the wig. "There's a switch here somewhere. Ah, there we go. No more talking now. Your costumes were made for the theater. They have built-in microphones, and I'm turning them on." He paused to flip the switch on Alfie's mic as well. "When the grub asks, I want you to give it a proper mummy roar. And, Charlie, I need you to shriek as loudly as possible. Do you think you can do that?"

Charlie and Alfie both nodded. The contents of Charlie's stomach were churning. He worried that more than just air might come out with his scream.

"Well, then wait until everyone's listening and let 'er rip," Meduso instructed. "Not too loud, though, or you'll bring the whole building down."

When the three of them reached the front of the line, the giant grub held up one of its six tiny legs and brought them to a halt. "You two are awfully cute for nightmares," it noted in a bizarre baby-doll voice.

Charlie said nothing. He could tell by the way Alfie's fists were clenched that he was offended.

"I don't believe yurei possess the power of speech, madame," Meduso offered helpfully. "And the mummy's tongue may have been removed as part of the embalming process."

The guard remained unimpressed. "My supervisor's gonna need to have a closer look at you two." She held a walkie-talkie up to her mouth. "Excuse me, ma'am? Can you come over for a second? We have a couple of nightmares here who are looking awfully *precious* to me." She sneered when she said the word *precious*.

Charlie gaped at the supervisor, who was heading their way. She was a bright blue goddess with four arms and a necklace made of human fingers. Her name tag read *Kali*.

"A mummy and a girl ghost? How adorable," Kali droned, as if she'd already seen it all. "You two better put on an impressive performance or we'll have to turn you over to *them* for an examination."

Charlie's eyes followed the goddess's gaze. Three goblins were standing on the side, exploring their nostrils as they waited to see what the pint-sized nightmares would do. Charlie took a quick look at Alfie and held up five fingers. Alfie nodded. On the count of five, he let loose a terrible roar.

"MMMRRRRRAAAAAAAWWWWWRRRRRR!"

And Charlie released what may have been the loudest screech of all time.

"EEEEEAAAAAAAAAAAAAAEEEEEEEKKKKKKK!"

The combined sound rocked the entire building. It rattled Charlie's brain and made his knees quake—and for once, it wasn't with fear. The little glass left in the courthouse's windows shattered and fell to the floor.

"Good enough," announced the supervisor, still looking bored. "You guys enjoy the trial."

Inside, the massive courtroom was packed. But it wasn't until they located Dabney at the front of the room that Charlie's eyes went wide. The battered clown was chained to an office chair, and a goblin guard stood beside him, plucking bright red hairs from Dabney's scalp one at a time. Suddenly Charlie got a sense of how much was at stake. There was no telling what the goblins might do to Dabney after the trial. And just like Jack's kidnapping and Alfie's terrible nightmares, Dabney's arrest was Charlie's fault. It was his duty to rescue him. But looking around the room at the fearsome creatures in attendance, Charlie wasn't sure that was something he'd be able to do.

"Out of the way!" someone ordered.

Charlie stepped to the side as the president's entourage pushed past Meduso, making room for their leader. President Fear was wearing a pair of gorgon shields, as were the members of his goblin posse, who almost shoved Alfie to the ground as they hurried to keep up. When the president arrived at the front of the courtroom, the audience broke into applause.

President Fear towered over most of the nightmares. His perfectly cut suit and rigid posture demanded deference, yet he would have been just as terrifying without them. It was his pitiless expression. And the smile that appeared whenever someone was suffering. President Fear was truly a classic nightmare, Charlie realized. He not only made the ideal school principal, he also would have been perfectly cast as a boss, bully, or prison guard—any role designed to make a person feel weak and helpless. The president had probably starred in a million bad dreams.

"Thank you. Thank you," Fear said solemnly, and a hush fell over the crowd. "Before we begin our official business this morning, I have some unfortunate news to report. There are two human children loose in the Netherworld."

Charlie, Alfie, and Meduso immediately dropped into seats before anyone noticed that the mummy and ghost weren't quite fully grown.

"Loose?" a banshee shrieked. Nightmare creatures began checking under their chairs, as if children might be hiding beneath them. Charlie was careful to look under his too.

"That's right. Loose!" The president pointed a finger at Dabney. "And this clown and his friends are responsible."

"Traitor!" someone shouted. A tomato flew through the air and splattered against Dabney's chest. It was quickly followed by three eggs and a beet.

"You guys sure throw a lot of food here," Charlie whispered to Meduso, wincing as a cabbage exploded near Dabney's head.

"What else are we supposed to do with it?" Meduso asked. He reached into his robes and pulled out a tomato. "Mother's idea," he said when he saw Charlie watching.

Charlie was about to ask for an explanation when the president held up one hand.

"Your attention, please!" he said, and the food stopped flying. "I'm sorry to say that the news only gets worse."

"What could be worse than disgusting little children infesting our world?" moaned the cockroach seated next to Charlie.

President Fear took a step toward the audience, as if he was preparing to share a secret. "I was hoping to make the following announcement in a more festive setting, but I have no choice but to make it now. For the last few months, I have been working on a special project—one that could benefit every creature in the Netherworld. The clown and his fellow rebels have put that project in jeopardy." The president's eyes glowed the red of bubbling lava. "I have found a way into the Waking World."

The crowd went silent. Charlie could see that the

announcement had taken them all by surprise. A mean-looking pixie raised her hand. "Um, excuse me? Why would you want to go *there*?"

"Let's see if Phyllis can answer that question," the president said. He was approaching a member of the audience.

Phyllis appeared to be a vampire. Aside from the size of her pointy incisors and her unusually pale complexion, she was an attractive creature with jet-black curls and ruby lips. "What? *Me*?" She searched the seats around her for another Phyllis. Then the president took her delicate hand, and Charlie almost felt sorry for her.

"You're just not as scary as you once were, are you, Phyllis?" he asked.

"Well, I'd like to think . . . ," the vampire started to argue. Then her spine sagged and her head dropped. "No," she admitted. "The last few humans I've visited have *wanted* me to drink their blood. They don't even scream when they see me. They start asking questions instead. Last night, a little girl actually asked me if I sparkle in the sunlight! Can you *imagine*?"

President Fear shook his head sadly and gave the vampire's hand a tender pat. "Now that you're no longer frightening, you'll be facing an important choice soon, won't you? You can either decide to become a new nightmare— or you can opt to retire from service. Have you figured out which it will be?"

"No," Phyllis whimpered. A blood-red tear trickled from one of her eyes.

"I know, it's a terrible choice, isn't it?" President Fear asked, and Charlie shuddered. The giant looked creepiest when he was trying to make a show of sympathy. "Well, what if I told you that you might not have to decide at all?"

"That's not possible," Phyllis said sadly. "All of us have to choose."

"We do today. But that may be something we're able to change," the president said. He looked up at the audience. "The Waking World humans fear us at night, but they leave us behind every morning. They wake up to see the sun shining and hear the birds chirping. And over time, we simply stop scaring them. But if we were to conquer the Waking World, we could make humans live in fear all the time—day and night. None of us would ever need change. And none of us would ever die."

"We could do that?" Phyllis asked in astonishment. "We could take over the Waking World?"

It was only when Charlie heard Alfie gasp that he realized he hadn't been breathing.

President Fear let go of the vampire's hand. His voice rose as his eyes passed over the crowd. "Yes. We *can* conquer the Waking World. I've discovered a portal between our world and theirs. It's located in a town called Cypress

Creek, and I've already begun preparing for invasion. But in order to continue, I must find the two boys who went missing last night. One of them is essential to my plans. It was his fear that opened the portal. Unless we keep him terrified, the doorway could close before we're ready."

Charlie shrank down in his chair, worried that his heart was thumping loud enough for everyone in the room to hear. The situation was worse than he'd ever imagined. The Waking World was on the verge of being invaded by monsters, and he, twelve-year-old Charlie Laird, was the one who had allowed it to happen.

President Fear snapped his fingers and three goblins scampered to his side, carrying a giant easel, the top of which was covered with a black drape. The president whipped off the cloth, revealing a simple whiteboard with big black letters.

1. FIND THE BOY
2. KEEP THE PORTAL OPEN
3. CONQUER THE WAKING WORLD
4. TRY A KRISPY KREME DOUGHNUT
5. NEVER DIE

"The plan, my fellow nightmares, is simple. One—find the boy. Two—keep the portal open. Three—conquer the Waking World. Four—try a Krispy Kreme doughnut. Five—never die."

The crowd whispered excitedly.

"Will it really be that easy?" asked a skeleton with a booming voice.

"Nothing could be simpler, my boy," the president assured it with a gruesome smile.

"I'm a *lady*," replied the skeleton with a huff.

"And what a lovely set of bones you have, dear," the president replied without batting an eye.

Then the remains of an Old West outlaw stood up. He took off his hat to address the president, exposing a hole in the center of his forehead.

"You say we gotta keep this kid in a state of terror. Well, I've scared a lot of folks over the years, and it's a tricky business. If you're not horrifying enough, they stop coming here to see you. But if you're too terrifying, it really messes 'em up. How are you gonna make sure we don't push the kid over the edge?"

President Fear's grin made him look like a demonic game show host. "What wonderful timing you have, Tex! That's the question I was hoping to hear! How do you keep a human scared—without driving him completely insane? Allow me to introduce you to the Terrorizer 3000." The president held up a rectangular object with a dull gray metal case and a shiny black screen. "It's a revolutionary new device invented by yours truly. It gathers data from sensors that are placed on a human and makes it possible to monitor the person's fear levels at all times. I try to keep the dial set between three and eight. An eight will make humans empty their bladders. A nine will make them pass out. And that's as far as you'll want to take it. Only in the most extreme situations should you ever turn the dial to ten."

"What happens when you hit ten?" someone asked.

The president ignored the question. "Perhaps a demonstration is in order. I have a guinea pig next door just waiting for the show to begin. Lights!"

The lights in the courtroom dimmed and a video image was projected on a white wall behind the president. A tiny blond girl in a pink nightgown was pacing back and forth across an empty room.

Alfie gasped. "Holy moly, it's Paige!"

Charlie sat up straight in his chair and squinted at the screen. He refused to believe it. "How could it be Paige? She's not scared of anything."

"You still don't get it, do you?" Meduso chided him. "Everyone is scared of *something*."

ᗫ CHAPTER NINETEEN ᗫ

WHO'S AFRAID OF THE DARK?

"You've probably noticed that many of the children of Cypress Creek have begun spending their nights here with us," President Fear told the captivated crowd. "Terror is spreading quickly throughout the town. The sun hasn't shone on Cypress Creek in weeks, and it's already beginning to look a lot like the Netherworld. Children are always the first to succumb to fear, but it won't be long before the adults fall prey to it too. Soon I will be taking some of you with me to the other side. Once Cypress Creek is under our control, we can expand our operations. We'll conquer the Waking World house by house, town by town.

"Those of you who are wondering how we can keep humans frightened twenty-four hours a day, please allow me to demonstrate. Our guinea pig today is a young girl by the name of"—he paused to check the screen of his device— "Podge."

"Podge?" Alfie whispered.

"Podge is in a room at a testing facility next door. Right now her fear level is hovering right around two. Let's see if we can bump that up to a respectable six or seven."

In the video, the lights went out, and a scream cut through the air. The camera filming Paige switched over to night vision, and the audience in the courthouse saw the tiny blonde standing in the center of the empty room. Completely blind in the darkness, she stretched her arms out in front of her, feeling around for a wall. Only, each time she got close to one, the room would expand. Within seconds, Paige was frantic. Her arms flailed and tears poured down her cheeks. She was walking in circles.

"It looks as if Podge's fear level has reached a healthy five," said President Fear without an ounce of concern for the suffering girl. "But I think we can do a little bit better, don't you?"

The door of Paige's room creaked open and a shadowy figure tiptoed inside. It was sleek and black, without eyes, mouth, or features. Its long, tendril-like fingers stroked the air. Paige stopped, held her breath, and listened as the figure's soft footsteps grew closer and closer. She wrapped her arms tightly around herself. Charlie could see her chest heaving. Watching Paige suffer was far worse than any nightmare he had ever had. Whatever the consequences, he had no choice but to help her.

"I'm going to put a stop to this," he whispered, rising from his seat. Alfie stood with him.

"Sit down!" Meduso grabbed their costumes and yanked both boys back down.

"But Paige needs us!" Alfie whispered.

"That room is under heavy surveillance," Meduso hissed. "If you're caught on camera, it will put our whole mission in jeopardy. Your friend is just having a very bad dream. If you insist, we can rescue her as soon as the clown is safe. But we came here for Dabney, remember? He's the one who's really in danger."

Charlie's eyes landed on Dabney, who was mesmerized by the video just like

everyone else. Even with paint on his face, the clown's horror was clear. Somehow Charlie knew that Dabney would have wanted him to save Paige.

"Shall we crank it up to six?" the president announced from the front of the room.

A few in the crowd cheered him on. But most of the nightmare creatures in the courtroom appeared shocked by the demonstration. They didn't seem to enjoy watching a child suffer. Even the giant cockroach next to Charlie squirmed in her seat as she watched the video.

On the screen, the dark figure took a step toward Paige. It bent down, its featureless face just inches from the girl's. Charlie could tell that Paige sensed its presence. She could probably feel its breath on her skin as well. But she still couldn't see it.

"What *is* that thing?" Alfie whispered, shifting uncomfortably.

"That, my friends, is the oldest nightmare of all," Meduso replied solemnly. "Most of your kind call him the Dark."

"Paige Bretter is scared of the Dark?" Charlie couldn't believe it. The Paige he knew was the coolest customer around. She was the kind of girl who could save a group of kindergarteners from a rabid skunk—or use her own sweater to put out a fire.

"Haven't you learned *anything* since you got here?" Meduso asked, keeping his voice low. "The important thing

isn't *what* Paige is scared of. It's *why* she's scared of it."
He pointed to a harmless-looking old lady sitting in the
front row. "Doesn't seem very scary, does she? But there's a
reason someone dreamed her up. Nightmares are humans'
fears in disguise."

Nightmares are fears in disguise. Where had he heard
that before? Charlie wondered.

"So do either of you have any idea why Paige might be
afraid of the Dark?" Meduso asked.

Charlie would have sworn he knew everything about
Paige, but he had no idea why she'd be so terrified of something she couldn't even see.

"She never told you she's scared of the Dark, did she?"
Meduso asked, and the boys shook their heads. "That's
how fear grows. When you keep it locked inside and never
let it out, it starts to eat you alive."

"I've had enough!" It was the cockroach beside Charlie.
He swiveled to face her, expecting to be scolded for whispering during the show. Instead, he saw the bug gathering
her things. "I can't watch this anymore. It's not supposed
to work like this," she muttered to herself. "You're supposed to give the humans a good scare, then let them wake
up. Nightmares aren't meant to be *torture*."

Charlie saw his opportunity. "I couldn't agree more,
ma'am," he told the cockroach. He grabbed her handbag
and offered her an arm. "Allow me to escort you out."

"Thank you, sweetheart," the cockroach said. "It's nice to discover there's *some* decency out there. You know, young lady, I don't imagine you're old enough to remember the horrible things the goblins used to do to humans. Let's just say that we had very good reasons for kicking them out of the Netherworld. And now they're back and we're torturing children. It's a shame, I tell you. I shudder to think what this land is coming to."

"Charlie! Where do you think you're going?" Meduso demanded as Charlie and the bug squeezed around him, making their way to the aisle.

"To get Paige," Charlie told him.

"Then I'm going too," Alfie said.

"No." Charlie pushed his friend back down in his seat. "Stay with Meduso. He'll need your help saving Dabney."

Charlie hadn't noticed the testing facility next door to

the courthouse. It must not have been there while he was waiting in line for the trial, because it wasn't the sort of place he'd forget. The dull gray building was overgrown with poison ivy, the leaves shining in the dim Netherworld sunlight. With its entrance flanked by marble columns and tattered shades hanging in its many windows, it appeared to be an abandoned asylum. Charlie was willing to bet it was home to hundreds of ghosts.

For most people, the first step inside the structure would have been their last. The stench of rot and mold was overpowering. The place even *smelled* haunted. But fear had no power over Charlie now. The old hospital could have been filled with witches of every variety and he would still have rushed inside.

He raced down corridor after corridor, hurdling piles of debris. The hallways were lined with doors. Most opened to reveal chambers decorated with dust-covered furniture and rusting bed frames. There were also examination rooms filled with terrifying contraptions. Finally, in the farthest reaches of the third floor, Charlie found a single closed door. An engraved nameplate on the wall identified the patient locked inside: BRETTER.

Charlie was already turning the doorknob when he remembered what he was wearing. Paige was probably too fragile to endure any more fear. Seeing a yurei appear out of nowhere might scare her to death. So despite all the cameras trained on Paige's room, Charlie tore off his black wig and revealed his face. The president of the Netherworld would soon know exactly where to find him.

The moment the door opened, the Dark silently slipped out. Charlie found Paige sitting in the middle of the floor, her knees drawn up to her chest and her arms hugging her shins. His heart cracked. He'd never seen her in such a state before. Paige had always been the tough one in the group. Now she didn't even look up when light spilled into the room. She just kept rocking back and forth, singing a lullaby to herself.

"Paige." Charlie crouched beside her. "It's me."

It took a while for his friend to respond. Paige seemed to be lost somewhere inside her own head. When she finally looked up, her eyes were bloodshot and their rims red.

"Charlie." She immediately wrapped her arms around him and held on tight.

"Why didn't you tell me your nightmares had gotten so bad?" he whispered.

Paige let go of Charlie. Her chin dropped to her chest. "I didn't want you to think I might be like her," she muttered.

Charlie didn't need to ask who she meant. He and his friends all knew that Paige's mom sometimes went for weeks without leaving her bedroom. And when the sadness became too much to bear, Mrs. Bretter would check herself into a hospital. During these times, Paige had to take care of herself while her parents coped with her mother's illness. The experience had made Paige mature beyond her years. She knew how to do things most twelve-year-olds didn't—like fix a broken television or make nachos in the microwave without scorching the cheese. And Charlie knew Paige was proud of the things she had taught herself to do. But he also knew that the knowledge had come at a terrible price.

Charlie gave the room another look and realized where they were: in a nightmare version of the hospital where Paige often went to visit her mom.

"Your mom is the one who's sick, Paige," Charlie consoled her as he peeled Terrorizer sensors from her skin. "You're perfectly healthy. You're just having a nightmare."

Paige's eyes roamed the room. "Are you sure?" she asked. "This all seems so real."

"It *is* real," Charlie told her. "But so am I. Can you tell?"

Paige reached over and pinched him. "Yes," she said.

"So you're not alone," he said. "And I can get you out of here."

He had just helped Paige to her feet when a familiar voice echoed through the halls of the hospital.

"CHARLIE LAIRD AND PODGE BRETTER! WE

HAVE THE BUILDING SURROUNDED! YOU'RE UNDER ARREST!"

Charlie winced. In his race to get into Paige's hospital room, he'd forgotten to come up with a plan for getting *out*.

"Am I crazy or is that Principal Stearns?" Paige grabbed Charlie's hand and squeezed it tight.

"It's a long story," Charlie muttered just as the doorway filled with goblins.

"Well, well," said President Fear. "Look what the goblins dragged out."

The crowd from the courthouse was gathered outside the hospital, waiting for a glimpse of the fugitives. Even Dabney, still bound to an office chair, had been wheeled outside for the spectacle. The goblins delivered Charlie and Paige into the grub guard's custody.

"Thought you could trick me, eh?" the grub asked, grabbing Charlie by his costume and Paige by the back of her nightgown.

The grub seemed to have grown even fatter since their first encounter. And there was no denying her strength. She swung her two prisoners around like rag dolls.

"A little mummy came in with the ghost," she told the president. "Didn't you say there were two small humans on the loose? Find the mummy—he's the second fugitive."

A shriek was heard at the center of the mob. The crowd parted to reveal a boy-sized mummy. Alfie stood there, his arms at his sides. Charlie knew he must have been scared to death, but he showed no sign of it. He didn't even look like he had to pee.

"That was easy," the president said. "I suppose you're the Turtle we've all been hunting?"

Alfie nodded.

"Too frightened to talk?" President Fear mocked him.

This time Alfie shook his head.

"No?" The president laughed. "You should be. I'm sure my goblins have something quite special planned for you tonight. Is there anything you'd like to say before they take you away?"

Alfie nodded.

"Then what is it?" the president snapped, growing tired of the game.

Alfie opened his mouth.

"MMMMMMMMMMMMMMMMMMMRRRRRRRR-RRRRRRRRAAAAAAAAAAAAAAAWWWWWWW-WWWRRRRRRRRRRRRR!"

The roar rippled through hairdos and shook the guard's fat. It bounced off the walls. And it shattered every remaining bit of glass in sight—from the windows in the abandoned hospital to the mirrored lenses in the guard's gorgon shields.

In an instant, Charlie knew what his friend was planning. With their gorgon shields destroyed, the goblins and guards would be helpless against Meduso. "Close your eyes," he ordered Paige. "Don't open them again until I say it's okay."

Unfortunately Charlie wasn't the only one who realized what was about to happen. "Gorgon alert!" a creature shouted. But the grub guard didn't get the message in time.

"What the . . . ," she started to say, just as her body turned to stone. The little arms holding Charlie and Paige cracked under their weight and crumbled to bits, setting the two fugitives free.

All around them was chaos. Half of the nightmare creatures were flailing about with their eyes closed, bumping into those standing in place, shielding their faces with paws or tentacles. President Fear and his goblins were all running for cover. No one dared risk getting a glimpse of the gorgon.

A figure in a Grim Reaper's robe dragged Charlie to his feet. "Take your friends and get out of here before someone decides to take a peek," Meduso ordered.

"Who is that? Can I open my eyes yet?" Paige asked.

"Go ahead," Charlie told her. "Paige, meet Meduso. Meduso, meet Paige."

"A pleasure to make your acquaintance, my dear," Meduso said gallantly.

"Wow." She gasped at the sight of the Grim Reaper. "This would probably give me nightmares if I wasn't already in one."

"You'll be surprised how fast you get used to it," a mummy said. Paige nearly shrieked when it tried to give her a hug.

"It's Alfie! Tell her it's me, Charlie!" the mummy cried.

But Charlie was too busy scanning the crowd. On the other side of the square, a clown chained to an office chair was spinning around as creatures raced past. "We can't leave without rescuing Dabney," he said.

"Who said I'm leaving?" Meduso asked. He reached into his Grim Reaper robes and pulled out the tomato Charlie had seen him holding. Then Meduso grabbed a skeleton who was running past. "May I borrow this?" he inquired, plucking a small bone from the skeleton's hand. Meduso stuck the bone into the tomato and hurled it at Dabney.

"Why did you do that?" Charlie asked as Dabney opened his mouth and caught the fruit like a pro. Then the clown tilted his head back and let loose a fountain of tomato juice.

"Skeleton key," Meduso said.

"But how's he going to . . ." Charlie glanced back at

Dabney, only to see that one of the clown's hands was already free.

"Even nightmare clowns go to circus school," Meduso said. "And that's not the only trick he's got up his sleeve. Now go find your witch, Charlie. I'll catch up with you soon. What are you waiting for? Run!"

CHAPTER TWENTY

LATE TO DINNER

When Charlie and his friends reached the nightmare forest, Charlie charged right in. But his newfound confidence didn't last very long. Even with Alfie and Paige by
his side, his fear grew with every step he took. After a few
minutes of walking, Charlie stopped and looked back the
way they had come. All he could see behind him were trees.
It felt like the woods had swallowed him alive.

Paige and Alfie didn't look frightened until their eyes
landed on Charlie's face.

"You okay, Charlie?" Paige asked.

He wasn't. He could feel the thing in the forest—the one

that had been stalking him since his bad dreams began. It was closer than ever. He desperately wanted to turn tail and run. But when he thought about Jack, he made himself keep on walking.

"I'm fine," Charlie lied as he began to jog. The jog quickly turned into a sprint.

"Charlie," Alfie panted. "Is there a reason we're running?"

"Is something chasing us?" Paige asked nervously. "What's out here?"

Charlie could tell he was scaring her. He slowed down, but his heart kept racing. "Nothing," he lied.

Dizzy and disoriented, Charlie wondered how he'd find the strength to keep going. Then suddenly, as if by magic, the bell tower appeared between the trees. His forest had shrunk, Charlie realized. When he'd first arrived in the Netherworld, it had been so vast that it would have taken him days to cross it. Now he'd been able to reach the heart of the woods in just a few short minutes. No wonder the thing had felt so close. There were barely any trees left to hide it.

While Alfie and Paige gazed up at the stone building in awe, Charlie sprinted the rest of the way to the bell tower. Dizzy with a mixture of hope and terror, he burst through the door. He hoped to find his brother alive and well, but he knew there was a chance he might make an awful discovery.

"Jack!" Charlie shouted. The fear surged inside him when there was no answer. The only sound he heard was the pounding of his own two feet. He charged up the stairs and into the bell tower's filthy parlor. The Venus flytraps had dried up and died. The witch hadn't been there in a while.

"Jack!" Charlie cried as he ransacked the rest of the house, his panic building as each room turned up empty. The cage held no prisoners. Even the dungeon was abandoned.

Charlie was sitting in the dungeon next to the witch's cauldron when Paige and Alfie found him. He was on the verge of tears. Because he'd stopped to help everyone else, he'd missed the chance to save his own brother.

"The witch must have gotten word from the president that we were on our way," Paige said. "Looks like she took Jack someplace else."

"Or maybe she ate him." The thought was the worst Charlie had ever had.

"Calm down, Charlie," Paige said, trying to comfort him. "Don't jump to conclusions."

"So I guess this is your nightmare?" Alfie asked, taking in the soot-blackened walls of the dungeon and the pile of bones beside the cauldron. "I can see why you're so scared."

"The witch has been bringing me here every night since I moved into the purple mansion." Charlie had seen his friends' nightmares, but it was strange to have them visit his. He felt uncomfortable and exposed—like he'd been caught dancing in his underwear. "There's a cage at the very top of the bell tower. That's where she wants to lock me up so I'm out of Charlotte's way."

Alfie held up a hand. "Hold on. Stop right there, Charlie. You still think *Charlotte*'s involved in this?" he asked skeptically.

"You know what happened! I accidentally opened the portal and the witch came over to our side," Charlie said. "She must have brought Charlotte through with her."

Charlie caught Paige and Alfie trading looks. "What?" he asked.

"It doesn't make any sense." Alfie tried to break the news gently.

"The portal is inside the purple mansion, right?" Paige added. "That means you opened it after you moved there."

"So?" Charlie asked.

"You met Charlotte before you moved to the mansion," Paige said. "She couldn't have come through the portal. She's a human like us, Charlie."

"No, she's a witch—just like the one from my nightmares!" Charlie insisted. "The two of them even look alike!"

"Do you think you might have made your nightmare look like Charlotte because you're afraid of her?" Paige asked cautiously.

"I'm afraid of her because SHE'S A WITCH!" Charlie shouted at the top of his lungs.

"Okay, okay!" Alfie said. "But remember what Meduso told us? It's not *what* you're afraid of. It's *why* you're afraid of it. Nightmares are people's fears in disguise."

"What does that even mean, anyway?" Charlie cried in frustration. He just didn't get it. He was scared of the witch because witches were horrible. Especially when they wanted to lock you in a cage and eat you.

Alfie sat down beside Charlie on the pile of bones. "I've been trying to figure it all out since we escaped from the Colosseum. I kept wondering why my nightmares are about being bad at sports. The truth is, I don't really mind being a terrible athlete. I have a big brain to make up for it. I think what *really* bothers me is when people laugh at me. It makes me wonder if being smart really matters. And I start feeling as small on the inside as I am on the outside."

"You should feel sorry for the people who laugh at you." Paige was sitting on the cot on which Charlie had passed many a miserable hour. "Only weak people need to make others feel small."

Alfie's face brightened. "I guess I never thought of it that way," he said. "So what about you, Paige? Why are you afraid of the dark?"

"I dunno. Isn't everybody a little bit scared of the dark?" Paige asked, trying to sidestep the question.

"Not me," Charlie offered miserably.

Alfie got up and took a seat next to Paige on the cot. "The place where you had your nightmare looked a lot like a hospital," Alfie said gently. "Do you think your bad dreams might have something to do with your mom?"

Paige's chin fell to her chest. She stared at the floor until she was able to speak. "My mom says that when she's sick, it feels like she's trapped all alone in the dark. She wants to escape, but she can't. I heard a doctor tell my dad that the problem might be hereditary. Which means I could end up with it too. So I guess that's what scares me about the dark. It's that I might not be able to find my way out. I could get lost in it and end up all alone too."

Alfie put an arm around Paige and gave her a squeeze. "It doesn't matter where you go," he told the girl. "There are three guys who are never going to leave you alone."

Paige laughed and wiped a tear from her eye. Charlie wanted to hug her too. But he couldn't bring himself to move.

"Charlie?" Alfie asked. "Have you thought about why you're so scared of the witch?"

"I don't want to play this game." The darkness was rising quickly. He could taste its bitterness and it almost made him gag.

"Because you're afraid to find out what really scares you?" Alfie asked.

Charlie had already figured it out. "I'm afraid Charlotte will take my father and brother away from me. There. Are you satisfied now?" But that was just one of his nightmares. He couldn't bring himself to mention the other one. The one that was out there in the forest, searching for him.

"You lost your mom," Paige said. "And you were worried you might lose the other people you love too."

"And I did lose them!" Charlie almost shouted. "The witch took my little brother. She tricked me into following her through the portal, and that's how I got stuck here. Charlotte wanted my dad all to herself, and now she has him."

"But, Charlie," Alfie said in his most reasonable voice. "I thought we determined that Charlotte couldn't possibly be a—"

"Hey, wait a second." Paige jumped up from the cot. Charlie recognized the look on her face. She'd just had a flash of genius. "How do you know the witch really took Jack? Did you actually *see* her kidnap him out of his room?"

"No," Charlie said defensively. "I heard her running up the tower stairs. When I got to the portal, I saw her carrying Jack through the forest."

"But you never saw the two of them together in the real world."

"What are you trying to say, Paige?" Charlie demanded.

"I get it!" Alfie announced, bouncing up and down with excitement. "Remember, Charlie? Meduso said that you had to come through the portal of your own free will."

"So?" Charlie asked, feeling a little slow.

"*So* the witch couldn't have stolen the real Jack! She couldn't have taken him through the portal against his will. Whatever she was carrying wasn't your brother. It was all just a trick to get you here!"

Charlie was about to ask what she meant when he remembered the body he'd seen thrown over the witch's back. He'd assumed it was Jack, but he hadn't actually seen his brother's face. It could have been practically anyone—or anything.

"Maybe you're right. But what if you're not?"

"There's one way to be sure," Alfie said. "President Fear said most of the kids in Cypress Creek are having nightmares these days. If Jack's one of them, we might be able to find his nightmare. And if only his spirit is here in the Netherworld, we'll know that his body is still back on the other side, safe in its bed."

"But I have no idea what Jack's nightmare might be." Charlie groaned at the thought of another puzzle to solve. "I don't even know if he ever has any. He's always seemed perfectly happy to me."

"*Always?*" Paige asked pointedly.

"Yeah. Jack likes all of his teachers. He doesn't have any enemies. He even gets along great with Charlotte. He's just a happy little kid who goes around wearing a Captain America . . ." Charlie's voice trailed off. He'd had a vision of the last time his little brother had worn the costume. He could see himself standing with Jack in front of their school. Then he saw his brother's spine soften and his shoulders slump. And he knew there was only one person who could frighten Jack Laird.

"What is it?" Alfie asked. "Do you think Jack's nightmare might have something to do with Captain America?"

"No," Charlie said. "But I just figured out what might give my brother bad dreams."

"What?" Paige asked.

It hurt to even think about the answer to her question.

"Me," Charlie replied. "We're going to have to check out our school."

∞ CHAPTER TWENTY-ONE ∞

NIGHTMARE SCHOOL

There was no real day or night in the Netherworld. In some terror-tories, the sun never set. In others, it never appeared to rise. From what Charlie had observed, Netherworld nightmares worked in shifts, depending on when their humans were sleeping. As he and his friends made their way along the road that cut through the forest, they passed nightmares who were on their way home. Charlie ducked behind a bush and waited for two monstrous kangaroos to hop by. A trio of big-eyed aliens raced past on bicycles. Flying foxes formed dense, swirling clouds overhead. Were-wallabies waddled through the woods in packs, some still in their human forms.

"Are you sure we're going the right way?" Paige asked Charlie once they were back on the road.

"Yes," Charlie said. He could feel it in his gut. The school was close.

Soon, blazing lights broke through the leaves. When Charlie reached the edge of the woods, he found a desolate wasteland stretched out before him. The ground was so parched that it had cracked into pieces. No trees or plants would ever sprout from that dead, dry soil. In the center of the lonely expanse stood a brick building with a playground behind it. From the side, the school would have looked just like Cypress Creek Elementary if it hadn't been for the iron bars on the windows and the padlocks on every door. Inside the school, dozens of faces were pressed against windows—and all of them belonged to kids.

At first Charlie wondered if they might be props, like the spectators in Alfie's Colosseum dream. But the closer he got, the more obvious it became that the horror on the kids' faces was very real. They weren't figments of anyone's imagination. Half of Cypress Creek Elementary's students were trapped in one big nightmare.

Charlie led his friends toward a group of four boys who were peeking out a broken pane of glass on the first floor.

"What's going on here?" he asked a redheaded kid who looked like he might have been Jack's age.

"There are six of us trapped in the boys' room," the kid replied in a quavering whisper. "There are more kids being held captive in other parts of the school. The principal has the whole place locked up tight. We can't get out, and there's something terrible roaming the halls. It eats anyone it sees."

"What is it?" Paige asked.

"An abominable snowman," the redhead replied. "I can smell it from here."

"It's not a snowman!" A blond boy behind him sounded outraged. "It's a swamp thing."

"You guys are crazy!" a dark-haired kid yelled. "It's a giant pig!"

"How many Nightmares are in there?" Charlie asked. The school's halls would be pretty crowded if there was a creature for every kid.

"We don't know for sure," the redheaded boy confided.

"Well, have any of you *seen* the monster?" Alfie asked.

When no one in the crowd spoke up, the kid with red hair shook his head. "Guess not," he admitted.

Alfie pulled Charlie to the side for a brief consultation. "Just as I suspected," he said. "They're all imagining their worst nightmare—but none of them have actually encountered a monster. Fear is what's keeping them all locked inside."

Charlie wondered what he would have imagined wandering the halls. A witch—or something worse?

"Hey! The dog that bit me in the park is waiting outside the bathroom door! He wants another taste of me. You've got to get us out of here!" pleaded a fourth boy, who was so short that Charlie could only see his eyes and the top of his head. "Did you come here to take the test too?"

The test? There was no time for tests, and no time to ask what the boy meant. "I'm looking for my brother," Charlie said. "Does anyone here know Jack Laird?"

"I do!" called the dark-haired boy at the back of the group. "But I haven't seen him at all. Maybe he's one of the kids who got eaten."

Charlie tried to push the thought out of his mind. He couldn't let it take root in his head. "Anyone else see a kid in a Captain America costume?" he asked.

"Ask the test taker," the redheaded boy suggested. "He's been here from the very beginning."

"The test taker?" Paige asked before Charlie could.

"He's around the corner. On the front lawn of the school. You can't miss him."

"Thanks for the tip," Charlie said. He had a hunch that the test taker was someone he should meet. But he was pretty sure it wouldn't be Jack.

"Tell him we're rooting for him!" the blond kid said.

"And bring us some food too!" the dark-haired boy shouted as Charlie and his friends hurried away. "We can't get to the cafeteria, so we've been eating nothing but bugs for as long as we can remember!"

Outside the school, on a patch of dirt where grass should have grown, stood a wooden desk. A boy with black hair sat behind it, hunched over a sheet of paper, a number 2 pencil clenched in his hand. Just a few feet away, at the top of a short set of stairs, the school's front doors were held shut by thick metal chains that were threaded through the handles and fastened with sturdy locks.

Inside the school, dozens of pairs of eyes were peering down at the boy behind the desk. He seemed to be busy filling in little circles on a test, but he spent more time erasing than he did writing. The ground around the desk was littered with test papers marked with giant red Fs.

Charlie groaned when he saw that his hunch had been correct: Rocco was the test taker. President Fear had a real gift for finding each person's secret weakness. Monsters wouldn't have scared Rocco Marquez. He'd have happily battled a hundred nightmare creatures to rescue the kids. But every knight has a chink in his armor. The only thing that could scare Rocco was a test.

"Rocco!" Charlie called.

The boy's head shot up. His face was so twisted with terror that for a second Charlie barely recognized his friend.

"How did you guys get into my nightmare?" Rocco asked. "Has the president kidnapped you too?"

"Shhh!" ordered a voice. A man with slicked-back hair and cadaver-gray skin was watching over the scene like a proctor. "There will be *no* talking during the exam!"

"Why is Rocco taking a test out here in front of the school?" Paige whispered. "And why is everyone watching?" Charlie shrugged and continued to make his way toward the desk.

The proctor checked his watch. "Keep working, Mr. Marquez," he ordered. "You have ten minutes left."

Rocco began filling circles in even faster. Then he stopped, erased a whole page of answers, and started all over again.

"Do you need some help?" Alfie whispered to Rocco before Charlie could stop him.

"Alfie!" Charlie and Paige groaned in unison.

"Cheating!" announced the test proctor. The way he spat out the word, he made it sound worse than murder or treason. "Test over, Mr. Marquez! Put your pencil down!"

"But I didn't take answers from anyone!" Rocco argued desperately.

"Perhaps not, but it's the thought that counts," said the

proctor. He chose a combination lock from a large pile beside Rocco's desk and clipped it to the chains on the school's front door.

"One lock will be added for every test you fail. One will be removed for every test you pass."

"I know! I know!" Rocco cried.

Charlie glanced over at the chains. Judging by the number of padlocks, Rocco was on a long losing streak.

"Excellent," said the proctor. "You have exactly three minutes until the next test begins."

Charlie, Alfie, and Paige formed a circle around Rocco's desk.

"What are you guys doing here, anyway?" Rocco stared up at them in confusion. "And why is Charlie wearing a dress?"

Charlie looked down at the white kimono he'd worn to Dabney's trial. It was surprisingly comfortable, and he'd forgotten he had it on. "Long story," he told Rocco.

"So this is your nightmare?" Paige asked Rocco.

"Same one I've been having for the last two weeks," Rocco confirmed. "Every night I come here and try to save all the kids by passing the tests, but I can't do any better than an F."

"Well, we're here to bust you out of this dream," Charlie told him.

"I can't leave!" Rocco moaned. "These kids are

depending on me! The principal locked them all up. There's something awful inside. It's eating them one by one, and I'm the only person who can stop it, but I'm just making things worse. I'd give anything right now to be smarter!"

Alfie snatched one of the test papers off the ground and had a quick look at it. "You know, most tests don't measure how smart you are," he proclaimed. "They just measure how good you are at taking tests."

Alfie handed the page to Charlie. Charlie scanned two of the questions and felt like his head might explode.

"Wow, this test is impossible." He let the piece of paper flutter back to the ground. "Even *Alfie* couldn't pass it. Look, we've all been friends since we were five, Rocco. You think the rest of us would hang around with a dummy?"

"You guys are just being nice," Rocco replied miserably.

"Not me," Alfie said, shaking his head. "I'm a nerd, not a saint."

Charlie knew he had to get Rocco out from behind the desk. The tests weren't passable, but Rocco would keep trying forever rather than leave his trapped schoolmates behind. "Come with us. We'll find another way to save these kids," he promised.

"Yeah, we'll cook up a plan that doesn't involve taking tests," Paige added.

"Why? Are you saying I'll never be able to pass one?"

Rocco tried to stand up, but his chair was attached to the desk and the whole thing went with him. "Thanks for the vote of confidence, Bretter."

Charlie started to defend Paige, but Alfie jumped in first. "I think what Paige was trying to say is that you might have more success at freeing the kids if you found a way to use the many skills you possess."

"That's just a fancy way of saying I'll never pass the test!" Rocco slammed his fist on the desk.

"Stop!" Charlie knew how frustrated Rocco felt, but arguing wasn't going to get them anywhere. "We need to stay calm, okay?"

Then a foul odor invaded Charlie's nostrils. It was the stench of roadkill on a hot summer day. The smell of meat so putrid it would make a maggot vomit. The aroma of the soup at the bottom of a garbage can behind the worst taco joint in town. It was absolutely nauseating, and it was getting stronger by the second.

"What is *that*?" Paige was pointing at a zombie lumbering toward the school. Its bloated face was the color of a fresh bruise. It wore a top hat, a moth-eaten suit, and a pair of old-fashioned glasses with dark lenses. An axe appeared to be wedged in the undead gentleman's neck. But worst of all, he was carrying a large black duffel bag with an arm dangling from its open zipper.

When it became clear that the zombie was heading their way, Paige and Alfie prepared to run, but Charlie held them back. "Just wait," he said, stifling a smile.

"I thought you were supposed to be looking for the witch!" the zombie whispered when he reached Charlie.

"Meduso?" Alfie asked, looking like he might collapse.

"Of course!" Meduso snapped. "I walked all the way to Mother's house to hide Dabney and procure new costumes for you. Then I hiked all the way to the belfry smelling like a slaughterhouse, only to discover that you weren't even there!" Finally Meduso noticed the newest member of their party. "Who's this?" he demanded. "Please tell me you haven't rescued *another* one of your friends."

"Meduso, meet Rocco Marquez," Charlie said, performing the introductions. "This is his nightmare. He needs to pass a test to free the kids trapped inside the school, but he doesn't think he's smart enough."

"To be honest, I'm beginning to wonder if you're all bumbling idiots," said Meduso.

"*Excuse* me?" Alfie sounded terribly offended. "I'll have you know—"

"You're all supposed to be hiding from the president of the Netherworld, so you decide to visit the school he runs? I suggest you get out of here as quickly as possible. If I found you, I guarantee President Fear isn't far behind."

"I'm not leaving," Rocco said, digging in his heels. "If I go, the kids are all going to get eaten!"

"No, they won't," Charlie insisted. "This is the Netherworld. If they all get eaten, there won't be anyone left to be afraid."

Charlie could tell Rocco didn't get it. He had yet to learn how the Netherworld worked.

"Maybe they won't *all* get eaten," Rocco admitted. "Maybe it will just be a few. How many kids should I let the monsters have, Charlie? What's a good number for you? Two? Three?"

The roar of an engine approaching saved Charlie from answering. But before he could say a word, Meduso shouted, "Hide!"

Charlie led his friends around the side of the school to escape the headlights. The only place to hide was a maintenance shed next to the playground. The five of them ducked inside, but Charlie knew it was only a matter of time before they were discovered.

He kept the door cracked, watching as a long line of limousines emerged from the forest. Within seconds, the school was completely surrounded. Charlie carefully closed the door.

"Do you see what just happened?" Meduso demanded angrily. "Your arguing distracted you. If you intend to make it out of the Netherworld, you have to stick together! In times of trouble—"

"—four will always be stronger than one," Charlie finished for him. His mother's words had grown powerful within him.

Meduso stared at the boy in surprise.

"Lookss like he'ss learned ssomething," Charlie heard Fernando hiss.

"What are we going to do?" Paige was on her tiptoes, looking out at the schoolyard through a crack between two boards. "There are about a hundred of those nasty *things* out there. Is there anything in here we can use as a weapon?"

While Paige rooted through the tools, Meduso put his eye to the crack. "Goblins," he announced. "And I'd say a hundred is a very conservative estimate. It's a good thing *one* of us took the time to come up with a plan." He opened the bag he'd been lugging and pulled out two perfect goblin costumes, along with Alfie's pajamas and the jeans Charlie had been wearing when he'd first arrived in the Netherworld.

"But you only brought two costumes!" Alfie cried.

"Well, how was I supposed to know that you were planning to rescue your entire town?" Meduso snapped.

"No arguing!" Paige reminded them. "Okay. Who gets to wear the costumes—and what are the rest of us going to do?"

Charlie wished he had an answer. But it looked like two of them would soon be the goblins' prisoners. And since it was his fault that President Fear had set his sights on the children of Cypress Creek, Charlie knew he had no choice but to volunteer. He'd just cleared his throat when Rocco spoke up.

"If I can get us out of here, do you guys promise we'll come back for the kids?"

"Of *course*," Charlie said.

"Okay then. You and I are going to pretend to be captured," Rocco ordered, taking charge. "Charlie, take off that dress and put on your jeans. Paige and Alfie—you're going to dress up like goblins. You'll say you found Charlie and me hiding in the maintenance shed. Make a big fuss about it. We'll need everyone out there to be distracted long enough for Meduso to get behind the wheel of one of the limos. Then you'll march Charlie and me to the vehicle and we'll all make our getaway."

"You know, that might actually work," Alfie marveled.

"Ssmart," hissed Fernando.

"We'll ssee about that," Larry replied.

"If you don't have a better idea, then pleasssse shut up," Meduso mocked the snake as he passed Charlie his jeans.

"Hey, Rocco, you just came up with the solution," Charlie pointed out as he stepped out of his dress and into his pants. "Are you sure you're really dumb?"

"My solution doesn't have anything to do with being smart," Rocco replied, though he looked rather proud of himself. "I just watch a lot of movies."

"Then let's hope the goblins don't," Charlie joked. When he pulled his jeans up, he could feel something in the back pocket. He reached inside and pulled out a folded piece of paper.

It took him a moment to remember where he'd gotten it. It was one of Charlotte's drawings—the one Charlie had picked up off the floor of the tower the night he came through the portal. *The Netherworld Mansion,* it was captioned. But there wasn't time for another look, so he put it back in his pocket and steeled himself for what was about to happen.

≈ CHAPTER TWENTY-TWO ≈

THE GREAT ESCAPE

They waited until they heard goblins right outside the shed.

"Everyone ready?" Rocco whispered. Charlie nodded along with the others. "Then let's rock and roll."

Rocco kicked open the door. Paige and Alfie, dressed as goblins, pushed Charlie and Rocco out into the schoolyard. Meduso stayed behind, waiting for a chance to slip away unnoticed.

It didn't look as if that was going to be possible. The schoolyard was lousy with goblins. They were sniffing around the playground and hunting through garbage cans.

Charlie spotted a particularly stupid one turning over tiny rocks in the drive, just in case there might be a kid hiding underneath. A handful of goblins caught sight of the two humans being forced from the shed and scuttled over to investigate.

"Get back!" Alfie screeched at the creatures. "We found the fugitives! They're ours to hand in!" His cries drew the rest of the goblins, and soon they had all gathered around.

"Excellent," said a familiar voice. A hunchbacked creature in torn-off pants pushed to the front of the group. Charlie's insides turned to ice. It was the head goblin from the Colosseum—the smart one with the cruel smile. "How did you manage to capture these children so quickly?"

"Detective work?" squeaked Paige.

"Of course," said the goblin. He paused to dig inside his nose. "And since you're such excellent detectives, perhaps you can tell me what happened to the other two."

"The other two?" Alfie asked meekly.

"Are you daft?" the head goblin snarled. "We're still missing a girl and a Turtle!" Then he stopped and his eyes lit up. He took a step toward Alfie and sniffed the air around him. "Any idea what we should do to them when we find them?"

"I know! Let's take all their clothes and make them run through a cactus farm!" a potbellied goblin shrieked.

"Let's put them in a pool with a shark and a sewer gator!" suggested a beak-nosed creature merrily.

"Let's make them judge a Bigfoot body-odor contest!" a third squealed with delight.

"What do you think?" the head goblin asked Paige and Alfie. "What should we make them do?" All Paige could offer was a nervous laugh and a shrug.

The jig was up, Charlie thought. The head goblin was toying with them. Somehow he knew that Alfie and Paige were impostors. Charlie was about to surrender and plead for his friends' freedom when a bright red object fell from the heavens and hit the goblin square on the head.

The creature's eyes went blank, and it was on the ground before it even let out a yelp. Charlie took a step forward to investigate the red missile, which had rolled to a stop. It was a can of Sloppy Joe mix—the same kind that was used in Cypress Creek Elementary's cafeteria.

Charlie turned to find out who had thrown it. He

looked up to see children of all shapes and sizes standing by the school's windows. As Charlie's eyes passed over possible candidates, a streaming roll of toilet paper hit the ground beside him. Its long white trail reached all the way to a window on the third floor.

"Run, test taker!" shouted a kid. "We've got you covered!"

Suddenly toilet paper was flying from every bathroom window. Outside, the ground looked as if it were covered in snow. Several goblins had been transformed into short, scrawny snowmen. Books, globes, and science equipment rained down on the president's men. Charlie saw a goblin pick up a math textbook that had just hit one of his colleagues.

"I always wondered what these things were for," the creature marveled before he was knocked out by another flying can from the cafeteria. Charlie watched as a nearby goblin was taken down with Cheddar-Flavor Cheese Powder. Another was

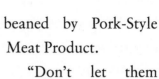

beaned by Pork-Style Meat Product.

"Don't let them capture you, Rocco!" someone yelled.

"STOP IT THIS INSTANT!"

Charlie saw that the back door of one of the limos had opened. All nine feet of President Fear emerged from the vehicle, leaving Charlie to wonder how he'd ever managed to fit inside. The storm of toilet paper paused. Hundreds of children watched quietly from above as the fearsome giant marched toward the school. "STEP AWAY FROM THE WINDOWS!"

No one budged. All eyes were fixed on the president of the Netherworld.

"Haven't you learned your lesson?" President Fear demanded. "How many of you need to be eaten before you finally decide to obey? Shall I send in more monsters?"

The only response to his question was a stream of red liquid from one of the cafeteria windows. Within seconds, the president's face and suit had been spackled with ketchup.

"THAT'S IT!" he bellowed, wiping the tomato sauce

from his eyes. "A child from every class gets eaten! Goblins, gather the most terrifying creatures in the Netherworld!"

"Bring 'em on," snarled a second grader, and the storm began again. Everything the kids could find was being hurled at the giant and the goblins outside.

"Stop!" shouted Rocco. "Don't get yourselves in more trouble!"

"You tried to save us!" cried a kid. "Now let us save you!"

A bucket full of something that looked like apple juice and smelled much worse flew from a bathroom window, soaking the president and two nearby goblins.

In the midst of the confusion that followed, a zombie appeared at Charlie's side. "The kids have you covered. Now go!" Meduso urged. "Take your friends and run!"

"But where?" Charlie asked. He was tired of running.

"The mansion," the gorgon said. "I've been waiting for a chance to tell you. I passed it on my way here. The witch has the tower lit up like a lighthouse. She hasn't been hiding, Charlie. She's been waiting for you to come find her."

Charlie had suspected this moment was coming, but he still didn't feel prepared. "But how are we going to get to the mansion without you?" Charlie argued, trying to buy a little more time.

"Don't worry. You can't get lost," Meduso said.

"What do you mean we *can't*—"

"Look." Meduso raised his arm and pointed over Charlie's shoulder. "You can see the mansion from here."

Charlie turned around. There in the distance was a mansion on top of a hill.

HOME, SWEET HOME

Standing at the base of the hill, Charlie felt as if the house had been waiting for him all along. The front door was open, and though the rest of the mansion was dark, the tower was ablaze with lights.

"You sure it's the right place?" Rocco asked skeptically. "That house isn't purple. It's *black*."

The mansion wasn't just black, Charlie thought. It was the color of darkness itself. Still, he would have known it anywhere. "Yes, that's my house," he said, surprised to hear the words come out of his own mouth. He'd never called it *his* house before. Charlie looked at his friends.

"The witch is inside." He could feel her presence. Goose bumps sprang up along his arms, and his heart was already beating a little bit faster.

"I'm dying to see what she looks like," Paige said as she and Alfie removed their goblin costumes.

"No," Charlie said firmly with a shake of his head. Cypress Creek and the entire Waking World were in danger—and the trouble had all started with him and his witch. He repeated to himself what Meduso had once told him: *There are no shortcuts in the Netherworld.* Charlie knew that to save the world from President Fear, he'd need to deal with the witch first. "I have to go in alone."

"Are you *sure?*" Paige asked.

Charlie bit his lip. It made him nervous to think the witch might want him to find her. That meant there was something in the mansion she wanted him to see. Paige and Alfie were convinced that the witch couldn't have brought Jack's body through the portal. But they'd never met the witch. They didn't know what she could do.

Charlie shuddered. What if the witch and her cat were inside having *dinner?*

"We're here for you if you need us," Rocco said.

"But if you're too scared . . . ," Alfie began to tell him.

Paige took Charlie by the arm and pulled him to one side. "Are you going to be okay?" she asked, searching his face for signs of uncertainty.

"Yes," Charlie said. And as soon as he said it, he knew it was true.

Charlie climbed the hill to the mansion alone. At the top, he turned around and saw his friends watching him down below. Charlie gave them a wave before he stepped onto the front porch. His confidence began to crumble as he forged his way through a jungle of overgrown plants. By the time he reached the front door, he was certain his heart would pound through his chest. Somewhere between the Venus flytraps and the flowering belladonna, Charlie had caught a whiff of something cooking.

The scent filled Charlie's head with images too terrible to describe. Most featured an enormous cauldron and what was bubbling inside. Charlie wanted to race back to his friends. But he didn't. He took a deep breath. Then he stepped over the mansion's threshold and into the darkness beyond.

He felt for the light switch, but as his fingers brushed the wall, he could sense little things moving beneath them. He snatched his hand away. In the distance, he heard the clatter of a pot hitting the floor. The witch was in the kitchen.

With only his memory to guide him, Charlie made his way through the pitch-black mansion. As he drew closer to the kitchen, he saw a thin strip of light beneath the door. That was when he felt something large brush against his leg.

"Hello, Charlie," Agatha the cat purred. "Feeling hungry?" She tried to trip him, but Charlie managed to push her out of his way. Then he summoned every bit of his courage and stepped into the kitchen.

The witch was standing at the stove, wearing Charlotte's favorite black dressing gown, her red curls pulled back in a ponytail. He watched her pour a stream of green batter into a waffle iron, and he suddenly felt queasy. He hadn't touched a waffle in about three years. They had been his mother's special dish—the one she made to kick off big days. The last batch she'd cooked had been for Jack's graduation from kindergarten, a few weeks after they'd found out she was sick. Sadness began to fill Charlie like concrete. His legs wouldn't move, and his lungs felt so heavy that he wasn't sure he'd be able to take another breath.

"Can I have another one, Mom?" It was Jack's voice. He was holding out his plate for another batch of green waffles. The word *Mom* hit Charlie hard.

"I'll have another too, sweetheart," called Andrew Laird. "I can't even remember the last time I ate waffles this good."

Charlie's attention was drawn to the breakfast nook, where his father and Jack sat shoveling forkfuls of food into their mouths. Even from a distance, he could tell they were props. But Charlie couldn't help himself. Now that he was inside his own nightmare, it felt all too real.

"What do you think you're doing?" he asked the witch. Aside from her mirrored eyes and green complexion, she was a perfect replica of Charlotte DeChant.

"What does it look like?" she replied. "I'm making breakfast for my family."

"They're *my* family, not yours," Charlie growled.

"No," the witch corrected him. "They *used* to be your family, but they don't want you anymore. Can you blame them? You wouldn't let them move on. When you weren't moping around, you were doing your best to make your brother's life miserable. So now Jack and your father are mine. Don't they make wonderful pets?"

The witch grabbed a plate full of waffles and delivered them to the breakfast nook. "Here you go, my little piggies," she sang as she slid into a seat next to Jack.

Charlie rushed toward the table. Up close, Jack and his father looked like department-store mannequins. Their hair was too perfect and their skin was as smooth as plastic. But Charlie missed them both so much that it hardly mattered that they were just figments of his imagination. He wanted to sit down to join them, but the table had shrunk. There was no longer room for Charlie. So he stood at the end and watched his father and brother eat breakfast without him.

The darkness returned, and with it the anger. The waffles clearly meant nothing to them. Charlie's dad had syrup in his beard, and he wouldn't stop smiling. Jack was letting the witch muss his hair. They'd forgotten Charlie's mom. And the witch was right. They didn't want Charlie anymore either.

Charlie ran out of the kitchen and up the stairs. He searched for his room, but it was no longer there. His boxes were gone. All evidence of his existence had been removed. So he opened the door to Jack's room and lay facedown on the bed.

It was then that he remembered the folded piece of paper in the back pocket of his jeans. He opened it up and examined the drawing on the front of the page. *The Netherworld Mansion.* Charlie flipped the sheet over. There on the back was another strange poem Charlotte had written.

The next lesson to learn is one that takes guts,
But not against punches or scratches or cuts.
For nightmares, I'll tell you, have only one power:
To scare you for minutes, which soon become hours.
The strength you must find is to stand and stop
 running.
When your courage is gone and the creatures keep
 coming,
Just know in your heart you can win if you fight.
Face your fears and defeat them.
Beat your nightmares tonight!

Charlie Laird felt like an idiot. Charlotte DeChant wasn't a witch. Whatever she'd been writing was about *facing* one's fears. Charlie thought back to the commotion he'd heard in the tower room the day he'd found Charlotte's illustrations scattered across the room. It had been President Fear who'd broken into the desk. If he was planning to take over the Waking World, he wouldn't want a story like Charlotte's being read.

"Hey! Why are you in my room?"

Charlie tucked the paper into his pocket and rolled over to find Jack looking down at him, his Captain America mask pushed back on his head.

"Jack?"

"What?" the little boy demanded warily. As soon as he said it, Charlie knew it was a different Jack from the one downstairs. This one had freckles, and hair that looked like it hadn't been brushed in a week. This was the real Jack. And the real Jack was scared.

Charlie hopped off the bed to give him a hug. But Jack held one hand out and pulled his mask back down with the other. "Get back. I'm not taking the mask off."

And suddenly Charlie figured it out. He'd found his way into his little brother's nightmare. A witch hadn't taken him. The Netherworld mansion was where Jack spent his nights, defending himself from his mean older brother.

"What were you doing in my bed?" Jack demanded.

"Sorry." Charlie smiled. "I was lying down to think a few things through."

"Well, Mom wants you to bring your bike in," Jack announced in his Captain America voice.

The word *Mom* felt like another punch to the gut, but Charlie didn't strike back. "Okay," he said. "Tell Charlotte I'll be down in a minute."

"That's it?" Jack asked cautiously, as if Charlie's good

humor might be a trap. "You're not going to yell or any-thing?"

"Nope," Charlie said. "But can I ask you a question?"

The boy didn't move a muscle. He just stood there star-ing at Charlie. "Sure, I guess," he finally replied.

"Do you remember much about our real mom?" Charlie asked.

Jack pushed his mask up. "She made this," he said, tug-ging on the hem of his Captain America shirt.

"She did," Charlie said, beaming from ear to ear. His brother hadn't forgotten after all.

"And I remember the song she used to sing when she tucked me in at night." Jack looked down at his feet. "I still know all the words."

"Well, if you ever have any questions about her, you can always ask me," Charlie told him. "I remember everything."

Jack grinned. "I know," he said. He stood in the mid-dle of the room, shifting his weight from foot to foot. He seemed confused about what to do next.

"Do you like having Charlotte as a stepmom?" Charlie asked.

Jack froze again.

"You can tell me," Charlie insisted.

"Yes," the little boy reluctantly confessed.

"Do you love her?" Charlie asked.

The boy hesitated, then nodded.

"I'm really glad," Charlie said, and he actually was. "'Cause you deserve to have a good mom, Jack. And you don't have to be afraid of me anymore. I'm going to be a better brother from now on. I promise."

Outside the window, a pale golden light had appeared on the horizon. Jack took off his Captain America mask. The nightmare seemed to be over. It had turned into something else.

"You deserve one too," Jack said. "Come with me for a second."

He motioned for Charlie to follow him.

"Where are we going?" Charlie asked once they reached the hall.

"Upstairs to the tower."

"What are you going to show me?" Charlie asked.

"I can't tell you," Jack said. "You just have to see it."

When they reached the tower room, Charlie found himself looking into what seemed at first to be a giant mirror. Then he realized it was the portal, and on the other side was a room that was almost identical to the one they were in. But instead of empty blackened walls, there were jars of seeds and dried plants on the shelves. Instead of cobwebs, there were colorful illustrations. And in the center of the other room, a woman was sleeping with her head on a desk.

"Charlotte?" Charlie asked in astonishment.

"She's hardly moved in two whole days," Jack told him. "She's been right there since she figured out where you went."

"What's she doing?" Charlie asked.

"Waiting. She sent a friend to find you. She's going to sit there until he brings you back. Dad thinks she's crazy. He can't see the portal the way we can. Charlotte can't either—not anymore."

"But you can see it?" Charlie asked.

Jack nodded. "Charlotte told me we're special. She even let me look at pictures she drew of the things that live here in the Netherworld. Some of them are pretty crazy. The guy who's been looking for you has *snakes* for hair."

Charlie nodded. "Meduso." He should have realized that his stepmother was his mysterious benefactor. "So Charlotte's really been worried about *me*?" he asked.

"She's worried to death," Jack said. "She keeps saying it was her fault. That she should have told you about the portal sooner. She thought she'd know if it opened, but for some reason she can't see it the way she used to."

"This isn't her fault," Charlie said. "It's mine. I started all this because I didn't want Charlotte to be part of our family. I tried to convince everyone that she was a witch."

"You were scared that Charlotte wanted to replace our real mom," Jack said. "But she doesn't. She and Mom used to be friends, you know."

"Charlotte told me," Charlie said. "But I guess I didn't listen."

The sun had risen on the other side of the portal. Light poured into the tower. When a beam fell across Charlotte's face, she mumbled in her sleep.

"She's going to wake up in a minute or two," Jack said. "I should probably wake up too. Will you be okay?"

"Yes," Charlie promised. "I'll be home soon." And for the first time, Charlie truly felt that Charlotte's strange purple mansion *was* his home.

"If you aren't," Jack said as he faded away, "I'm coming to get you."

The windows glowed in the morning light as Charlie made his way downstairs. The sun painted the black walls and furnishings a cheerful shade of purple. He was almost out the door when he heard movement in the kitchen.

He found the witch sitting alone at the breakfast table. Her eyes were black now. The mirrored lenses had been removed. A red wig lay in front of her, and without it, she looked nothing like Charlotte.

"I thought you'd be gone," she said when she saw Charlie.

"I was just thinking the same about you," Charlie replied.

"Things don't move that fast around here," the witch

explained. "You don't get a new job just like that. I've got to wait to be reassigned. And believe me—I'm not looking forward to my next assignment."

"Why not?" Charlie asked.

"This was a high-profile job, and I screwed it up," the witch said. "I guess my heart just wasn't in it. You seemed like an okay kid to me. I took it too easy on you. I'll probably be on probation for the next couple of centuries."

"Or you could retire," Charlie told her.

The witch shook her head. "Retiring means dying," she said. "I may be tired of this nonsense, but I'm not ready to shut down the whole show."

"President Fear says nightmares die when they quit," Charlie said. "But I don't think it's like that at all. I believe that when nightmares retire, they turn into *dreams*."

"Yeah, right," the witch scoffed. "And what would a washed-up witch like me do if I were a *dream*?"

"I dunno," Charlie said. "Just be yourself, I guess."

"Humph," the witch said skeptically. "Never been asked to play that role before. I'll give it some thought. But just so you know—you aren't going to be dreaming about *anybody* until you're finished with that other nightmare of yours. Might take you a while. From what I can tell, it's a doozy."

Charlie's knees went wobbly and he grabbed hold of a chair. "My *other* nightmare?"

"Yeah—the big one," the witch said. "The portal is still open. That means you aren't done yet. You really thought your *stepmom* was the thing that scared you most?"

No. Charlie had always known there was something else. "What is it?" he asked.

"Oh dear," the witch said. "I think you better have a look outside."

When Charlie opened the front door, he expected it to be there waiting for him on the porch. Instead, all he found were his three best friends. But judging by the expressions on their faces, they could see something he couldn't.

"What's going on?" Charlie asked. "Why did you guys hike all the way up here to the mansion?"

His friends looked at each other.

"We saw someone come out of the forest," Alfie said. "We think she's looking for you."

Charlie would have rushed back inside the mansion if Paige hadn't stepped forward.

"It's okay," she tried to assure him. But the gentle way she took his arm told him to prepare for a blow. "Come with me."

Paige guided him to the edge of the porch and pointed down the hill. Below, the houses of Cypress Creek were all still and dark—like an empty movie set. Except for one house several blocks away. It seemed to be lit by a rare ray of sunshine. And there was someone moving around in the front yard. Charlie recognized the house in an instant. It was the one he'd lived in as a little kid.

"There's someone in the yard," he told Paige. His worst nightmare had come for him.

Paige took Charlie's hand and squeezed. "Yes, and we're pretty sure it's your mom," she said.

ꙮ CHAPTER TWENTY-FOUR ꙮ

CHARLIE'S WORST NIGHTMARE

Charlie found her in the front yard of the old house. She'd spent so much time there, weeding and planting and tending her garden. Now she was kneeling down, inspecting a group of little mushrooms that were rising from the soil around the stump of an old oak tree.

"Charlie!" she called to him. Somehow she'd known he was there. "I've been looking all over for you! Come here and have a look at this."

Charlie didn't know if he could. The pain was almost too much to bear. He had missed her so much. He couldn't stand to have his mom back for a few minutes—and then have to let her go again.

"Charlie?" his mom called once more. And this time she turned around.

Her jeans and T-shirt were covered in dirt. Her hair was pulled back in a messy ponytail. She wasn't wearing a bit of makeup. And yet she was the most beautiful person Charlie had ever seen. He ran to her and threw his arms around her. For a few long, wonderful seconds, everything was exactly the way it was supposed to be.

"Hey now," she said, wiping Charlie's tears away with the hem of her shirt. "Let's not waste our time together being sad."

But Charlie couldn't stop. It felt like he was being torn apart. His mom wrapped her arm around his shoulders and held him close to her side.

"Can I show you something?" she asked.

All he could do was nod.

His mother pointed down at the tree stump. There were a dozen little mushrooms circling it. Each had a bright red cap speckled with tiny white spots.

"Do you remember when we had to cut our old tree down? Then a while later you and I found these toadstools in the yard?"

Charlie sniffed. He could recall the day perfectly. It had

been one of the last times he and his mom had spent a few hours alone.

"Remember what I told you back then? When the tree died, it helped bring the mushrooms to life."

"You also said that type of mushroom is deadly poisonous," Charlie mumbled.

"Only if you eat them," his mom said. "Otherwise they're just beautiful."

Charlie looked up at her. "Mom?" he asked. "Can I stay here with you?"

His mom just smiled.

"I'm really here," Charlie told her. "I came to the Netherworld on my own—through the portal in the purple mansion. I can stay forever if I want."

"Without your friends or your little brother?" she asked. "Without your dad and Charlotte?"

"You know Dad married Charlotte?" Charlie must have looked startled, because his mother chuckled.

"Of course," she said. "You're the only one who's never come to see me. And whenever I tried to look for you here, you always ran away."

"I'm really sorry. I . . ."

His mom squeezed his shoulder. "You don't have to apologize, Charlie. I'm just glad we're together now. There are a few things I never got a chance to tell you. Why don't we have a seat in our old spot."

They sat side by side on the stairs of Charlie's old house. Charlie could see the purple mansion high on its hill. The windows in the tower sparkled in the sunlight.

"So you found the portal," his mom said. "I guess I always knew you would. I felt the same way about the tower when I was your age."

"I wish I'd never gone inside," Charlie said. "I should have known the purple mansion was bad."

"The mansion's a lot like the mushrooms," his mom said. "It can be good *or* bad. It just depends on how you look at it. You know that house has been in Charlotte's family for almost two hundred years? Her great-great-grandfather Silas DeChant built the place. He was the man who first opened the portal. Has she had a chance to tell you the story?"

"No," Charlie said, feeling as though one of the world's biggest secrets was about to be revealed.

"Well, when Silas was a young man, he inherited a fortune from his father," Charlie's mom said. "But he never learned to enjoy his wealth. Instead, he began to wonder if his friends only liked him because he was rich. Silas even convinced himself that his fiancée wouldn't have loved him if he'd been a poor man. He became terrified that his loved ones would desert him if he ever lost his money. In Silas's worst nightmares, he was all alone. And can you guess what happened next?"

"Silas ended up all alone." His nightmare came true, Charlie realized.

"Yep," his mom confirmed. "He wrote in his diary that it felt like a black cloud was hanging over him. Then the cloud found its way inside him, and it made him mean and bitter."

"I know just how he felt," Charlie said. "I call it the darkness."

His mom pulled him closer. "I've felt it too, and I'd say that's a very good name for it. And once the darkness was inside Silas, it started to spread to his family and friends—it even got to his dog. So in order to save them, Silas left the people he loved and traveled far, far away. He built his house on top of a lonely hill, and for almost a year, he lived in it all alone."

"I think I know the next part," Charlie said, remembering what Meduso had told him about the portal in the purple mansion. "Silas let his fears take over his life. For him, there was no difference between the Netherworld and the Waking World, so a door between the two worlds opened up in his house."

"That's right," his mom said. "And it would have stayed open if something amazing hadn't happened."

"What was it?" Charlie asked.

"One day there was a knock at the front door. Silas must have been pretty surprised, because his house was in the middle of nowhere. The nearest neighbor lived hundreds of miles away. When Silas opened the door, there was the fiancée he'd left behind. He'd always imagined that she'd married someone else. But that wasn't what had happened at all. The day after Silas had disappeared, she had loaded her belongings onto a wagon and set off in search of him. It had taken her a year to find the mansion. And when Silas saw her standing on the front porch, he realized how hard it must have been to find him. That's when he knew he would never be alone."

"Wow," Charlie said. He'd left his friends standing on the very same porch. He knew they would have come looking for him too.

"And after they were married, guess what Silas's wife did first?" Charlie's mom leaned over, as if whispering a secret into his ear. "She painted the whole darn place purple."

"She thought it was a happy color," Charlie said, remembering what Charlotte had told him.

"Yep," his mom confirmed. "Then she sent letters to all of their friends, inviting them to move to the town that she and her husband had decided to found. A whole bunch of them came and built houses. And that was the start of Cypress Creek."

"I don't understand," Charlie said. "If you knew all this, why didn't you tell me when I asked you about the place?"

"Because that's the nice part of the story. I didn't want you to think the house is totally harmless. It's not. I knew someday you'd explore it, and when you asked, you were still too little to know everything. I planned to tell you as soon as you turned eleven. That's how old I was when I took my first trip to the tower with Charlotte DeChant."

"So you and Charlotte really were friends?" Charlie asked.

"Oh yes. Best friends. You can't help but be close to someone once you've been inside her nightmares. We shared a pretty amazing adventure."

"Can you tell me about it?" Charlie almost begged.

"I don't need to," his mom told him. "Charlotte wrote the whole story down for you."

"For me?"

"And for your brother too. It's important that you both know what happened. You and Jack can see the portal and travel through it. Those are very rare gifts. The DeChants always thought they were the only humans who possessed the abilities. That's why they've worked so hard to keep the house in the family. Every generation, one of the DeChants lives in the mansion to guard the portal. Now Charlotte's the only DeChant left."

"What's going to happen after her?" Charlie asked. "Charlotte doesn't have any kids."

"Yes she does," Charlie's mom told him.

Charlie started to disagree and then gasped. "Wait— you're talking about me and Jack?" That was what Jack had meant when he said the Laird boys were both special. "We're going to be the portal's guardians?"

"Charlotte will tell you more about that," his mom said. "Now I think it's time for you and your friends to go home. Your dad must be worried sick about you."

A wave of panic nearly knocked Charlie over. "No, Mom," he pleaded. "Don't make me leave. Just a little while longer." He threw his arms around her and held on for dear life. *"Please."*

Charlie's mom kissed the top of his head. "Listen to me, Charlie. I'll always be right here in this house. Anytime you need me, you'll know where to find me."

"In the Netherworld?" Charlie sobbed.

"If you can say goodbye to me now, I won't be your nightmare. I'll just be a dream. This is your fear, Charlie. You have to face it."

"But, Mom!"

"You have a father and brother and friends who love you," his mother said. "And I promise, Charlie Laird, it may not always be easy, but you *will* be okay without me."

Charlie looked up at the purple mansion. His friends were still waiting for him. And he knew that what his mom said was true.

"They'll need your help getting out of here," his mother said. "Do you think you can do it?"

"Yes," Charlie said.

"Then say goodbye."

Charlie took a deep breath and wrapped his arms around his mother as tight as he could. "Goodbye, Mom," he said.

"Goodbye, Charlie." She pulled him even closer. "I'll see you in your dreams."

CHAPTER TWENTY-FIVE

NO ESCAPE

Charlie stopped halfway up DeChant Hill and turned around for one last look at the house he'd grown up in. Now that it was no longer host to a nightmare, the terrortory was shrinking. The front lawn was just a thin strip of grass, and the little garden was already gone. Charlie's mother had left for the Dream Realm, where she belonged. And this time she wouldn't be back.

Charlie was sad, but the darkness was gone. And for the first time in ages, he wasn't afraid. Without fear weighing him down, he felt lighter. Charlie Laird was finally free.

"How did it go?" Rocco asked quietly when Charlie reached the mansion's porch.

"I said goodbye," Charlie said, taking a seat next to Paige. She put her arm around him and rested her head on his shoulder. Even in the Netherworld, her hair smelled of strawberries.

"So your nightmare is over?" Paige asked.

"I guess so," Charlie told her. "I'm not afraid anymore." He was *worried*, of course, but he wasn't *scared*. And now he could see the difference between the two.

"Ummm, Charlie?" Alfie asked, sounding as though he'd rather keep his mouth shut.

"Yeah?" Charlie responded.

"If your fear was keeping the portal open, does that mean it closed when your nightmare just ended?" Alfie asked.

Charlie felt like he'd stuck a fork in an electric socket. If the portal was shut, there might not be a way to get his body back to the Waking World. He was on his feet in an instant. "I've got to get to the tower!"

Charlie's friends were on his heels as he raced up the stairs. When he reached the tower room, he found Meduso resting in a chair, smiling broadly as he studied a sheet of paper. There was no sign at all of the portal. Charlie carefully patted down every wall in the octagonal room. All

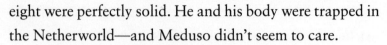

eight were perfectly solid. He and his body were trapped in the Netherworld—and Meduso didn't seem to care.

"The portal is closed!" Charlie yelped.

"Oh, don't be such a worrywart!" Meduso announced with a chuckle. "We'll find a way to open it again."

"How did you even get here?" Charlie asked.

"How do you think?" Meduso asked. "I *walked,* just like you. By the way, you really should have a look at this." He didn't seem very concerned that the boy he'd been sent to help might be stuck on the wrong side of the portal. "It's really quite remarkable work. And I'm not just saying that because it's a portrait of me."

Meduso held up the page for Charlie and his friends to see. On the front was a drawing of Meduso in natty safari attire. He held a pith helmet in his hand, and his three snakes fanned out from his head.

"That's one of Charlotte's drawings!" Charlie exclaimed. "How did you get that?"

"She gave it to me, of course." Meduso tapped the bottom of the page. "Look, it's even inscribed: 'To my favorite nightmare—Love, Charlotte DeChant.'"

"You missed the besst part!" Larry poked his head out from beneath Meduso's fedora.

" 'And to the sweetest snakes in the Netherworld, Larry, Barry, and Fernando.' "

"Sso kind," said Fernando.

"Meduso!" Charlie yelled. "Did you go through the portal while I was saying goodbye to my mom?"

"Certainly," Meduso confirmed. "I owed Charlotte an update. She's been so distraught, the poor dear. She took a big risk sending her own nightmare to find you. She worried you might refuse my help."

"So you really are Charlotte's nightmare?" Charlie asked.

"I used to be. In fact, Charlotte and I met when she was about your age. That's when she came to live in this mansion. But we didn't become friends until she visited the Netherworld with another little girl."

"Was the other girl my mother?" Charlie asked. "Was her name Veronica Salas?"

Meduso laughed. "As a matter of fact, it was. Such a feisty little thing! I don't think she'd ever been scared of anything aside from clowns. As a matter of fact, your mother was the one who introduced me to Dabney. He'd been her nightmare, but by the time I met them, they were thick as thieves.

"You know, it was Dabney who convinced me that nightmares could help humans. It's lucky for you that I learned that lesson. The old Basil Meduso would *never* have helped you escape from the Netherworld."

That reminded Charlie of the reason he had come. "How am I going to escape if the portal is closed?" He pointed at the wall where the door between the worlds had once been. "How are we all supposed to get home?"

"Your friends needn't worry. They didn't come through the portal," Meduso pointed out. "Their bodies are still asleep on the other side. All they have to do is wake up."

"What about me?" Charlie asked.

"I don't know yet," Meduso admitted. "I thought you'd be able to open it by yourself. But clearly you haven't learned how to use your abilities. Give me a little time and I'll figure something out."

Charlie must have looked as miserable as he felt.

"Hey, aren't we all forgetting something?" Rocco asked. "None of us can go back to the Waking World right away! We promised we would go back for the kids in the school. They helped us escape!"

"And don't forget *our* nightmares," Alfie added. "The rest of us haven't faced our fears yet. If we wake up now, we'll just be back here again tomorrow night."

His friends were right, Charlie realized. He'd been thinking only about himself. Even if the portal were open, it wouldn't be right to use it. Charlie had fixed his own problems. Now he had to get everything else working again.

"Okay," Charlie announced. "We'll let the gorgon worry about the portal. We've got people to save."

⚐ CHAPTER TWENTY-SIX ⚐

THE TURTLE SWIMS

Nightmare Elementary had changed since Charlie had last seen it. A wide moat now encircled the school. Just beyond the moat was a barbed-wire fence topped with loops of razor wire. Fierce dogs patrolled the area between the fence and the school building. And looming over the grounds were six guard towers, each manned by goblins.

"Guess the president knew we'd be coming," Charlie heard Rocco note miserably.

"Yeah, so he built the world's deadliest obstacle course," Paige added.

"Welcome, young humans!" The voice on the loud-speaker rattled their ears. "It's back-to-school time!"

Dark clouds crept past, and it began to drizzle just as Charlie looked up to find President Fear stationed in the crow's nest at the top of the nearest guard tower.

"The portal is closed," Charlie shouted up at him. "You'll never conquer the Waking World now. You should let all the kids in the school go free."

"And why would I want to do that? Children's screams are music to my ears," said President Fear, and as if on cue, a bloodcurdling shriek issued from the building. "Sounds like one of your schoolmates may have just been eaten."

"He's lying," Alfie whispered. "I don't think there are any monsters in there. Remember when we talked to those kids who were hiding in the bathroom? None of them had actually *seen* a nightmare creature. Their fear is what's keeping them trapped inside."

Charlie hoped it was true, but he wasn't going to risk it. And neither, it seemed, was Rocco.

"If you won't let the kids out, we'll find a way in!" Rocco yelled up at the guard tower.

"Then allow me to make you an offer you can't refuse," the president replied. "I will let Turtle Boy have a go at my obstacle course. If he makes it to the school doors in one piece, the rest of you may join him there."

"And if he fails?" Charlie demanded.

President Fear glared back at them. "Then the four of you will be locked up with the other brats. And you, Mr. Laird, will open the portal again."

Charlie had just opened his mouth to refuse the offer when Alfie stepped forward. "Deal!" he shouted.

Standing beside Charlie was the same short, bespectacled kid he'd known his entire life. From the outside, nothing about Alfie had changed. But Charlie could see that his friend was different now. Somewhere in the Netherworld, Alfie had discovered his own secret power.

"You sure you really want to do this?" Charlie whispered to Alfie.

"Heck yeah," Alfie said as he stripped out of his clothes. "Don't you see? This is my nightmare. I think I'm finally ready to beat it."

"You *think*?" Charlie asked. "Alfie, you gotta be *sure*."

"A DEAL WAS MADE! MOVE AWAY FROM THE TURTLE!" the president yelled. A rotten melon hit the ground beside Charlie, splattering him with stinking seeds. He was still wiping them from his face when Alfie stepped up to the edge of the moat. "ON YOUR MARK, GET SET . . . SWIM!" bellowed the president.

Charlie watched Alfie position his arms over his head—and winced when his dive ended as a belly flop of epic proportions. Foul-smelling water splashed Paige and a piece of rotting seaweed slapped Charlie across the face. The laughter from the guard towers above was deafening.

"TURTLE! TURTLE! TURTLE!" chanted the goblins.

Charlie felt like he was back at the Colosseum, but this time there was nothing he could do to save his friend. Alfie was the silliest-looking swimmer he'd ever seen. He fought the water like a cat in a bathtub. And yet, Charlie suddenly realized that while Alfie's technique was anything but elegant, it wasn't entirely ineffective. While the goblins were busy shouting insults, Alfie was quickly approaching the opposite side of the moat.

Up in his guard tower, the president had noticed Alfie's progress as well. "Release the piranhas!" he ordered the goblins.

A metal gate opened at the base of the guard tower and thousands of snapping piranhas set off in search of a meal.

"Cheater!" Paige shouted.

"I'm sorry," the president replied. "When exactly did I promise to play fair?"

The obstacle course was hard enough by itself, Charlie thought miserably. If the president was going to cheat, poor Alfie was a goner for sure.

Then he heard Rocco yell, "Look! He's out! Alfie's safe!"

Alfie was climbing the stones on the far side of the moat, two feisty piranhas attached to the seat of his underwear.

Alfie reached back and ripped the fish from his backside, leaving a pair of holes in his boxer shorts.

Sopping wet and trailing long strands of seaweed, Alfie quickly arrived at the second obstacle—a twenty-foot-high fence with razor wire coiled along the top. Vicious dogs hurled themselves at the other side, eager for a taste of the treat heading their way.

"What's he doing?" Charlie muttered to himself. Alfie had dropped to his knees, and his head seemed to be bowed in defeat. But then he started to dig. His hands tore at the ground beside the fence, and a steady stream of dirt flew out from between his legs.

The goblin guards roared with laughter.

"HE'S NO TURTLE. HE'S A *GOPHER!*" one cried.

"GOPHER! GOPHER! GOPHER!"

The speed at which Alfie scooped dirt was astounding. But there had to be a more dignified way to dig, Charlie thought. No wonder the goblins were laughing.

On the other side of the fence, the six dogs crowded together. They were all jet black, with coats that glistened in the light. Their twelve blood-red eyes were fixed on the hole where Alfie had disappeared. Fangs bared, they licked their lips and waited for their dinner. Just one of the dogs could rip the boy apart. If the six of them got ahold of him, there'd be nothing left at all.

"GET THE GOPHER! GET THE GOPHER! GET THE GOPHER!" the goblins chanted.

The tension was eating at Charlie's stomach, but he wouldn't turn away. Then he saw another hole opening up a few feet behind the dogs. Alfie had tunneled right under the beasts. But there was still at least a hundred yards between him and the school gates.

"THERE HE IS!" a goblin yelled, and the rest howled when they saw the little dirt-covered creature rise from the earth. Within seconds, the dogs had caught scent of their prey. Charlie waited for Alfie to do something spectacular. But he didn't. There was no more slapstick. No dazzling displays of genius. This time, Alfie Bluenthal just *ran*.

Charlie watched Alfie's arms pumping back and forth. Even in the Netherworld, the kid wasn't particularly fast, but at least he'd had a good head start. Charlie realized that the guard towers were silent. Suddenly no one was laughing at Alfie anymore.

"GO, ALFIE!" Paige yelled, and Alfie put a little more distance between himself and the dogs.

"YOU'RE ALMOST THERE!" Charlie called, and by the time the words were out of his mouth, Alfie *was* there.

Charlie almost collapsed with relief when he saw the school gate close safely behind Alfie, shutting out the vicious dogs. The boy sprinted up the stairs to the front entrance. All around him, the obstacle course had started to vanish. The moat dried up until it looked like little more than a ditch, and soon the dogs had disappeared and there was nothing left of the fence.

Charlie, Paige, and Rocco ran to Alfie's side. As they drew closer, they could hear cheering and applause. The kidnapped kids of Cypress Creek Elementary were gathered at the windows. They'd all witnessed Alfie's remarkable feats.

"Incredible!" a girl their age called down. "You're a superhero!"

"The Amazing Turtle!" someone else added.

"I kind of like that," Alfie said thoughtfully. "It's got a nice ring to it."

"You've earned it," Paige told him. "You just passed the president's fitness test. When I saw you start to run, I thought you'd never . . ." She stopped herself from saying any more.

"Don't worry," Alfie replied with a modest shrug. "I wouldn't have thought I could do it either. But when

President Fear turned the obstacle course into my night-mare, I knew I didn't have to be physically fit to win."

"You didn't?" Rocco asked.

"Nope, that wasn't what my nightmare was about. I wasn't afraid of being a bad athlete," Alfie said. "I was afraid of being laughed at. Then I realized that making them laugh could give me an advantage. If I let them under-estimate me, I could take them all by surprise."

"I don't think you have to worry about anyone here underestimating you again," Charlie assured him.

"And now that you've beaten your nightmare, you can wake up whenever you want," Paige said.

"What—and miss all the fun?" Alfie replied. "Are you kidding?"

"The fun stops here, Mr. Bluenthal," President Fear boomed as he crossed the schoolyard. He looked more livid than ever. "You pests may have made it to the front of the school, but the doors are sealed tight. And the crea-tures inside the halls are ready for dinner."

An earsplitting shriek came from the other side of the school's front door. President Fear's red eyes glowed a bit brighter. Charlie could have sworn he even looked taller. Fear was feeding on the terror inside.

⚘ CHAPTER TWENTY-SEVEN ⚘

THE TEST

"Help!" A girl who'd been watching from a first-floor window had vanished. Then the rest of the children who had gathered on the other side of the building's main doors disappeared in a matter of seconds. Charlie heard running and screaming in the halls.

"Take a look," President Fear said with a nasty smile.

Charlie pressed his face against a window. Peering between the bars, he could see the first-floor hallway. Most of the seventh and eighth graders' lockers were open, and the contents were strewn across the floor. It looked as if terrible things had taken place in the corridor. But there was no trace of any nightmare creatures.

Charlie and his friends spun around to find President Fear. "There are only two beings in the Netherworld who possess the power to open those doors," he said. "I'm one of them, of course. The other is Mr. Marquez."

"Me?" Rocco turned a sickly shade of gray.

"You never finished taking your exam, did you?" President Fear stepped aside, revealing Rocco's school desk. Standing next to it was the oily-haired proctor with a stack of papers in his hands. "This time, you only get one chance to pass, and it's the only way to free your schoolmates."

Rocco's legs started to wobble, and for a moment Charlie wondered if the boy might collapse. He grabbed one of his friend's arms. Paige took the other. Together they dragged Rocco a few yards away.

"This may be my nightmare, but I don't know if I can face it," Rocco said once they were out of the president's earshot. "You saw the last test I took. I'm pretty sure most of it wasn't written in English."

"Maybe there's another way to rescue the kids," Alfie muttered. "The school doors are locked and the windows are barred. Is there any other way to get inside?"

"What about that giant trash chute in the cafeteria?" Paige asked. "It goes from the kitchen to the Dumpsters outside. Last week I saw a lunch lady toss a whole box of moldy turnips down it. I bet the chute's big enough for the four of us to climb up."

"I hate to be a spoilsport," Alfie said, "but I'm pretty sure the chute has to be opened from inside the kitchen. Do you think we could get one of the kids to do it?"

"What's the point?" Rocco groaned. "What would we do if we got into the school anyway? The whole place is filled with monsters."

"The exam will begin in exactly seventeen seconds," the proctor interrupted. "Take your seat, Mr. Marquez."

Charlie sighed. Their time had run out. "Looks like you're just going to have to take the test," he told Rocco.

"If I can beat my nightmare, you can too," Alfie said, trying to encourage Rocco. "Remember how you saved us all from the goblins?"

"That was nothing but dumb luck," Rocco replied miserably as he squeezed into the little wooden desk.

The proctor plopped a giant stack of paper down in front of Rocco. Alfie snuck a peek at the top page, and when he looked back at Charlie and Paige, Charlie could tell he was horrified.

"Keep your distance!" the proctor snapped at Alfie. "Do not approach this desk again or you will all be punished for cheating!"

Charlie, Paige, and Alfie backed away. The only place to watch was among the goblins that had formed a large circle around Rocco's desk. Inside the school, some of the children had returned to the windows, where they clung to the bars. Those who had been imprisoned the longest had started to look a bit like monsters themselves. Their hair was matted, and dark circles hung under their bloodshot eyes. They watched Rocco with a mixture of hope and terror.

Rocco stared down at the paper, pencil in hand. He still hadn't made a single mark. Then his hand twitched and his lips formed silent words. When Rocco looked up at the assembled crowd, Charlie saw inspiration in his eyes.

"Excuse me!" he called out to the proctor. "I have a question."

"No questions!" the proctor responded. "Your friends can't help you now."

Rocco shook his head. "Not for them. For *him*." His arm rose, and he pointed at the president.

President Fear looked surprised. "I'll allow it," he said with a smirk and a glance at the ticking clock.

"What's he doing?" Paige whispered.

"Beats the heck out of me," Charlie replied.

"The kids inside the school must be afraid of different things, right?" Rocco asked the president.

"Of course," the president replied.

"So if they're all afraid of something different, does that mean there's a nightmare for every kid in that school?"

"That's right," President Fear answered a bit more cautiously.

"Well, then the school must be packed with nightmares. Why haven't we seen any of the creatures?"

President Fear's evil grin disappeared in an instant. "No more questions! Get back to your test!"

It was Rocco's turn to smile. "You're just a big bully, aren't you?" Then the boy's head dropped again, and he began to write furiously.

"He must have figured out a few of the answers." Charlie felt his hope growing.

"I don't think so," Alfie groaned with a shake of his head. "I saw the test. It's multiple choice. Rocco shouldn't be *writing* at all."

And yet Rocco appeared to be on a roll. He scribbled words on each piece of paper. When he finished with a page, he would flip it over and slap it facedown on the desk. By the time he'd gone through the entire stack, there was still fifteen minutes left on the clock. Rocco grinned in triumph. Then he picked up the first piece of paper in the pile and began to fold it. First in half. Then at the edges.

Charlie couldn't believe what he was witnessing. It was the same thing that had gotten Rocco into trouble in countless classes with countless teachers. Under ordinary circumstances, it would have been funny. Now it looked as if Rocco had lost his mind. "He's making a paper airplane," Charlie said.

Rocco finished the first airplane and set it aside. The goblins snickered, and the president looked overjoyed. By the time Rocco had finished, a pile of paper airplanes covered the desk. Then he stood up, aimed carefully, and launched one into the air. It swooped, soared, and flew between the bars on one of the school's windows.

"Mr. Marquez!" cried the proctor and the president in unison. But Rocco didn't seem to hear them. He was too busy sailing paper airplanes into the school. Rocco's arm was so agile and his aim so excellent that every last one made it into the hands of a student.

"You fail!" President Fear announced.

"Not yet," Rocco said. He sat back down with a single sheet of paper in his hands. "The rules are the rules. There's five minutes left on the clock."

When the bell finally rang, President Fear marched up to Rocco's desk and snatched the paper out of the boy's hands. He took one look and began to laugh. Then he held the page up so the goblins could see it. There were no circles filled in. No test answers had been selected. The only thing Rocco had written was a giant A with a plus sign beside it.

Charlie groaned.

"If you really believe you deserve an A-plus for this pathetic excuse for a test paper," the principal said between guffaws, "then you're even dumber than I ever imagined!"

"I earned that A-plus," Rocco insisted, showing no fear or embarrassment. "You told me I had to use that test to free the kids. So I did."

"Oh really?" the president asked. "Then where are they?"

"Right there," Rocco said. Marching around from the other side of the school were dozens of children. "They beat your nightmare," Rocco said. "That means they're all free to wake up and go home."

"How?" It was the only word the president seemed to be able to utter.

One of the children marched right up to him—a girl without an ounce of fear in her eyes. "Here," she said, thrusting a paper airplane at him.

"Can I see that?" Charlie asked a boy who was holding an identical plane.

He unfolded the page and read it.

THE ONLY MONSTER IS OUTSIDE THE SCHOOL. HIS NAME
IS FEAR. DON'T LET HIM BEAT THE KIDS OF CYPRESS
CREEK. STICK TOGETHER AND HEAD FOR THE CAFETERIA.
SLIDE DOWN THE TRASH CHUTE AND MEET US OUTSIDE.

Charlie held the paper up in the air. "You lose again," he told President Fear. "Looks like Rocco aced the test."

"But this isn't—" President Fear started to say.

"Hey," Rocco jumped in. "When did I ever promise to play fair?"

Charlie and the gang gathered around Rocco to celebrate.

"How did you know that the kids wouldn't get eaten on their way to the cafeteria?" Charlie asked.

"Well, I was thinking about how afraid I was, and that's when I put it together. None of the kids had actually seen a monster in there—they were just taking Fear's word for it. That's when I knew—the president was just bluffing."

"And what if you'd been wrong?" Paige asked.

"Yeah," Rocco replied thoughtfully. "That would have been a big bummer."

"Hey, listen," Alfie said, calling their attention to the whispers passing among the goblins in the crowd outside the school. It was clear the beasts weren't pleased.

Charlie was already nervous when a tiny girl tugged at his shirt. It took one look at her upturned face to tell she was upset.

"What's wrong?" he asked the child.

"My friend Amber isn't here," the girl whimpered. "She got locked in a bathroom and she couldn't get out." The girl pointed skyward. Sure enough, a hand was waving a toilet-paper flag from a third-floor bathroom.

The president started to laugh once again. "It seems as if your plan had a flaw, Mr. Marquez," he said. "You didn't save everyone, did you? If there's still one child inside, that means you failed. Either they all get rescued—or none of them do. Goblins! Round up all these children and escort them back inside the school."

And at what might have been the worst moment in Charlie's existence came the most beautiful sound he'd ever heard.

☙ CHAPTER TWENTY-EIGHT ❧

ALONE WITH THE DARK

Ahhhbleeeewgah! Ahhhbleeeewgah! Ahhhbleeeewgah!
A tiny yellow car appeared on the horizon. As it raced closer, Charlie could see Dabney behind the wheel—and Meduso squeezed in beside him. But as welcome as the sight may have been, Charlie's attention was quickly drawn to the creatures racing alongside the car. Most were on foot. Others flew or hopped or slithered. Hundreds of the scariest nightmares ever dreamed up were all headed in their direction. The Cypress Creek kids huddled together. A few gasped or whimpered softly, but no one bolted.

"Gorgon alert!" shouted one of the president's goblins. "Meduso is here! Get your gorgon shields on!"

By the time the yellow car skidded to a halt in front of the school, the president and his minions were all sporting protective sunglasses with mirrored lenses.

"Well, well," said President Fear. "Isn't this my lucky day. Seize the gorgon and the clown!" he shouted at the goblins.

Before the president's thugs could obey, dozens of nightmare creatures formed a circle around the clown car.

Charlie could barely believe it. The monsters were acting as Dabney's bodyguards.

A murmur passed through the goblin mob, and none of them made a move.

"I gave you a command!" President Fear shouted.

The goblins hung back as Dabney and Meduso pried their bodies out of the miniature vehicle.

"You! Bigfoot!" The president grabbed the arm of a Sasquatch. "Take the traitors into custody. And when you're done, round up all these children and send them back to school."

The Sasquatch growled and shrugged off the president's hand. "I'm not a goblin—I don't take orders from tyrants."

The other nightmare creatures began to gather around, and the president soon found himself trapped in the center of an angry crowd. Charlie and his friends squeezed between scaly shins and fur-covered thighs until they had a good view of the action.

"How dare you defy me!" the giant bellowed at the Sasquatch. "I'm the president of the Netherworld!"

Someone in the crowd began to giggle. Then the strange giggles became all-out guffaws. Charlie saw Dabney the clown step into the middle of the mob. "You call yourself *president*?" he asked once his laughter was under control. "You don't even follow our rules. We are nightmares, and our job is to scare humans. We make them scream and cry and sometimes wet their pants. But we do *not* torture them." Dabney turned to the assembled nightmare creatures. "Am I right?"

Charlie had to cover his ears as the creatures growled, roared, and stomped in agreement.

Dabney thrust a gloved finger at President Fear. "He says that nightmares can stay alive forever if we find a way to keep people frightened twenty-four hours a day. I'd call that torture, wouldn't you?"

President Fear spun around in a circle, searching for a friendly face in the crowd. For once, Charlie thought, it was the giant who looked intimidated.

"I'm trying to help our kind!" the president cried. "I don't want any more nightmares to die."

"Nightmares don't *die*," Dabney declared. "When we choose to retire, we turn into *dreams*."

"So you say, but where's your proof?" President Fear sneered, his confidence returning. "Are we supposed to take a washed-up circus clown's word for it?"

Charlie knew it was time for him to step forward. "The Dream Realm is real. My mother made the trip there tonight. And even if you don't believe me, you should listen to Dabney. His word is worth something. President Fear is a liar and a cheat."

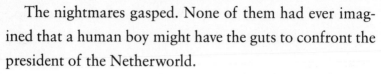

The nightmares gasped. None of them had ever imagined that a human boy might have the guts to confront the president of the Netherworld.

Charlie pointed at the school. "President Fear has been keeping dozens of kids locked up in this building," he told the nightmares. "Tonight, they faced their fears and escaped. But now the president is trying to lock them back up again."

The creatures in the crowd looked down at the children who were mingling among them—and the kids peered up at the nightmare creatures. Neither seemed to know what to do.

"If they conquered their nightmares, that hardly seems fair," said a monstrous scorpion.

"I'm afraid this is all just a big misunderstanding," President Fear insisted. "In accordance with Netherworld rules, the children who escaped will be allowed to go free. But there is one child left inside the school. And until she beats her nightmare, I'm afraid she'll have to return every night."

"That *is* how the Netherworld works," a buglike alien told Charlie. "We can't change the rules."

"But Amber can't face her nightmare!" Charlie argued. "She got locked in a bathroom. She hasn't had a chance to be brave!"

"Let me go get her," someone called out. "I'll unlock

the door." It was Paige. Charlie wondered what she was doing—until he realized that Paige still had her own nightmare to face.

The president considered Paige's offer. "Are you sure you want to volunteer, Miss Bretter? Don't you know what's waiting inside for you?" He lifted one beefy arm in the air. When he snapped his fingers, all the lights in the school shut off. "Are you ready to face the Dark?"

"Yes," Paige said, though she looked a bit queasy as she headed up the stairs to the school's front doors.

"Not so fast, Miss Bretter," President Fear called. He held out a hand and one of his goblins passed him a small camera with an elastic strap. "It wouldn't be much fun for the rest of us if we didn't get to watch."

He strapped a camera to her forehead. It made her look small and helpless.

"Can we wish her good luck before she goes?" Charlie asked.

"No," President Fear snapped. "From this point forward, Podge is on her own."

Paige stood in the doorway, a wall of darkness before her. She took a step inside, and the doors slammed shut. The camera feed began, and the front wall of the school became a giant screen. What must have been pitch-black to

Paige appeared fluorescent green to the audience. She was in the school's main hallway. The floor was still strewn with notebooks and empty toilet paper rolls and cans from the cafeteria.

Paige waded slowly through the debris, her arms held out in front of her. At least this time she knew where she was, Charlie thought, and she had some idea how to get where she needed to go.

The feed captured the sound of a locker opening. Paige flinched. She must have heard it too. She stopped in the middle of the hall and waited for some sign that a creature was stalking her. Her chest heaved as she gulped air. Paige was already terrified—and she couldn't see what the viewers outside saw. A figure in black had slipped out of the locker. Even though the Dark had no face, everyone watching the video recognized him at once. The Cypress Creek kids cringed at the sight of the creature with its featureless head and tendril-like fingers. Charlie saw one of the smallest kids move closer to Rocco. As the Dark crept up to Paige, the older boy put a reassuring arm around the little one.

The Dark examined Paige from every angle, brushing against her as it moved. She swept the air with her arms, but the Dark always managed to avoid her touch. It was taunting Paige. Toying with her. Charlie could barely stand to watch. It was only a matter of time before Paige ended up on the floor like she had in the hospital, her arms wrapped around her legs, too frightened to move. But to Charlie's surprise, Paige began to walk. One foot shuffled forward; the other followed. The Dark stood back, as if confused. Paige was at the base of the main stairway when it decided to take action.

A murmur passed through the crowd as the Dark began to expand. It filled the school's hallway with a blackness so impenetrable that even the night-vision camera couldn't see through it. For a few long moments, Charlie lost sight of Paige. Then the blackness seemed to burst. When the video returned to the screen, it was met with the screams of the children on the lawn. There was no longer just one Dark stalking Paige. There were dozens.

They circled and surrounded Charlie's friend, each taking a pinch of clothing or a strand of hair. And then they began to move her. Paige struggled to resist, but she was slowly being dragged toward a door beneath the stairs. Somehow Charlie knew that behind the door was the place the Dark called home. If it took Paige with it, she might never find her way out.

Charlie was on the verge of begging the president to call off his creature when a bloodcurdling scream brought him to a halt. It had come from the third floor of the school.

Everyone outside the school looked up. Like Charlie, they'd all been so busy watching Paige that they had forgotten about Amber, the girl trapped in the bathroom upstairs.

Charlie was certain the scream would be the last straw—the thing that finally drove Paige over the edge. But to his surprise, it had a different effect. Paige blindly grabbed at the stair railing, and somehow her fingers managed to wrap around it. As she pulled herself forward, the Darks' grips began to slip. Several of them let go altogether. When the girl screamed a second time, Paige suddenly broke free. She raced up the stairs. She didn't flail or stumble. She seemed to know her way. Then Charlie realized that Paige was using the sound of the girl's screams to guide her.

Paige found Amber huddled in a toilet stall.

"You're safe with me," Paige told the girl. Then she took her hand and led her down the stairs. The Dark was still there, but it stood back and watched. There was nothing more it could do. And when the front doors of the school opened, a roar of applause met the girls.

"You did it!" Charlie, Alfie, and Rocco surrounded Paige on the front stairs of the school and hugged her all at once.

"I didn't have a choice," Paige said. "I heard Amber scream and I knew there was someone who needed me. I stopped thinking about how scared I was and just followed her voice. It led me right out of the Dark."

It felt like a perfect ending, but Charlie couldn't help thinking that something was wrong. Then he figured out what it was. "Where's Meduso?" he asked his friends. The gorgon should have been with them to celebrate.

"He's right over . . ." Alfie pointed to an empty space at the front of the crowd. "Well, he *was* there."

"Looking for someone?" It was President Fear's voice. He joined the four children in front of the school. "Did your snake-haired friend leave without saying goodbye?"

A figure with a burlap sack over its head was being carried through the crowd by six of President Fear's biggest goblins. While everyone else had been watching the school doors, the goblins had used the distraction to capture Meduso.

"Just what do you think you're doing?" Dabney demanded.

"Arresting a menace to society," President Fear replied. "Meduso has turned too many innocent nightmares to stone. There's an entire dump filled with statues. And these"—he took off his mirrored sunglasses, tossed them on the ground, and destroyed them with the heel of his shoe—"were never my style."

Charlie heard the crunch of a hundred sunglasses as the goblins all followed the president's lead. Charlie looked out at the mob that had gathered at the school. More goblins must have arrived on the scene. Now the nightmare creatures and Cypress Creek children were outnumbered at least ten to one.

"The time has come!" the president shouted to his goblins. "Take the children and do whatever you like to them. They're just a little taste of the delights in store for you once we've conquered the Waking World!"

In an instant, the scene was pandemonium. Goblins snatched children as the nightmare creatures tried in vain to save them.

"You can't do this!" Dabney shouted.

"The kids earned their freedom!" Charlie yelled.

"What difference does it make?" President Fear responded. "The rules don't apply to me anymore. Without a gorgon, there's no way to stop my goblins."

Suddenly the doors of the school were thrown open. "STOP!" said a voice so deep and powerful that it made Charlie's brain vibrate. Every creature in the schoolyard froze, and all eyes turned to the building, where darkness filled the doorway.

"Who just said that?" Charlie heard Rocco ask.

"You can't see him because that's the Dark," Alfie said, sounding awestruck.

"RELEASE THE CHILDREN," the Dark boomed.

"Excuse me?" President Fear said. "Are you speaking to me?"

"THEY HAVE ALL FACED THEIR FEARS. YOU MUST SET THEM FREE."

"I'm afraid that's not going to happen," the president said. "You see—"

"THERE IS NOTHING TO SEE. RELEASE THE CHILDREN OR YOU WILL RECEIVE NO MORE ASSISTANCE FROM ME."

"I don't need you or any other nightmare to conquer the Waking World," the president said, growing even bolder. "All I need is my goblin army."

"YOUR RULE IS OVER. YOU HAVE MADE AN ENEMY OF THE DARK."

"You dare threaten me?" the president snarled as he stormed up the stairs. "You seem to have forgotten. I can get rid of you too."

He snapped his fingers and every light in the school blazed to life. In an instant, the Dark was gone. President Fear started to laugh. But he was stopped abruptly by the sound of someone clearing her throat.

"I won't be so easy to get rid of, Mr. President."

Standing in the doorway was Medusa. President Fear dug into his suit pocket, his fingers frantically searching for his gorgon shields.

"Looking for these?" Charlie asked, kicking a pair of smashed sunglasses toward the steps.

"I thought only losers needed glasses," Alfie taunted him.

They watched as Medusa grabbed the president by the ears, pulled his head toward hers, and stared deeply into his eyes. Every hair on the president's head went gray.

Within seconds, the most feared giant in the Netherworld had been turned to stone.

Medusa slid her stylish dark glasses onto their usual place on her face and then turned to address Paige and Amber, who were standing nearby. "Would you ladies be so kind as to give me a hand?" she asked politely.

The two girls rushed at President Fear and shoved him with all their might. The president's statue teetered and tottered—then fell face-first and shattered into smithereens.

"Now, goblins, be gone!" Medusa ordered. Her snakes writhed wildly around her head. "You're banished from this land. Any of you caught crossing the border into the Netherworld will be turned into a lawn ornament!"

At first none of the goblins budged. Then one at the back of the crowd turned tail and ran. Another followed suit. And another. Until a herd of goblins was stampeding toward the horizon.

Medusa adjusted her glasses and cleared her throat. "Dabney, darling, would you please free my son?"

The goblins had run off, leaving Meduso with his hands tied and a burlap sack over his head.

"Children," Charlie heard Medusa say. "Gather around."

The Cypress Creek kids looked to Rocco.

"It's okay," he assured them, and soon all the kids were

standing in a half circle around one of the most famous monsters in history.

"Take each other's hands," said Medusa. She looked over to see that Charlie, Alfie, Rocco, and Paige hadn't joined in. "You too, please."

Charlie did as he was told.

"You've faced your fears," Medusa told them. "But you also did something far more important. You stuck together. Now it's time for all of you to go home. I want you to close your eyes. Imagine your bedrooms. Picture yourselves asleep in your beds. . . ."

"Wait—this is it?" Alfie asked. "Is she going to make us wake up?"

"You heard her," Charlie said. "It's time."

"But what about you, Charlie?" Paige asked. "You're not asleep. What's going to happen to you?"

"Yeah, we can't leave without you," Rocco said.

"Yes you can," Charlie insisted. "I found my way here, and I'll find my way back. I need you guys to go home and let my family know I'm okay."

"Are you sure?" Paige asked.

"Positive," Charlie told her, wishing he really felt so optimistic. "Now close your eyes. I'll see you guys in the morning."

"I'm going to count," he heard Medusa say. "By the

time I reach ten, you'll all be back in your beds. One . . . Two . . . Three . . ."

Charlie watched as the children of Cypress Creek vanished one by one. Paige was last. Before she disappeared, she gave Charlie's hand a gentle squeeze. And then she was gone. Charlie was alone once more. But this time, it felt okay. Dabney put a hand on his shoulder.

"Don't worry," he said. "I know how to get you home."

Now that the children had returned to the Waking World, Medusa addressed the nightmares in the audience. "My fellow creatures, we must all learn from the events of today. Our job is to frighten. But we should always do so with a purpose in mind. A little bit of fear can be helpful. Too much is dangerous.

"We've all witnessed what fear can do. We were so scared of dying that we allowed the president to do horrible things. I cannot promise you that the Dream Realm exists. Each of us will have to find out on our own. But I believe in my heart that nightmares don't die. If we do our jobs well and help humans face their fears, we're rewarded by being transformed into dreams. But in order to enter the Dream Realm, we will need to show the same bravery the children of Cypress Creek have shown here today."

Meduso was making his way to his mother's side. Charlie could hear Larry and Fernando arguing as the gorgon passed.

"He can't be sseriouss!" Larry cried.

"Stay out of the way," Fernando ordered. "We both knew it would come to thiss."

When Charlie saw Meduso whisper in his mother's ear, he knew what the gorgon was about to do. The look of shock on Medusa's face transformed into one of sadness before it settled on something a lot like pride. She hugged her son and slithered back to give him center stage.

"I used to enjoy turning other creatures to stone," Meduso confessed. "It was more than a job—it was a passion. I didn't wait in a cave for people to come find me, the way my mother did. I set out to find and freeze as many as possible. I turned entire towns to stone and never thought twice about it. Then I met a little human girl named Lottie, and she taught me how wonderful it could feel to actually *help* someone.

"When I leave the Netherworld, the creatures I petrified will return to life. I've been wanting to retire for years. Until now, I've been too frightened. But I've witnessed amazing things in the past few days. I'd like to thank Charlie Laird and his friends for showing me what real courage looks like. Now I'm finally ready. It's time to be Lottie's dream."

Meduso slipped a hand into the pocket of his suit and pulled out a golden compact. Charlie recognized it from the vanity in Medusa's wardrobe room. That's where Meduso must have decided how his own story would end.

"Wait!" Charlie cried. He threw his arms around the gorgon. "Thank you."

"Thank *you*," Meduso told him. "Charlotte was right. You're a pretty good kid."

When Charlie let go, Meduso took off his glasses and gazed into the compact. A smile stretched across his face before it turned to stone.

"Will you miss him?" Charlie asked Dabney later as they made their way toward the purple mansion.

"Yes," said the clown. "Meduso and I didn't have much in common. If we hadn't been thrown together, we probably wouldn't have met. But sometimes that's how you make your very best friends."

They were halfway up the mansion's hill before Charlie worked up the nerve to ask the question he'd been saving.

"You were my mother's nightmare, weren't you?"

"Yes," Dabney said.

"What was she like when she was a kid?"

"A lot like you," Dabney told him.

"Oh yeah? Did she open a portal and almost let a monster destroy the Waking World?" Charlie joked.

"Not exactly," Dabney said with a giggle. "But if you

want to learn more about their adventures, you should read Charlotte's book. I hear it has some delightful pictures."

The clown opened the front door of the mansion.

"Are you sure I can get back to the Waking World?" Charlie asked.

"I have a hunch you will," Dabney said.

They took the stairs to the tower two at a time. Before Charlie even reached the top, he could see that the little room was awash with light. When he was finally there, he found himself looking through one of the walls and into an identical room. There was only one difference: on the other side were Jack, Alfie, Paige, and Rocco. They'd all come to get him.

"How did the portal open?" Charlie asked.

"Your brother," Dabney said. "His worst fear is that you'll never come home. Do you want to go back?"

"More than anything," Charlie said.

"Close your eyes. Are you scared?"

"No," Charlie said.

"Then take a step forward."

Charlie knew when he felt the arms around him that he was finally home.

EPILOGUE

"How's this?" Charlotte asked, sliding her latest illustration across the desk to her stepson.

Charlie examined the monster she'd drawn. It looked exactly like the giant grub he'd seen in the Netherworld. "It's perfect," he marveled. "I still can't believe how good you are."

"Lemme see!" Jack had been standing at one of the tower's windows, keeping squirrels away from a bird feeder with a slingshot and a handful of dried beans. He rushed over to the desk for a peek at the drawing. "That thing isn't so scary," he scoffed. "It looks like something you'd find in our yard."

"Oh yeah?" Charlie replied with a laugh. "Call me next time you turn over a rock out there and find a six-foot-tall worm."

Jack riffled through the other drawings strewn across Charlotte's desk. Among them were pictures of an old lady with tentacles shooting out of her mouth, a cockroach in a cocktail dress, and a were-wallaby. "These are so cool," Jack said. "When do *I* get to explore the other side?"

"Never, if you're lucky," Charlie said. He had no intention of ever going back. But he knew there was always a

chance that his brother or some other kid would end up making the trip. That was why Charlie and his stepmother were working together to finish the book she had started.

"And don't get any big ideas about trying to open the portal again, mister," Charlotte told Jack. "I don't have many friends on the other side these days. If you got lost over there, I don't know who I'd send to find you."

Charlie thought about his own nightmare guide. "How is Meduso?" he asked Charlotte. "Is he enjoying the Dream Realm?"

"When I saw him last night, he was wearing a Hawaiian shirt and drinking a piña colada," Charlotte said. "He couldn't be happier. Larry's even stopped complaining, and apparently he *loves* karaoke."

Suddenly Charlie heard a commotion downstairs on the first floor of the purple mansion. A dog was barking, a cat was hissing, and it sounded as if several lamps had been knocked over.

"They're at it again," Charlotte sighed. "Charlie, would you mind letting Rufus out?"

"Nope," Charlie replied, hopping off his seat.

"And while you're down there, give the pot a stir too, wouldja?"

"Sure thing," Charlie told her.

By the time he reached the kitchen, Rufus had cornered Aggie behind the trash can. After spending twenty-five years as a statue, Rufus always wanted to play. But as usual, the cat wasn't having it.

"Come on, boy," Charlie said, pulling the dog back by its collar. "Go take a run around the backyard."

The dog bounded out the back door, and Charlie headed for the stove. Aggie nuzzled against his legs as he took the lid off a pot on one of the front burners. Holding his nose, Charlie gave the bubbling potion inside a stir.

"What *is* that gunk?" Andrew Laird set a shopping bag and a pizza box down on the counter.

Charlie looked up. "Oh, hey, Dad," he said. "I think it's a cure for toenail fungus."

"Yep," Andrew Laird said, mussing his son's hair. "That's exactly what it smells like."

Another herbalist had recently opened a store in a nearby town, and Hazel's Herbarium had been losing business. Charlotte had heard through the grapevine that the other shop was selling some kind of miracle product—but she hadn't been able to find out much more.

"You guys sure have been working hard up there," Charlie's dad said. "When do I get to read your book?"

"Soon," Charlie promised, wondering what his dad would say when the truth was finally revealed.

"Well, why don't you give the others a shout and tell them to come down? I picked up dinner on my way home."

Charlie put the lid on the pot. When he reached the

base of the stairs, he stopped to admire the two portraits that now hung side by side on the landing. One was Silas DeChant. The other was Charlie's mother. It was Charlotte's best work. The painting captured Veronica Laird's spirit as well as her beauty. Now whenever Charlie needed to see her, his mother was always there.

"Jack!" Charlie shouted up the stairs.

"What?" screeched his brother in return.

"Dad brought pizza. Tell the stepmonster it's time for dinner!"

YOU THOUGHT THAT WAS IT?

Jason Segel and Kirsten Miller
team up again for book two in the
Nightmares! series.

THE SLEEPWALKER TONIC

FALL 2015

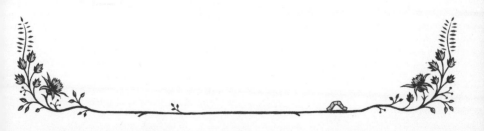

ABOUT THE AUTHORS

JASON SEGEL used to have nightmares just like Charlie, and just like Charlie, he's learned that the things we're most afraid of are the things that can make us strong . . . if we're brave enough to face them. Jason likes acting, writing, making music, and hanging out with his friends. Sometimes he writes movies. Sometimes he writes songs for movies. Sometimes he stars in those movies and sings those songs. You might know him from *The Muppets* and *Despicable Me*. Your parents might know him from other stuff. *Nightmares!* is his first novel.

KIRSTEN MILLER grew up in a small town just like Cypress Creek, minus the purple mansion. She lives and writes in New York City. She's the author of the acclaimed Kiki Strike books, the Eternal Ones series, and *How to Lead a Life of Crime*. You can visit her at kirstenmillerbooks.com.